NIGHT CALL

Visit us at www.boldstrokesbooks.com

What Reviewers Say About Radclyffe's Books

A Matter of Trust is a "...sexy, powerful love story filled with angst, discovery and passion that captures the uncertainty of first love and its discovery." – *Just About Write*

Shield of Justice is a "...well-plotted...lovely romance...I couldn't turn the pages fast enough!" – Ann Bannon, author of *The Beebo Brinker Chronicles*

"The author's brisk mix of political intrigue, fast-paced action, and frequent interludes of lesbian sex and love...in *Honor Reclaimed*...sure does make for great escapist reading." – *Q Syndicate*

Change of Pace is "...contemporary, yet timeless, not only about sex, but also about love, longing, lust, surprises, chance meetings, planned meetings, fulfilling wild fantasies, and trust." – *Midwest Book Review*

"Radclyffe has once again pulled together all the ingredients of a genuine page-turner, this time adding some new spices into the mix. *shadowland* is sure to please—in part because Radclyffe never loses sight of the fact that she is telling a love story, and a compelling one at that." – Cameron Abbott, author of *To The Edge* and *An Inexpressible State of Grace*

Lammy winner "...*Stolen Moments* is a collection of steamy stories about women who just couldn't wait. It's sex when desire overrides reason, and it's incredibly hot!" – *On Our Backs*

"With ample angst, realistic and exciting medical emergencies, winsome secondary characters, and a sprinkling of humor, *Fated Love* turns out to be a terrific romance. It's one of the best I have read in the last three years." – *Midwest Book Review*

"*Innocent Hearts*...illustrates that our struggles for acceptance of women loving women is as old as time—only the setting changes. The romance is sweet, sensual, and touching." – *Just About Write*

Lammy winner "...*Distant Shores, Silent Thunder* weaves an intricate tapestry about passion and commitment between lovers. The story explores the fragile nature of trust and the sanctuary provided by loving relationships." – *Sapphic Reader*

In *When Dreams Tremble* the "...focus on character development is meticulous and comprehensive, filled with angst, regret, and longing, building to the ultimate climax." – *Just About Write*

By the Author

Romances

Innocent Hearts

Love's Melody Lost

Love's Tender Warriors

Tomorrow's Promise

Passion's Bright Fury

Love's Masquerade

shadowland

Fated Love

Turn Back Time

Promising Hearts

When Dreams Tremble

The Lonely Hearts Club

Night Call

The Provincetown Tales

Safe Harbor

Beyond the Breakwater

Distant Shores, Silent Thunder

Storms of Change

Winds of Fortune

Honor Series

Above All, Honor

Honor Bound

Love & Honor

Honor Guards

Honor Reclaimed

Honor Under Siege

Word of Honor

Justice Series

A Matter of Trust (prequel)

Shield of Justice

In Pursuit of Justice

Justice in the Shadows

Justice Served

Erotic Interludes: *Change Of Pace*
(A Short Story Collection)

Stacia Seaman and Radclyffe, eds.:
Erotic Interludes 2: *Stolen Moments*
Erotic Interludes 3: *Lessons in Love*
Erotic Interludes 4: *Extreme Passions*
Erotic Interludes 5: *Road Games*
Romantic Interludes 1: *Discovery*

NIGHT CALL

by

RADCLY*ff*E

2008

NIGHT CALL

ISBN 10: 1-60282-031-7
ISBN 13: 978-1-60282-031-9

This Trade Paperback Original Is Published By
Bold Strokes Books, Inc.
New York, USA

First Edition: October 2008

CREDITS
EDITORS: RUTH STERNGLANTZ AND STACIA SEAMAN
PRODUCTION DESIGN: STACIA SEAMAN
COVER DESIGN BY SHERI (GRAPHICARTIST2020@HOTMAIL.COM)

Acknowledgments

I think it's safe to say that every medical professional dislikes night call. Those hours between dusk and dawn are lonely, stressful, unpredictable, and often filled with desperation and despair. On the other hand, I think we would all say that those hours are often filled with our greatest challenges and our finest moments. Whether we are in the operating room, the emergency room, on the patient floors, in the field, or piloting the rescue helicopter, we play a part in a drama that will affect lives forever. When I think back on the events that mark the milestones and turning points in my medical career, they always occurred at night.

In this book I have focused on a small group of emergency and critical care physicians, nurses, EMTs, paramedics, and medevac pilots and crew. The medical scenes are based primarily on my own experiences as a surgeon. I had the very good fortune to receive expert input from a ten-year Army veteran who flew helicopters for eight years, the last four of which she spent as an instructor at the Army's Helicopter Pilot School. Currently she flies a medevac helicopter in the civilian sector. Thank you, Jennifer, most profoundly—your technical advice and personal insight made this a far finer book. Any errors or misrepresentation are mine alone, and I apologize for getting any critical details wrong despite your patient and thorough explanations.

My thanks also go to my first readers Connie, Diane, Eva, Paula, and RB, as well as to my editors, Ruth Sternglantz and Stacia Seaman, and to the generous proofreaders at Bold Strokes Books for making this a better book.

Sheri, thank you for seeing into my head with such dead-on accuracy. Great cover.

To Lee, for being there in all ways, night and day. *Amo te.*

Radclyffe 2008

Dedication

For Lee
For the Wind Beneath My Wings

CHAPTER ONE

H ey, Holmes! I thought you were in Vegas?"
"Yeah, I was." Tristan sank down on the ugly green vinyl
sofa that occupied one wall in the OR lounge and propped her feet up
on a nearby chair. "But when I heard you all were having so much fun
back here, I left early."

Most of the Philadelphia Medical College surgeons and
anesthesiologists were in Las Vegas for a trauma meeting all week,
and only a skeleton staff remained at the hospital. Tristan had been
there too until she'd received an emergency call from her chief. Acute
staffing shortage, he'd informed her. Two of the senior anesthesia
staff were unexpectedly out of commission—one with a broken leg
following a collision with a goose while he was rollerblading through
the park along the Schuylkill River, and the other with a family crisis.
Since Tristan was the low man—or woman, in this case—on the ladder,
seeing as how she'd just started on staff only a few weeks before, she'd
gamely saluted and fallen on her sword for the good of her brother and
sister anesthesiologists. She'd taken the redeye back the night before
and gone straight to the hospital.

The only thing that made the premature return trip and no sleep
tolerable was the memory of the outrageous few hours she'd spent
with a woman who had taught her a couple of things about herself and
what she enjoyed in bed. For Tristan, that was a remarkable revelation,
because, although she didn't consider herself a player, she enjoyed the
company of women. And being twenty-nine and single and planning
to stay that way, at least for a good many more years, she enjoyed the

company of women frequently. So discovering that she liked being fucked senseless by a petite toppy femme in four-inch heels, while her hands were restrained over her head, ranked right up there with some of her most enlightening experiences. So much so she couldn't stop thinking about it—not the woman, who'd been easy to look at and interesting even when they weren't in bed, or the admittedly mind-blowing sex—but just how much she liked being completely *not* in control. She doubted anyone who knew her, including herself, would have ever described her as being happy with someone else calling the shots. But she'd been more than happy having Meg direct the action; she'd been exhilarated.

"So the meeting was a drag, huh?" Charlie Dixon probed.

"Oh yeah. Deadly boring." Tristan craned her neck and grinned up at the six-foot-four mocha-skinned trauma fellow before putting thoughts of hot blondes, power play, and multiple orgasms out of her mind. Charlie only had half a foot on her in terms of height, but he was svelte, the way some dancers were. He always made her feel like a clod with her solid build that required sweating three times a week in the gym and pounding the city streets for ten or twelve miles every few days to keep her body muscular and not just bulky.

"I hear Vegas is a swinging place," Charlie said mournfully as he slumped into a rickety chair at the round table in the center of the room.

"Couldn't prove it by me."

Charlie eyed her suspiciously, but Tristan refused to bite. She'd always found that the guys she worked with accepted her being a lesbian without much fuss, but they were still curious about how she made out with women. Sex was a popular topic around the OR, since there wasn't much to fill the long hours between emergencies most nights except talking about sex and sports. She didn't begrudge the guys their interest, but she didn't play to it either. Maybe she didn't want to spend a lifetime with the women she dated, but they weren't conquests or notches on her bedpost. And if she was seeing more than one woman at a time, she didn't make that a secret with any of her dates. She had nice, friendly, comfortable relationships with her girlfriends, and she wanted to keep it that way. So when the guys hinted for a little kiss and tell, she just smiled and shook her head.

"Say, Charlie," Tristan teased, "how's your wife?"

"Bitching that she never sees me," Charlie replied.

"Can't blame her. It's true, isn't it?" Tristan didn't really mind the long hours, especially now that she had a staff position. She kept an apartment a few blocks from the hospital in West Mount Airy for when she was on call and had fifteen acres of rolling farmland in Bucks County for the weekends when she wasn't. She'd grown up in the Philadelphia suburbs, so a few times a month she joined her parents and one or two of her siblings at their parents' club for dinner or some other social outing. Most of the time she was too busy to think about the fact that she hadn't had a relationship longer than a few weeks for more than a decade, and since she rarely had difficulty finding a date whenever she needed company, she didn't dwell on her chronic single status when she did. She loved her work, she loved women. Life was good.

"I keep telling my wife—one more year," Charlie said. "One more year and I'll be in the big time, just like you."

Tristan laughed.

"Yeah, and look what I'm doing in the middle of the night on a Sunday. Sitting on my ass in the OR lounge waiting for the next—"

Their beepers went off simultaneously, and Tristan grabbed for hers. "Shit."

"There goes the rest of the night," Charlie grumbled as the overhead announced a code red. "The chopper's going out. Bet it's a multiple MVA. Right time of night for it—drunks driving home or tourists coming back from the Shore for work tomorrow. Trying to make time in the middle of the night and then falling asleep. God damn it."

Tristan pulled the trauma beeper off the waistband of her scrub pants and frowned at a number she didn't recognize.

"Huh. Must be a mistake."

❖

At the sound of a knock on her door, Jett McNally, who sat with her back against the wall and her long legs stretched out on the bed, stuck her finger between the pages of the book she was reading and called, "It's open."

Linda, the flight nurse on Jett's medevac team, poked her head in. "Hey, Cap, we've got a scene request. I don't have the details yet, but the first responders are calling for a physician ride-along."

Jett shook her head in amused resignation. She'd explained to Linda she'd never been a captain, and she didn't have a rank anymore, *and* she didn't stand on ceremony anyhow, but Linda insisted on calling her Cap. Healthstar, the medevac company Jett flew for, received two types of requests—scene requests, usually accidents or some other trauma, or transfer requests, transporting patients from one hospital to another. Ordinarily, the medcrew consisted of a nurse and a paramedic, but Jett's EC-145 Eurocopter could hold nine, including the patient, if needed. Once in a while, a physician accompanied them if the patient's condition was extraordinarily precarious. Jett didn't really care what kind of flight she went out on, but she preferred emergencies to transfers. The adrenaline rush of racing against time, of beating the odds, gave her the satisfaction very little else could. When the stakes were high, she felt alive.

"How far away are they?" Jett asked.

"About thirty miles."

Jett tossed her book onto the single bed. When she had started her tour earlier that night, housekeeping hadn't yet been by to clean the flight crews' rooms, so she had changed the sheets and blankets herself. The cover was tucked in so tightly the book bounced. Her DI would have been proud. "See you on deck."

With her flight gear under her arm, Jett hustled down the hall and outside to the rooftop helo deck. One of the medcrew would get the rest of the pertinent medical information. All Jett needed to do was confirm they could fly and then prepare the aircraft. Even though she was flying civilian now, her routine was ingrained after thirteen years in the Army, including a tour in Afghanistan and one in Iraq. She saw no reason to change anything now, because she could go skids up in four to five minutes once the call came in, and whether it was a civilian emergency or combat, every second counted.

When she'd done her walk-around earlier at the start of her twelve-hour tour, she'd reviewed the aircraft's maintenance logs and run through as much of the preflight checklist as she could. She'd also determined that the weather was adequate for flying. Just the same, weather could change in six hours and she was responsible for the safety of her crew. She wouldn't fly in bad weather, even though there were injured to be evacuated. The rule was, you didn't risk three lives for one. She'd taken chances, sure—in combat. All of the pilots had, rather than leave their comrades behind. Those few times she hadn't been able to reach the wounded haunted her still.

Tonight the sky was nearly cloudless, a hot, hazy summer night. The flight was a go. By the time she had suited up, climbed into the cockpit, and run through the rest of her preflight check, Linda and Juan, the paramedic, were waiting, helmets in hand, ready to board.

"Where's the doctor?" Jett yelled from the cockpit.

"Should be here any second," Linda called back.

Jett disliked civilian physicians in her aircraft. They weren't used to flying and weren't used to taking orders. With one aboard, she had one more thing to worry about, but there was nothing she could do about it. The civilian world operated differently than the Army, where rank trumped everything, including education or perceived skills. Despite the fact that her medcrew was trained to handle anything out in the field, if the first responders wanted a physician, then a physician they would get.

At that moment, the double glass doors enclosing the elevator lobby in the far corner of the rooftop opened wide and a woman in pale blue scrubs sprinted out toward them. An assortment of beepers bounced on the waistband of her scrub pants, and a stethoscope danced around her neck. Jett gave her a cursory glance. She appeared young, probably a resident, her body muscular and fit-looking. Her collar-length brunette hair was thick and casually styled. In the harsh lights of the helo deck, her blue eyes stood out in startling contrast to her olive complexion.

"Make sure she gets squared away," Jett called to Linda before starting her engines. Out of the corner of her eye, she saw Linda grab the doctor by the arm, and all three ducked their heads, ran under the spinning rotors, and climbed aboard. After giving them a second to strap in, Jett took the helicopter up from the roof of the main hospital building and headed northwest toward the turnpike. She checked her watch. Four minutes and twenty-five seconds.

She was flying. Life was good, for these few minutes, anyhow.

❖

"What's going on?" Tristan shouted to the woman who had introduced herself as Linda as she pulled the safety harness across her chest. She didn't know either of the flight crew, and all she could see of the pilot was a strong profile, dark eyes, and thick sandy hair sticking out from under the back of her helmet. Tristan had a brief instant to register that the pilot was female and good-looking before her mind honed in on the question of what faced her. All she'd gotten from the paramedic who phoned her was that Healthstar needed a doctor, and Tristan's name was on the top of the roster tonight. She was double-boarded in anesthesia and critical care, like a lot of anesthesia docs, so when her new chief had asked her if she'd take trauma call, she'd said sure. She'd never been up in a helicopter before, and this wasn't exactly what she'd had in mind for her first time. A romantic ride with a beautiful woman around Manhattan, a view of the Statue of Liberty in the background, was more what she had pictured. Even though a glance out the window told her that the scenery from here would be pretty spectacular, knowing what waited for her—or rather, not knowing— definitely killed the mood. The two people beside her were better equipped to deal with most emergencies in the field than she was. Her expertise was hospital-based and most of what she did was in a room filled with high-tech equipment, a multitude of drugs, and sophisticated monitoring devices. "You have a report on the patient?"

"Details are sketchy," Linda replied, handing Tristan a radio headset with a microphone. "It's the governor's daughter-in-law. MVA. Reports are she's in bad shape."

"Shit." Tristan could see it now. Not only would they have to deal with a critically injured patient, they'd probably have news people crawling all over them, documenting everything they did or didn't do. It was a PR nightmare, and as the physician on scene, she was going to get all the attention.

"No kidding," Linda said.

"I'll take a quick look at her airway," Tristan said, "then you two concentrate on securing the victim, just like you would if I wasn't there. Anything you need me to do, tell me. I guess you know not to talk to anyone."

Linda grinned. "Oh yeah, we know all about that. HIPAA HIPAA hooray."

A lot sooner than she expected, Tristan realized they were landing at the edge of a field adjoining the turnpike. The accident scene below pulsed with a life of its own as the lights of a dozen emergency vehicles beat against the night sky. Two other helicopters were setting down simultaneously, hovering like menacing behemoths over the ring of patrol cars, ambulances, and fire engines whose headlights illuminated a jackknifed tractor-trailer and three mangled automobiles. Two forlorn, white-tarp-covered forms lay alone on the oil-stained highway while rescue workers swarmed around the wreckage, tending to the still-living.

The instant the helicopter touched down, Tristan jumped out behind Linda and Juan. Following Linda's directions, she helped unload a stretcher and rapidly piled emergency equipment on top. Then she set off running with them toward the scene.

"We're from PMC," Linda called to a man with a lot of gold braid on his uniform cap who Tristan figured was the incident commander. He held two radios and was waving emergency crews in various directions.

"Over there," he directed.

Tristan looked where he pointed. A cluster of emergency personnel knelt on the highway inside a loose ring of state police. Two news vans were angled on the shoulder of the road and a handful of reporters with television cameras strained against a temporary barricade of yellow crime scene tape, trying to get footage. The patient, assuming she was in there somewhere, was not visible.

"Jesus," Tristan muttered under her breath.

Juan cleared the way by announcing who they were, and the crowd parted enough to let them through. When she finally cleared the protective ring of cops and the assorted curious, Tristan saw a woman in her early thirties, unconscious, bleeding profusely from obvious facial injuries. Judging from the victim's position, Tristan surmised she'd been ejected from a vehicle—probably the overturned Lexus SUV covered with flame retardant foam that was now resting on the median. Her right leg was angulated, a portion of the femur protruding through a long rent in her once-white slacks. With trauma to both her head and lower extremities—bracket injuries—there was a good chance she had internal injuries as well. She already had IVs running in both arms.

Tristan dropped to her knees by the patient's head and placed her stethoscope quickly on both sides of the patient's chest, listening for breath sounds. She heard no air movement on the right. "Pneumothorax on the right."

While Juan positioned the backboard next to the victim, Linda opened the emergency equipment box and pulled out a thin trocar with an attached flexible polyethylene tube connected to a syringe. She pushed aside the remnants of the patient's bloodstained blouse, quickly swabbed a spot below her breast with antiseptic, and pushed the three-inch needle between her ribs. Then she slid the tubing in after it and used the syringe to evacuate the air from the patient's chest. As Tristan listened, breath sounds returned. It was a temporary measure, but it would do for now.

"Better," Tristan said.

Despite the improvement in airflow, the patient's breathing was labored. Fractured ribs. Tristan gently palpated her jaw. The mandible shifted beneath her fingers with a grating sensation. Fractured as well, and probably her mid-face too, if the amount of blood streaming from her nose was any indication. With this much hemorrhage and mobile facial fractures, her airway was very unstable.

"She needs to be intubated."

When Tristan glanced up, Juan already had a laryngoscope out and handed it to her. Using the portable suction, he cleared some of the blood out of the patient's mouth while Tristan inserted the scope's flat metal blade with a light at the end into the back of her throat. Moving the tongue aside and carefully lifting up on the jaw so as not to move the victim's head, Tristan squinted into the oral cavity, hoping to find some landmarks. Unfortunately, with the continued bleeding and massive swelling, she couldn't see a thing. Still searching for anatomical landmarks, she held out her free hand for the endotracheal tube and made a blind pass in the direction of the trachea—or at least where she hoped the trachea was. She really needed to get this tube in, because the last thing she wanted to do was an emergency trach in the field. Too much risk to the patient, especially one with an unstable neck. Tristan eased the tube in a little more. God, she hated blind intubations. *Please, baby, come on.*

Juan pressed his fingers to the patient's throat, and as Tristan continued to push, he nodded and said, "Feels like it's going through the cords."

Tristan persisted until only a few inches of the tube protruded from the patient's mouth. Then she took the ambu bag that Linda had connected to the oxygen tank and carefully hooked it to the end of the endotracheal tube. She squeezed the inflatable bag while Linda listened to the patient's chest.

"You got it," Linda announced with satisfaction. "Good breath sounds on both sides."

"All right then," Tristan said. "Let's get her on the backboard and go."

Tristan stabilized the head, Juan placed a cervical collar, and then on Linda's count, they rolled the patient, slid the backboard underneath her, and strapped her down. While Linda secured the IVs, O2, and other tubes, Juan splinted her leg. Within minutes, they were ready to go. As they worked, Tristan could hear shouted questions from the reporters.

"Is that Marsha Eisman?"

"How badly is she injured?"

"Does the governor know?"

"Is she going to die?"

Tristan ignored everyone. She'd have to face the reporters soon enough, but it wasn't going to be out here. She had far more important things to do than worry about the hospital's PR.

Jett checked her gauges in preparation for takeoff while she waited for the medcrew to return with the patient. She hated this part—the waiting. She wanted to be out there in the field, doing something. But her job was to get her crew out and back again as quickly and as safely as possible. She could and had assisted in retrieving the wounded. But that had been under different circumstances.

"Chief, you shouldn't be out here! Get back to the chopper."

The major had to scream in Jett's face to be heard above the rattle of small arms fire and the explosion of mortar rounds that came with such rapidity the air reverberated with the continuous roar.

"The incoming fire is getting worse. We need to get the wounded aboard," Jett shouted back. She helped the major roll an injured soldier onto the stretcher, grabbed the other end, and lifted. "Another few minutes and we might not be able to get airborne."

"If we don't have a pilot, it won't matter how long we take."

Since the major didn't actually order her to drop the stretcher, Jett just put her head down and ran for her Black Hawk. They loaded the injured and raced back for more. After that, there wasn't time for talk. The medevac crew finally cleared the field of injured and Jett somehow got them up and out in one piece. As soon as she'd landed at the field hospital and the wounded were off-loaded, she'd gone back out again. The hours ran together until finally she was off duty and she staggered, weak-limbed and numb, away from her aircraft for some much-needed food and rack time. She slumped down at a table in the mess tent and mechanically shoveled whatever was on the plate into her mouth, not tasting it, not caring, just knowing she needed it if she was going to wake up in a few hours and do it all again.

"Nice flying, Chief," a dark-haired major a few years Jett's senior said as she sat down across the table from her. She wore medical insignia in addition to her oak cluster, and Jett figured her for one of the medcrews.

"Thank you, ma'am," Jett said, trying to put a little enthusiasm in her voice. She was so tired she could barely see her plate.

"You ought to stay with your aircraft, though. We can't spare any of our pilots."

Jett recognized her now from the first run of the day, which seemed like a week ago after the night she'd had. "Sorry. I didn't recognize you, Major."

The major smiled, and Jett tumbled into the warm blue depths of her eyes. Quickly, she looked away.

"But not sorry you put yourself in the line of fire, is that it, Chief?"

"I was only thinking of the wounded."

"I know." The major extended her hand across the table. "Gail Wallace."

Jett took her hand. Her skin was smooth and warm. Warm like her eyes and her smile. Jett couldn't remember ever seeing anyone so beautiful.

She jolted back to the present as Linda rapped one hand on the side of the helicopter. "All set, Cap."

Jett watched the team lift the stretcher into the aircraft, and when she was sure her crew was secure, she took the helicopter up, Gail's face still vivid in her mind. She couldn't remember how many times she'd glanced back to see Gail behind her, tending the wounded or leaning out the door, manning a gun while Jett took off under fire. She didn't want to think about Gail, not now, not while she was flying.

Flying had always been her escape. As soon as she was airborne, she was free—free from the memory of her father's anger, her mother's misery, her own helplessness. Behind the controls, she *was* in control. Even in the midst of combat, she felt only exhilaration, not fear. She made choices, and no matter the outcome, she would live or die by them. No regrets. Except one.

Ignoring the familiar ache in the pit of her stomach, she gave herself over to the strong, steady hum of the rotors above her head, like the heartbeat of a lover in the dark. Even knowing it wouldn't last, she welcomed the few moments of peace and headed toward home.

Chapter Two

Jett circled the hospital rooftop, checking her speed, her angle of approach, and the wind direction. The trauma team ringed the circle of light below, waiting to converge on the aircraft. Gently, she set her aircraft down precisely in the center of the landing pad. The doors flew open and the medcrew jumped out, guiding the stretcher out as the trauma team raced forward to meet them, heads lowered beneath the sweep of the still-turning rotors. Within a matter of seconds, Jett was alone on the rooftop, her job done. Adrenaline still surged through her bloodstream, and her hands trembled as she locked down her aircraft. With her helmet tucked under her arm, she strode to the stairs and hurried down a level to the suite of rooms reserved for the flight crews. She had her own small on-call room and private bathroom. The door from the hall opened into the room on one side and, opposite, another door led to the lounge area where the pilots and medcrews waited until a request came in. In addition to her bed, her room held a dresser, a small TV with only intermittent reception, a single straight-backed chair, and a tall narrow bookcase. She propped her helmet on her dresser, stripped off her flight suit, and draped it over the back of the chair. Then she went into the bathroom, ran cold water, and doused her head and face.

"Tough flight?"

Jett lifted the tail of her Army-issue green T-shirt and wiped her face, then turned to find the major standing just behind her. "Hot and dusty."

Gail smiled. "Just routine, then."

"Yeah."

"How long have you been here?"

"Four months," Jett said. "This time."

"Regular army?"

"Yes. You?"

"Sixteen toward my twenty," Gail said.

A career Army officer. Jett had thirteen years in herself, but she'd come up a different route. She didn't often have casual conversations with other soldiers. She talked to her fellow pilots, but mostly about the flights or their aircraft. She'd always been a solitary person; living in close proximity with men and women with whom she couldn't be completely honest only made her more reluctant to make connections. That's why it was so odd that she felt comfortable talking to the major. Gail. Her name was Gail.

"Do you want to grab something to eat?" Gail asked.

Jett hesitated, uncertain if she wanted to say yes because a little friendly company would help take her mind off the horrors she witnessed every day, or because Major Gail Wallace made her heart beat faster. Because the last thing she wanted was to want something she couldn't have.

"I should probably catch some rack time," Jett finally said.

Gail studied her silently. "Another time, then."

Jett hesitated a beat or two as Gail turned away. "On the other hand, I can sleep later."

"Wonderful," Gail said, smiling back over her shoulder at Jett. "Come on, then. I'm buying."

A knock at her door brought Jett upright, icy water streaming from her face. She grabbed a towel on her way out of the bathroom.

"Yeah?" she called.

The door opened and Linda stuck her head in. "Do you want to pitch in for pizza? We ordered a bunch."

Jett rubbed her face vigorously and shook the water from her hair. "Okay. Sure. I'll be right out."

"Don't wait too long or there won't be anything left but the boxes."

The door swung closed and Jett sank down on the side of her bed. In the six weeks she'd been at PMC, she hadn't gotten friendly with anyone. The first few weeks she'd spent riding with other pilots to get used to the system and the crews, rotating shifts until her mandatory probation period was over. For the last few weeks she'd been on a regular rotation and flew with the same crew more often than not. Without the division of rank, the civilian crews were more relaxed and informal than she was used to in the military. Until now, she'd been able to avoid a lot of the socializing that went on, but she couldn't keep ducking the people she worked with without being rude. As much as she wanted to stretch out on her bed with her eyes closed and just wait, with her mind blank, until the next call out, she pulled the door open and stepped into the lounge. She could pretend to enjoy herself for a few minutes of meaningless conversation. She was good at pretending.

❖

Tristan piled her beepers and the rest of her gear on the dull brown metal cabinet that served as a bedside table in her on-call room. After calling the page operator with her extension, she kicked off her running shoes and socks, and crawled under the sheet, still in her scrubs. The adrenaline rush was tailing off, and she was hovering on that edge between exhilaration and exhaustion. She needed to get some sleep, but her mind was racing.

More reporters had been waiting when Healthstar arrived back at the hospital. Apparently someone at the scene had called the hospital's powers that be, too, and the chief of anesthesia had been rousted from bed and had met them on the roof with the trauma team. He was in the OR doing the case right now. Tristan wasn't insulted that she'd been bumped, since she would have had to call in backup if she'd gone to the OR. Considering the extent of the patient's injuries, she'd have been in the operating room all night long. Unfortunately, Tristan had been delegated to feed the reporters something so they wouldn't begin gnawing each other's arms off.

After fielding questions for fifteen minutes, she'd finally escaped. The state police had verified that the woman was indeed the governor's daughter-in-law, which meant this story was going to be top news for the foreseeable future. If she was lucky, someone else would have to deal with the press after tonight. With a sigh, she closed her eyes and tried to relax. She could feel her pulse racing, and with nowhere to divert all those jumbled hormones, her body channeled them elsewhere. She felt a familiar stirring between her legs. Great. Wired *and* horny.

If she'd been reasonably certain she wouldn't be interrupted, she might have been tempted to do something about the insistent thrum of excitement in the pit of her stomach, but the last thing she wanted to do was get even more worked up and then get called before she could finish. She'd just have to tough it out, and sooner or later, her mind would shut down and she'd fall asleep. She was just on the verge of drifting off when the phone rang.

"Holmes," she said.

"Hi, Dr. Holmes. It's Mary up in L and D. We need you up here right away."

"I'm on trauma call—I think maybe you want Jerry Edwar—"

"Nope, we want you. Dr. Maguire specifically asked for you if you were in-house."

"Quinn?" Tristan thought Quinn was still in Vegas. "What's she got to do with it?"

"Dr. Blake has been in labor since late last night. She might need to be sectioned and—"

"I'm on my way." Tristan dropped the phone into the cradle and rolled out of bed. After pulling on her socks and running shoes, she clipped her beepers back to her waist and took off at a jog. Labor and Delivery was all the way on the other side of the hospital and up two floors. The obstetricians needed their operating rooms near the newborn nursery and neonatal intensive care units. The doctors and nurses in obstetrics had very little to do with the other hospital staff, with the exception of the pediatric intensivists, who camped out in the neonatal intensive care unit taking care of the critically ill preemies.

Honor Blake is about to deliver. Jesus. Tristan tried to remember how far along Honor was in her pregnancy. Honor was chief of emergency medicine, but Tristan knew Quinn Maguire, Honor's partner, far better. Quinn was now the trauma chief at PMC, but before that she'd been a trauma fellow at the same hospital in Manhattan where Tristan had been an anesthesia resident. Tristan had been surprised along with everyone else when Quinn didn't stay on at St. Michael's in a staff position, but then she'd heard Quinn had fallen in love and settled happily in Philadelphia. Tristan had met Honor a few times when she'd been called to the emergency room. The ER at PMC handled surgical as well as medical emergencies, including trauma. Whenever she was on call, Tristan was down there at least once. Honor was smart and easy to work with, and the last time Tristan had seen her, very pregnant.

Tristan barreled through the double doors at L&D and saw Quinn, wearing rumpled navy scrubs, pacing in front of the nurses' station. From the looks of her, Quinn hadn't been to bed in quite some time. Her jet black hair was disheveled, and even from the end of the hall, her blue eyes appeared bruised. Tristan couldn't remember ever seeing Quinn so agitated. Unlike many surgeons, Quinn was the epitome of calm in the midst of crisis. She rarely raised her voice, almost never lost her temper, and had just about the fastest hands Tristan had ever seen. If *she* ever woke up in the trauma unit needing emergency surgery, she wanted Quinn Maguire to be standing over her.

"Hey, Quinn, I hear you're about to add another member to the family."

Quinn smiled, but it seemed forced. About Tristan's height, she ordinarily moved like an athlete, powerfully graceful. At the moment, she looked like all that power was about to roar down the hall with the force of a flash flood in a desert arroyo. Quinn was surrounded by so much nervous energy the air practically crackled. "Honor's been in labor twenty hours. The baby's holding up, but Honor's getting pretty tired."

Tristan clapped a hand on Quinn's shoulder. "Who's the OB?"

"Deb Brandeis."

"That's good news." Since Tristan spent a lot of time in OB and the NICU doing high-risk anesthesia procedures, she knew Deb well, and Deb was that rare mixture of highly competent and deeply caring. At that moment, a small redhead in baby blue scrubs popped out of a patient room and headed toward them like a whirlwind.

"Hi, Tris."

"Hey, Deb." Tristan grabbed Honor's chart off the counter and flipped through to the medical intake form. As she scanned it, she said, "How are we doing?"

"Moving along. Quinn," Deb said, clasping Quinn's arm. "We just had a dip in the baby's heart rate. It only lasted a few seconds but—"

"No more waiting." Quinn was already halfway down the hall. "Let's *go*."

Tristan watched her. "Jesus, she's wound up."

"Normal for the expectant partner at this point," Deb said easily. "Let me talk to Honor and tell the nurses to get the room set. Are you ready?"

"How's the epidural?" Tristan asked. It was standard to insert a catheter into the lower portion of the spinal canal and inject anesthetic directly around the cord to reduce the pain of the labor contractions. The mother remained awake, and the regional anesthetic avoided the need for potent sedatives that could adversely affect the baby's heart and respiratory rates.

"The block is working great. Honor's been pretty comfortable."

"Then I just need to get her to sign a consent. Anything else I need to know?" Tristan joined Deb on her way down the hall.

"She's healthy. No meds. No significant family history. She had one uncomplicated vaginal delivery about ten years ago."

"Piece of cake, then," Tristan said.

"Yeah, except both parents are doctors." Deb laughed. "Why do I get them all?"

Tristan bumped her shoulder. "Must be because you're the best."

"Must be."

❖

"Don't look so worried, baby," Honor said, mustering as much strength and positive attitude as she could. God, she was tired. She didn't remember this being so much work the first time she did it, but she'd been ten years younger then too. Younger and never touched by tragedy. Everything was different now, and remembering what made life so very good, she grasped Quinn's hand. "I love you. Everything is going to be fine."

"I know." Quinn squatted next to the bed, holding Honor's hand to her cheek as she stroked her damp, sun-streaked hair. Honor's collar-length waves were lusterless, her deep chestnut eyes shadowed with exhaustion. "Deb thinks you've about had enough hard work for one day. I agree."

"She said that dip in the fetal heart rate wasn't anything to worry about," Honor said, her eyes going to the monitor by the bedside that beat at a steady hundred and sixty a minute. "The baby's fine."

"Absolutely," Quinn said, her voice raspy. "But it's time for you to rest, sweetheart."

Honor sighed. "It will take me four times as long to recover if I have a C-section."

Quinn grinned. "Then I guess you'll be out of work eight days instead of two."

"I want to be able to take care of the baby when I get home."

"You will." Quinn leaned over and kissed her forehead. "You'll just need a little extra help for a week or two. Arly and Phyllis will love doing extra baby duty. So will I."

Honor frowned at the mention of their daughter. "Have you talked to Arly? Is she okay? She's not scared, is she?"

"Arly? Scared?" Quinn laughed. "I can't answer her questions fast enough, starting with, why can't she visit, followed by when can she see you and the baby. She's waiting by the phone for my hourly updates. Phyllis said she refused to go to sleep until Phyllis promised to wake her up for my calls."

"Thank God for Phyllis." Honor sighed. They'd all be lost without Arly's grandmother. "Don't tell Arly about the surgery. I'll explain that when I see her."

Quinn kissed her again, this time on the lips. "I won't "

Quinn looked over her shoulder at the knock on the door. Deb entered with Tristan right behind her.

"Honor, honey," Deb said. "It's time to get this little camper some daylight."

"Okay," Honor said, finally giving in to the inevitable. "Hi, Tristan."

"Hi, Honor." Tristan put Honor's chart on the bedside table and swung her stethoscope from around her neck. "Let me listen to your heart and lungs real fast, then I need you to sign this consent."

"I'll see you in the OR." Deb patted Honor's hand and disappeared. A moment later, Tristan followed her out.

"Don't go anywhere, okay?" Honor gripped Quinn's hand more tightly. She was used to being in charge, making hard decisions quickly, and accepting responsibility. She'd been alone, raising her daughter, for a long time before Quinn, but in the last two years she'd come to accept that having a shoulder to lean on when she was tired or frightened didn't make her weak. And that she could always trust Quinn to be there.

"I'll be right beside you the whole way," Quinn whispered.

Honor nodded and closed her eyes. She was safe. And she was ready.

CHAPTER THREE

Quinn stroked Honor's face as she watched over the sterile barricade that separated the operating field from Tristan and all her anesthesia equipment. The scene was as familiar to Quinn as her own face in the mirror, but everything this time was different. The operating field was Honor's abdomen, and as Deb made the first horizontal incision just above the pubis, the bright red blood was Honor's blood. Quinn looked down into Honor's face, trying to put every ounce of the love she felt into her eyes, aware that was all Honor could see. Tristan had allowed Honor to have one arm free so she could hold Quinn's hand, even though ordinarily both arms would be strapped to the supports on either side of the operating table. Quinn squeezed Honor's fingers.

"Everything looks great, sweetheart," Quinn whispered.

Honor smiled sleepily. "Can you see the baby yet?"

"Not yet. Soon."

"Go check. Make sure everything's okay…all the parts."

Quinn laughed quietly. "I will." She glanced at Tristan and raised an eyebrow, not wanting to ask aloud if Honor was doing all right. Ordinarily, she was too busy operating to worry about what anesthesia was doing, and she trusted them to do their job as well as she did hers. Now, with nothing to do but watch everyone else take care of Honor, she felt helpless. Useless. And more anxious than she could ever remember feeling.

"Mama is doing fabulously," Tristan said, leaning down so Honor could hear her.

"Wonderful stuff, whatever you gave me," Honor said, her voice slightly slurred. She frowned. "Shouldn't give me drugs."

Tristan laughed. "Don't worry, Dr. Blake, that baby is going to be out before any of what you're getting gets down there."

"All right then," Honor proclaimed. She blinked and frowned again. "Quinn?"

"Right here." Quinn pulled her gaze away from the surgical field. Deb had delivered the uterus, which glistened a deep purple under the overhead lights, into the field. Deb murmured something to the nurses that Quinn didn't hear, then made a one-inch incision in the lower portion of the distended muscle. Quinn bent down. "The baby's coming in a second, sweetheart."

"Go. Go look."

"Okay. I'll be right back."

Quinn stepped around the barrier and moved behind Deb to the end of the table where the scrub nurse waited with her instruments. "Can you toss me a gown?"

"Here you go, Doctor," the nurse said, holding up a sterile gown for Quinn to slide her arms into. The nurse handed off a packet of sterile gloves, which Quinn pulled on. Because she hadn't scrubbed first, she wasn't technically sterile enough to step up to the operating table, but she could get close enough to Deb to see, and she could hold the baby without any concerns. She watched over Deb's shoulder as Deb inserted a large pair of scissors inside the uterus and cut the rest of the way through the muscular wall. Quinn held her breath, knowing that occasionally the scissors would lacerate the baby as the baby moved around inside the uterus. Then a tremendous gush of blood-tinged fluid poured out. A second later a tiny arm poked out of the gap in the muscular uterine wall. Deb reached into the uterus with one hand, found the head and directed it up toward the incision, and the baby came swimming out on another spurt of blood and amniotic fluid. Quinn had seen cesarean sections dozens of times, but somewhere around the time the scissors had gone into Honor's uterus, she'd stopped breathing. Now her breath whooshed out in a gasp of relief. Then her stomach plummeted. The baby was blue and not breathing. Quinn struggled not to panic.

"Get the suction up," Deb said calmly to the nurse as she deftly clamped and cut the cord, freeing the baby from the placenta, which remained inside Honor's uterus. As soon as Deb inserted the suction catheter inside the baby's nose and mouth, the child cried. The scrub nurse scooped the baby up, turned, and handed it off to the waiting pediatric nurse, who carried the child to a waiting bassinet underneath a heat lamp.

"Is Honor okay?" Quinn murmured close to Deb's ear.

"Doing fine," Deb said. "Go see your baby."

My baby, Quinn thought, suddenly unsteady. How life had changed. A few short years ago she'd seen herself as the star of a big-city hospital trauma center, her life one adrenaline rush after another. She'd never been one for serious relationships, but she hadn't played around either. She'd focused on work. So she hadn't seen a woman in her future. All that had changed when illness had nearly derailed her surgery career permanently. Then, when she thought she'd lost everything, she discovered what had been missing in her life all along. A family of her own. Now she had Honor and Arly and Phyllis. And a new baby. From behind her, she heard Honor's voice, sleepy but clear.

"Quinn? Tell me."

Quinn stood next to the bassinet and looked down, amazed. They hadn't wanted to know the baby's sex until now, and that seemed the least important thing at the moment. "Sweetheart? Solid Apgars—all systems go. Ten fingers, all perfect. Ten toes. Equally perfect. Oh—and some extra little bits, also perfect."

"Little bits? A boy?" Honor laughed. "We have a boy?"

"Yep. Arly has a brother. You can see him in a minute." Quinn watched the nurse record the various vital signs, documenting the baby's neurologic and cardiovascular status. He was crying and waving his arms and legs. He had a thatch of hair, just a shade lighter than Honor's. His eyes were brown. "He's beautiful, sweetheart."

"Tris," Deb said, "can you push some more Pitocin, please?"

Quinn suddenly realized that the room behind her had grown very quiet. She turned, heart pounding. Her eyes went first to the monitor behind Tristan's head. Honor's heart rate was 140, her blood pressure was down, her O2 saturation below normal. For one dizzying second, the room spun, and then Quinn's mind snapped into sharp focus and she took three rapid strides back to the operating table. "What's wrong?"

"She's bleeding and the Pit doesn't seem to be working," Deb said, kneading the uterus between her hands, trying to coax the sluggish muscle to contract. The vessels supplying the uterus were as large as

Quinn's thumb, having increased in size during pregnancy to meet the demands of the growing fetus for blood and nutrients and oxygen. Now the inner surface of the uterus had been stripped of the placenta, and if the muscle didn't contract, closing off the open ends of the vessels, the vast volume of blood that had gone to supply the baby would simply pour out through the opening of the uterus. At this rate, Honor would bleed to death in a matter of minutes.

Quinn wanted to push Deb out of the way and grab a clamp, a suture, anything to stop the river of blood pooling in Honor's abdomen. She forced herself to move to the head of the table, to Honor. Honor's eyes were closed, and she was very pale.

"It's okay, sweetheart," Quinn whispered, kneeling so her face was close to Honor's. "It's going to be okay."

Honor didn't answer.

❖

"You want me to tube her, Deb?" Tristan waved to the circulating nurse to get her attention. "Get an anesthesia tech in here STAT."

God damn it. She hated when an easy case went bad. She hated it *whenever* that happened, but it was always so much worse when it was someone she knew, or the family or friend of someone she knew. This time, she couldn't even think about Quinn just inches away, fear seeping from her pores. Quinn had pulled off her sterile gloves and had one hand on Honor's face. Her fingers trembled, something else Tristan had never seen.

Tristan checked the O2 saturation. It had fallen dangerously low. Now the call was hers, not Deb's. "I'm going to intubate. Where the hell's the tech?"

"I can help," Quinn said, straightening up. "What do you need?"

"Get me a number seven ET tube. Second drawer in my cart," Tristan said without bothering to look up from her drug box. She pulled out ampoules and drew up the medication to paralyze Honor so she could insert the breathing tube into her trachea. "Did someone call down for blood?"

"Do we have a type and screen on her?" Deb called out. "Someone hook up another suction. I can't see anything in here."

"She's A positive," Quinn said. She held the tube next to Tristan's right hand while Tristan inserted the laryngoscope into Honor's mouth to hold her tongue out of the way and expose her epiglottis.

"Nice clear view for a change," Tristan muttered, taking the endotracheal tube lightly between her thumb and first two fingers and easing it past the epiglottis, through the vocal cords, and into the trachea. "Blow up the balloon. Eight cc's."

When Quinn fumbled with the thin plastic tube attached to the balloon at the end of the trach tube, Tristan realized Quinn was in no shape to be assisting her. Carefully, she extracted her laryngoscope while supporting the tube with her other hand. "Here, I'll do it."

"I got it," Quinn said gruffly. "Eight cc's, right?"

"Right."

Quickly, Tristan connected the endotracheal tube to a ventilator, cycled in the appropriate amounts of general anesthetic and oxygen, set the volume on the respirator, and started to relax just a little. There wasn't much she could do now but wait, which was never easy, but Deb was a good surgeon on top of being a good obstetrician. "How are things going over there, Deb?"

"Slowing down, but not enough. How is she?"

"She needs volume, but otherwise looking good."

"Quinn," Deb said, her attention still on the surgical field.

"Yes?" Quinn said sharply.

Tristan felt Quinn stiffen beside her. Someone probably should've gotten Quinn outside, but Tristan wasn't quite certain how anyone would have.

"If I can't get this bleeding stopped in another minute, I'm going to have to do a hysterectomy," Deb said. "You're next of kin. Do you consent?"

"I..." Quinn drew a shaky breath. "Honor and I haven't talked about more kids...I don't know what she wants."

The room was silent except for the sound of the suction removing the blood that continued to flow. Tristan understood that in that moment, Quinn Maguire was no longer a calm, cool, collected trauma chief. She was a woman faced with losing everything that mattered to her, vulnerable and alone.

"You and Honor have two kids, Quinn," Tristan said quietly. "They need Honor. So do you."

Quinn met Tristan's eyes, hers filled with misery.

"Quinn?" Deb repeated.

"Yes," Quinn said firmly. "Yes. Do it."

❖

Tristan stepped off the elevator onto the top floor of the parking garage and blinked in the early morning sun. For a few seconds, she struggled with the disorientation of returning to the normal world, where most people were on their way to work on Monday morning while she was on her way home to bed. At least, she should be on her way home to bed, but she knew she wouldn't be for a while. She'd barely finished with Honor when she'd been called back to trauma admitting. Healthstar had made another run and brought in a second patient from the turnpike accident. Until Tristan's relief had arrived at eight, she'd been in the operating room with a nineteen-year-old girl who'd been trapped in the front seat of her Mazda Miata underneath the back wheels of the tractor-trailer for forty minutes before the EMTs could extricate her. She'd lost her right leg below the knee and might lose the other, if she didn't bleed to death from a ruptured spleen, fractured pelvis, and lacerated inferior vena cava. Her blood pressure had bounced from 40 to 200 with the rapidity of a ping-pong ball in a championship match, keeping Tristan constantly on edge.

Now she was so keyed up she felt sick, and sleep was the last thing she wanted. If she were a drinker, she'd go home and open a bottle of aged Burgundy, but even though her internal clock was upside down, she didn't want a drink. If she had a girlfriend waiting for her, she'd break speed limits to get home and entice her lover into being late for work. Sex always took the edge off her post-call nerves. But if she wanted something quick and easy, she'd have to start calling her sometimes-girlfriends, and the chance of catching any of them at this time of day was unlikely.

She thought back to the woman she'd recently spent the night with—well, part of the night before she'd been called back to Philadelphia. Meg. Meg provided sex for money. The concept wasn't all that strange to Tristan, particularly at the moment. Being able to release the energy that raged along her nerve endings at the same time as she obliterated the images of a devastated body from her mind was something she'd gladly pay for. The problem was, she didn't know where to go or how to go about it. In Las Vegas anything was possible. Unfortunately, Vegas was a long ways away.

She was so busy thinking about Meg, and how it felt to be completely powerless while Meg took her pleasure, she almost walked into the very nice ass bent over the front of a beat-up Jeep that looked like it had been to hell and back, recently.

"Jesus, sorry," Tristan blurted.

A slender woman with thick, sandy hair and midnight blue eyes regarded her without expression. At second glance, she wasn't so much slender as wiry. Her arms, bare below the rolled-up sleeves of her blue shirt, were deeply tanned and corded with muscle. Her hands were flat and broad, her fingers almost blunt with short, neatly trimmed nails. She stood, shoulders squared, her wide full lips compressed into a tight line as she observed Tristan wordlessly.

"Car won't start?" Tristan asked.

"It will, eventually."

Tristan probably should have kept going, because the woman obviously wasn't interested in conversation. But she didn't want to climb into her car alone and go home alone and get into bed alone. She didn't want to *be* alone, not just yet. The night's tragedies, and rare triumph, were too fresh in her mind. So, still pumped up, still wired, and not inclined to be brushed off, she stood her ground "Work in the OR?"

"No."

"Cath Lab?"

A head shake.

"ER. No, I would've seen you down there." Tristan held out her hand. "I'm Tristan Holmes. Anesthesia."

"I know."

The woman shook Tristan's hand while Tristan waited for a name. For more information. For something she couldn't even identify. As if finally remembering what was expected of her, the woman said, "I'm Jett McNally. I fly for Healthstar. I flew the run you were on earlier tonight—out to the turnpike."

"Oh, sorry," Tristan said. "I didn't recognize you without the helmet."

"No need to apologize."

"Some mess out there tonight."

"Yeah."

"How many runs did you end up doing?"

"Three."

Silence fell again. Tristan knew she should leave. But she didn't have a good reason to, having nowhere to go, and no one waiting. And this pilot and she had something in common—they'd shared something meaningful without even knowing each other's names—the patient they'd treated, the devastation they'd witnessed out on the turnpike, and maybe the aftermath of tragedy they'd helped avert. The pilot wasn't anything at all like the women Tristan usually gravitated toward—the fun-loving, outgoing, sparkling kind of women who you could tell just from looking at them enjoyed a good time. This woman's eyes were wary. Everything about her sent out "keep your distance" signals.

Funny, Tristan thought, that she should meet two women in the course of just a few days' time who telegraphed *stay away*, and really meant it. But she had persisted with Meg and those few hours had been more exciting, and more satisfying, than all the easy connections she'd had in the last few years. This pilot wasn't actually running away, as Meg had at first. She didn't need to. The barriers around her couldn't have been more visible if they'd been constructed of stone, and Tristan couldn't help but wonder what she might learn if she broke through them. She inclined her head toward the Jeep and the open hood. "You need a ride somewhere?"

"No, I'm fine. Aren't you just coming off shift?"

"Yeah. Long night."

"You're probably ready for some rack ti—you must be tired."

"I'm not. Are you?"

"No." Jett closed the hood and dusted off her hands before sliding them into the pockets of her loose, faded green fatigue pants. "Wide awake."

"Me too." Tristan grinned. "My car's over there. How about some breakfast?"

Jett looked like she was going to refuse, and she glanced at the sky as if expecting something to appear. After a few seconds she met Tristan's eyes. "Coffee would be good."

CHAPTER FOUR

A s she awoke, Honor was aware of three things. Her throat was very dry, a sharp pain lanced through her abdomen each time she took a breath, and wherever she was, it was very very quiet. Shouldn't the delivery room be noisier? Why wasn't the baby crying? God, the baby! She jerked and tried to sit up. A hand on her shoulder restrained her.

"Hey, take it easy, sweetheart," Quinn whispered. "Everything is okay."

Honor struggled to focus on Quinn's face. "Where's the baby?"

"He's in the nursery, all tucked up, nice and warm. He's fine."

"Where am I?"

"You're in your room, on the maternity ward."

Honor frowned. "I don't remember getting here."

"You've been asleep for a while."

"How long is a while?" Honor reached for Quinn's hand and could barely raise her arm. She was more tired now than she'd been after twenty hours of unrelenting labor. "Baby, you look terrible. Is he really all right?"

"Yes," Quinn said immediately. "I wouldn't keep something like that from you. You know that." Quinn grinned. "He looks just like you."

Honor laughed, then stopped abruptly as her incision screamed in protest. "You can't possibly know that. Babies are all generic at this age."

"He is not. He's got your hair and your eyes. I think he's got Arly's chin, though."

"She's going to love that. Be sure to tell her."

"I already did. Three times."

"Have you had any sleep at all?"

"I've been taking naps," Quinn said, but she looked away when she answered.

"You are *such* a terrible liar," Honor said.

"Okay. I've been thinking about taking a nap." Quinn leaned over and kissed Honor on the forehead. "How are you feeling? Sore?"

"A little. I'm so angry about needing this damn C-section. I didn't have any problem with Arly."

"Well, it was hardly your fault," Quinn said gently. "Deb thought the head became disengaged during labor and shifted out of the birth canal. That's why you couldn't deliver him vaginally."

"At least it's not the way it used to be. A C-section doesn't necessarily mean I'll need one the next time. If we have another one." Honor laughed and gripped Quinn's hand harder. "If you don't lose your mind the first couple of years. You had it easy coming on board when Arly was eight."

"Don't worry, I'm up for it," Quinn said, her voice rough.

Honor studied her, then shifted over, moving slowly and carefully. She patted the bed beside her. "Sit down and tell me what's wrong."

When Quinn looked like she was going to protest, Honor said, "Please, Quinn."

Sighing, Quinn settled on the edge of the bed and leaned over, her arm on the far side of Honor's hips. She was careful not to put any weight on Honor's body. "You had a lot of bleeding after the baby was delivered."

"How much bleeding?" Honor kept her voice steady but she knew Quinn could feel her trembling.

"Five units' worth."

"God." Honor closed her eyes for a second. "Did I get blood?"

Quinn nodded.

"What about Hep C or HIV? Quinn, am I going to be able to nurse?"

"We used the two units you had banked and made up the difference with saline. They're crossing a unit from me against yours right now." Quinn caressed Honor's hip. "I should be ready to give you another unit in a few days, but you're going to be light-headed if you try to get out of bed right away, no matter what."

"But I can breastfeed?"

"Yes. Deb wasn't happy about not giving you more blood, but I knew how much you wanted to nurse the baby."

"Thank you." Honor kissed Quinn's fingers. "I'm glad you were there."

When Quinn didn't answer, Honor got a sinking feeling in her stomach. "There's more you're not telling me."

"No," Quinn said. "I'm glad I was there too."

"But something else happened."

Quinn sighed. "Listen, they're going to bring the baby in soon. All that matters is that he's fine and you're fine."

"Do you really think that's going to work?"

"Not really. But I thought you might be tired enough that I could sneak it by you."

"You're the one who's really tired if you believe that," Honor said with a weary smile. "So give me the rest of it."

"Tristan did a great job of stabilizing you while all this was going on, but you were bleeding pretty heavily. Deb thought you needed a hysterectomy."

Honor caught her breath. "Oh, Quinn."

"No! No, Honor." Quinn leaned down, cupping Honor's face with one hand. "We didn't do it. She was just about to. I…I told her to go ahead. Then the bleeding just stopped." She closed her eyes. "I'm sorry, Honor."

"Baby," Honor whispered. She threaded her fingers through Quinn's hair and stroked her neck. "You don't have anything to be sorry about. You made the right decision. I'm glad Deb didn't need to do it, but if she had, it would have been okay. The most important thing is being with you." Quinn turned her face away, but not before Honor saw her tears. "Lie down next to me."

"Honor, I'll hurt you," Quinn said, her voice raspy.

"You could never hurt me. And I need you. Just for a minute. Please."

Quinn stretched out on her side on top of the covers. Honor stroked her face as Quinn buried her face in the curve of Honor's neck. "I love you so much. I was afraid…"

"It's all right," Honor soothed. She knew firsthand the agony of having love wrenched from her grasp. She didn't want Quinn to feel one moment of that pain. "I'm right here, and everything is all right."

"I can't even imagine being without you," Quinn gasped. "I don't know how you…"

Honor knew what Quinn didn't want to say. They had talked about Terry, the love Honor had lost, many times, and each time they talked about her, Honor's pain lessened. She would never get over the pain of losing her, but the agony of living without her diminished with each day she spent loving and being loved by Quinn. Honor loved Quinn even more because Quinn suffered for her loss, even though Honor didn't want her to. "You don't have to think about it, baby, because I'm here with you. And I hope you never have to think about it." She kissed the top of Quinn's head. "But you would have Arly, like I did, and for a while that would be enough reason to go on. And now you'll have…what's-his-name too."

Quinn laughed and sat up, rubbing her tears away with the bottom of her scrub shirt.

"If you think I'm too weak to notice that you don't have anything on underneath that shirt, pull it up again and see what happens to you," Honor said. When Quinn wasn't coaching softball or soccer or some other sport, she was working out at the gym, and her body was beautiful. Honor constantly found herself turning around in the morning and catching a glimpse of Quinn naked, and being suddenly overcome by a wave of unmitigated lust. It was a wonderful thing to experience after countless mornings of waking beside her.

"Maybe I should take my shirt off altogether before I tell you what I did," Quinn said.

"Trying to distract me?"

Quinn nodded.

Honor shook her head. "It won't work. I can do two things at once, and even though it's hard for me to think when I'm looking at you naked, I'll manage."

"I let Arly pick the baby's name."

"Say that again."

"She was really excited, and I could tell that she felt left out, and..."

"Oh my God," Honor whispered, imagining calling her son Beavis or SpongeBob or something equally horrifying for the rest of his days. Of course, they hadn't signed a birth certificate yet, so there was still time to change things. But Arly would be so upset.

"She picked Jack."

"Jack?" Honor asked quietly.

Quinn nodded.

"Jack was Terry's father's name."

"I know. When Arly picked her grandfather's name, Phyllis cried."

"Oh, Quinn," Honor said. "We talked about naming him after *your* father if it was a boy."

"Phyllis is Arly's grandmother and a big part of the family," Quinn said. "We wouldn't make it a week without her. I think naming our son Jack is just fine. If my father is upset, which he won't be, we can just have another one."

Honor started to cry, something she never did. But she didn't mind the tears, because all she felt was happy. "That's easy for you to say."

Quinn leaned down and kissed her. "I love you. What do you say I go get Jack?"

"Yes, but hurry back. I already miss you."

Jett watched Tristan out of the corner of her eye as Tristan drove, trying to figure out what it was about her that had made her say yes to an offer from a virtual stranger. It wasn't as if she longed for company. She didn't. She had an apartment in a sprawling complex on Lincoln Drive, where she could go for days, even weeks, without speaking to anyone and not minding. When she arrived home after her shift, she was usually too wound up to sleep right away, but she'd gotten used to that after spending months in the desert where sleep was something to be squeezed in between flights, if the heat wasn't too bad and she could actually stay inside a tent for an hour or two. She'd learned to stay awake, running on adrenaline and caffeine and nerves. Unlike some of her fellow soldiers, she avoided drugs except for a drink now and then, and even that she monitored. Her father had been a mean drunk, and she'd often borne the brunt of his discontent. She wasn't going to be like him, even if she did sometimes have to ride the whirlwind of her own wild temperament with nothing to blunt its force. If she was careful, if she kept tight control, she'd be fine.

In the Army there was always more work. Now when she had to take time off and she couldn't sleep and she couldn't shut off the pictures in her head, she restored antique timepieces. She preferred watches because the mechanisms were so small that she had to focus all her energy on manipulating the tiny parts. She couldn't think about anything else then—not about where she'd been, or where she was going, or what she'd lost.

Flying was the same. Her aircraft, her crew, and her passengers required every bit of her concentration, and while she was flying, she had no past and no future. Only the now. No memories to expunge, no dreams to discard. In between flights, she waited for those moments to come again.

Maybe she'd said yes to this adventure because Tristan hadn't been put off by her shields. Even now, Tristan seemed content to drive and allow silence to fall between them. Jett was grateful for that. She wasn't any good at small talk. She had never understood the point of discussing things that had no meaning, and now, other than her job, nothing much had meaning for her. She wondered what would happen when the silence no longer protected her.

Tristan turned right onto School House Lane. She rented the second floor of an old Victorian, half a block down the street from Honor and Quinn. Quinn had actually found the listing for her right after Tristan had accepted the position at PMC. She hadn't had time to take Quinn up on her offer of dinner at Quinn and Honor's home, even though they were practically next-door neighbors. But she *had* agreed to help Quinn coach a soccer team. That seemed like the least she could do to say thanks for all Quinn's help. The fields where she was due to start coaching soccer in another week were a quarter of a mile in the other direction. Despite being within the city limits, the residential area had an old-fashioned neighborhood feel to it. She recognized the cars parked on her street, and the kids who ran up and down the sidewalk in the late afternoon, and the women carrying shopping bags back from the Super Fresh, and the guys with six-packs tucked under their arms. The working-class neighborhood was nothing like the enclave where she'd been raised, with manicured lawns and circular drives guarded by stone animals. She liked it much better where she was now.

"This is it," Tristan said as she pulled into the curb in front of the sprawling three-story white structure with a wide front porch at the end of a flagstone walkway.

Jett looked out her window and frowned. "This looks like your house."

"Yes." Tristan turned off the engine and pulled her keys from the ignition. "I've got coffee and some frozen coffee cake. Hungry?"

"You didn't say you were going to cook."

Tristan grinned. "I was afraid to scare you away. Besides, I'm not cooking. I'm microwaving."

Jett hesitated but Tristan was already out of the car and headed around to the sidewalk. At the very least, Jett had to get out of the vehicle, and when she did, she couldn't just walk away. Wasn't really sure she wanted to. Despite Tristan's super-confident, take-charge manner, Jett didn't feel manipulated. Tristan pushed, but she was so casually open about it, Jett was more curious than wary.

"I don't want you to go to any trouble," Jett said, climbing out and closing the door behind her. She glanced up the street, pretty certain she knew where she was. Probably no more than a mile or two from her apartment complex. She could easily walk. She could say she was more tired than she'd realized, thank this woman for the ride, and just walk away. That would be the smart thing to do. She didn't move.

Tristan tilted her head and regarded Jett thoughtfully. She seemed ready to bolt. Tristan couldn't tell if it was simple shyness, or something else. Jett didn't look like the shy type. Women who flew medevac helicopters weren't usually shy and retiring, any more than surgeons or anesthesiologists were. When you measured life or death in seconds, there wasn't much room for uncertainty. "It's no trouble. As I recall, I invited you."

"Just the same."

"Just the same, let's go get some coffee." Tristan turned and walked away.

Left with no choice, Jett followed her up the sidewalk, noting her long, powerful strides. Her hair shimmered like black gold in the sunlight, and her broad shoulders, narrow waist, and muscular hips and legs made Jett wonder if she was a swimmer. She had the body for it. The thought was disconcerting because Jett wasn't accustomed to noticing women's bodies. In the service, she'd trained herself not to. She slowed as she approached the white stone steps that led up to the porch, thinking about all the times in her life she'd been faced with the choice between stepping into the unknown, or retreating into safety. She almost always chose the riskier path because the excitement of challenge, the rush of danger, satisfied her in a visceral way. The only other thing that came close to the intensity of that feeling was sex, and she hadn't allowed herself that in a long time. There was danger, and then there was foolhardiness.

"So," Tristan said, already across the porch and holding open the door for Jett, "I'm on the second floor."

Once again, the choice seemed clear. Jett climbed the steps and went through the door into a long hallway carpeted in a faded, dark floral print, with a staircase at the far end. She climbed up one floor and waited for Tristan on the landing.

"Where did you learn to fly?" Tristan asked as she extracted her keys.

"The Army."

"No kidding. How long have you been out?"

Jett didn't answer and Tristan decided it wasn't the time to push. She slipped past Jett to open the door to her apartment. When she did, their bodies briefly touched. Instantly, her system went on full alert. All the pent-up urgency and excitement of the previous night coalesced into a simmering knot of arousal in the pit of her stomach. She'd been thinking about sex since she left the hospital, and this pilot was one attractive woman. Of course, she had no idea what Jett's interests were, and why she was even thinking about it, she wasn't sure. Jett hadn't given off a single vibe in that direction, but telling her body that was pointless. Mentally sighing, Tristan opened her door and stepped inside. She smiled at Jett. "Come on in."

❖

"I'm awake," Honor called at the soft knocking on her door. She smothered a smile when she saw her best friend Linda and frowned at the small, trim blonde instead. "Oh sure, now you show up. When all the hard work is done."

Linda, in jeans and a sleeveless yellow blouse, glanced around the room. "Where's Quinn?"

"I finally got her to leave. She promised to take a nap in the trauma call room until the next feeding. Did you hear?"

"Uh-huh. A boy." Linda perched carefully on the foot of Honor's bed. "That's wonderful, honey."

"I wish you could've been here."

"I'm sorry. I would have been, but this flu or whatever is going around has knocked out half the staff and I got called to work last night. Then it was a zoo. We spent all night in the air."

"Right, and we all know how much you hate flying around in that helicopter." Honor wasn't really angry, or even hurt, but it still bothered her a little bit that Linda had left the emergency room after years of being one of the senior charge nurses to join the medevac crew when the hospital had been approved as a flight base. She missed Linda. Not just her competence, but her friendship. Even though they lived right around the corner from each other, their schedules often didn't match, and even when they did, Linda had a toddler of her own at home, which made impromptu socializing difficult.

"Well, the scenery is nice," Linda said, grinning.

Honor groaned. "Do you still have the hots for that new pilot?"

"Only metaphorically. You know I'm completely faithful in mind and body."

"I know you can't walk past a good-looking butch without feeling a tingle."

"Wait just a second." Linda lifted her wrist and pretended to feel for her pulse. "Yep. Still got one, so I guess you're right."

"You are so full of it. So, are you still flying with her?"

"The mysterious, and yummy, Jett McNally?" Linda gave a satisfied smirk. "Not only am I still flying with her, I got her to eat pizza with the gang last night."

"Why are you so bound and determined to get her to socialize?"

Linda suddenly looked serious. "She seems sad. I hate that."

"I love you, you know that? But you can't fix everyone."

"Maybe, maybe not. Sometimes it's just a matter of giving fate a helping hand."

"Oh no." Honor knew Linda's penchant for matchmaking and

thought ahead to the pre-playoff softball bash Linda and Robin always hosted. "Don't tell me you invited her to the party?"

"I didn't," Linda said with a note of excitement. "But it's a really good idea. After all, it worked with you and Quinn."

"And just exactly who do you plan on fixing her up with?"

"I haven't worked that out yet. Mandy?"

At the thought of the much younger, incredibly well-built, seductive blonde, Honor felt her temperature climbing. "If you bring *her* within five miles of my lover, there will be bloodshed."

Linda laughed. "Like Quinn would even notice."

"The problem is, Quinn *doesn't* notice. Even when Mandy is practically molesting her. And God, she just won't quit."

"Well, it hasn't even been two years. Obviously, Mandy is slow."

"One thing she isn't is slow," Honor snarled.

"All right. Don't get worked up. It's not good for the baby when you're breastfeeding."

"That's an old wives' tale," Honor muttered, fussing with her covers and feeling decidedly fat and frumpy all of a sudden. "And now with this damn incision, it's going to take twice as long before we can have sex."

Linda leaned over and whispered dramatically, "For *you* to have sex. Not for Quinn. Even right after the babies are born, Robin always manages to take care of m—"

"All right," Honor interrupted sharply. "I get the picture."

"You can't really think Quinn minds?"

Honor glowered. "I mind. Do you have any idea what it's like watching her walk around in the morning and not being able to do anything about it?"

"Oh God. I wish." Linda patted Honor's leg. "Let me go check with the nurses and see if it's time for Jack's feeding. I want to watch."

"Pervert." Honor relaxed as Linda started for the door. "You're the best medicine I could possibly have, next to burning up the sheets with Quinn, that is."

Linda turned from the door and waggled her eyebrows. "Always glad to take care of a woman in need."

CHAPTER FIVE

Here you go." Tristan handed Jett a cup of coffee, set the coffee cake she'd nuked on a side table, and stretched out on a lounge chair next to the one Jett occupied on the small porch off her kitchen. The second-story porch overlooked a grassy backyard. A large old oak grew beside the house, its massive branches shading the area where they sat.

"Thanks."

Tristan leaned her head back and sighed. The sky, visible through the canopy of green, was robin's egg blue and crystal clear. In two hours, the day would have surrendered to the July heat, but right now, she felt the slightest hint of a breeze. She was almost too tired to think, and her mind wandered in the midst of her pleasant torpor. She remembered all those carefree, lazy summer days of her youth, when the greatest crisis in her life was whether a particular girl might be interested in her "that way." Now, what seemed like a lifetime later, she lay next to a woman still wondering the same thing. All that had changed was her—she still asked the question, but somewhere along the way she'd stopped looking for anything beyond the simple answer. If it was yes, they'd share a few hours' pleasure. If no, she'd move on. And right now she was too damn tired to wonder why that was.

She turned her head and regarded Jett's face in profile. Her hair was a mix of dark blond verging on golden brown, but she bet when she was younger it was cornsilk yellow. Up close she could make out the fine lines around her deep blue eyes. Those and her dark tan indicated a lot of time in the sun. "Where are you from?"

If the seeming non sequitur bothered Jett, she didn't give any indication. She answered, "New York."

"City?"

"State. Up near the Vermont border."

"Farmers?"

Jett shook her head and sipped her coffee. "In a way. My family has an upland apple orchard. Been in the family for a couple of generations."

"But you didn't want to be a farmer?"

"No," Jett said softly. "I wanted to fly."

Tristan drew her leg up onto the lounge chair and turned on her side, curling one arm under her head. The bones beneath Jett's smooth, bronzed skin were sharply carved, the hollows beneath her cheekbones shadowed even in sunlight. Her nose was strong and straight, the bridge high, nearly Roman. She wasn't beautiful, or handsome, but her face was captivating. "How did you know that? That you wanted to fly?"

"I went up in a crop duster with one of the neighbors when I was seven. She—"

"She?"

Jett nodded, a faint smile breaking the straight line of her mouth. "She worked for herself out of a barn and a tiny airstrip down the road from us. She let me take the rudder the first time we went up."

When Jett didn't continue, Tristan said, "And that's all it took?"

Jett sipped her coffee. "Yeah."

"What did you like about it?"

"Why are you asking?"

Tristan wasn't put off by the question, because Jett sounded more confused than put out. "I was just thinking about how oblivious I was when I was young, and how all the things I thought were important weren't really."

Jett laughed. "Are you feeling mellow post call?"

"Yes," Tristan murmured. "How could you tell?"

"Sometimes when you get stripped down to the bone, you look around and everything feels different, doesn't it?"

Tristan recognized the wistful edge of pain in Jett's voice and knew it came from having seen too much tragedy. "You were in the war, weren't you?"

"Two tours."

"How long have you been back?"

"A couple of months." Jett placed her coffee cup on the table and her expression became remote.

The movement had an edge of finality to it, and Tristan recognized once again that the subject was off-limits. "You didn't tell me what hooked you on flying."

Jett didn't think anyone had ever asked her that before. When her brothers realized how much she loved to go up in the rickety single-engine plane with Elenor Brundidge, skimming low over miles of green while spraying the cornfields, they'd tried to convince her father not to let her go. That had been one of the few times she could ever remember her mother taking up for her in the face of the angry, sullen men in the family. Then in the Army everyone was too busy making her prove she could do the job to care why she wanted to. Other pilots had their own reasons for loving to fly and rarely discussed it.

Jett glanced at Tristan. She looked a little sleepy, lying there in the sun, her hair tousled and her gently questioning dark eyes regarding her steadily. Tristan's arm still curled beneath her head, but when she smiled lazily, Jett almost sensed Tristan reaching out to touch her. She'd never felt anything quite like the pull of that invisible caress. Maybe that was why she answered.

"The very first time I went up, I had the feeling I could keep going forever and never touch down."

"An adventurous spirit?" Tristan watched Jett gesture with her hands as she spoke—gentle, eloquent movements in sharp contrast to the strength evident in her wide palms and muscular fingers. Tristan remembered the helicopter hurtling through the dark only hours before, only now she could imagine Jett guiding it with those powerful, commanding hands. Her stomach tightened at the image of those hands stripping her bare, those fingers demanding and sure. Tristan took a long breath and banished the fantasy. She couldn't help what her body craved, but she really wanted to know why Jett loved to fly, because she sensed that was a big part of who she was. And she wanted to know who she was. "Wanderlust?"

"Maybe. I never felt like I really fit in where I was." Jett laughed shortly, sounding raspy, as if she were out of practice. "More likely I wanted to escape my two older brothers. Somehow, I always ended up doing half their chores."

From the bitter edge to her words, Tristan suspected there was more she wanted to escape, but she didn't probe. When Jett fell silent, Tristan missed their brief moment of connection. "I understand the sibling thing. I've got three sisters, all beautiful, all successful, all super straight. We didn't have that much in common."

"You can't be that much different than them," Jett said, turning slightly to face Tristan. "You've got two of the three covered."

Tristan had been hit on enough times in her life to know when she *wasn't* being hit on. She might have been disappointed except for the unexpected surge of pleasure at Jett's words. She rarely thought about her own appearance or how women looked at her. She wasn't often called beautiful, although her appearance did sometimes elicit comments. She had her Greek mother to thank for her dark Mediterranean hair and skin coloring and her English father for her blue eyes. Either parent could be responsible for her fiery temperament. Her mother blamed her father for her *womanizing*, as she called Tristan's lack of a regular girlfriend, which only made her father laugh. For his part, he insisted her stubbornness came totally from her mother. They both claimed credit for her brains and her passion. They hadn't always been happy about her choices, and it hadn't helped that her sisters all led storybook lives.

"I love them," Tristan said, "but I wish I'd discovered airplanes when I was younger. There were plenty of times I wanted to disappear." Aware that Jett was still watching her, Tristan tried to sound casual. "Did I mention that I'm a lesbian?"

"No."

"I am."

"Was that a problem for them?" Jett asked. "Your family, I mean."

"I pretty much knew the way I felt when I was in high school, so I told them. It didn't exactly go over well. It took me quite a while to convince them it wasn't a phase." Tristan thought back to the heated discussions with her parents, who were convinced that she was just trying to be different from her sisters. And her sisters all wanted her to be like them. But she wasn't like them, and never could be. "The first few years were interesting. My sisters kept trying to fix me up on dates until I was almost out of college. When they didn't wear me down, we all reached a truce."

"So you still see them?"

"My family?" Tristan nodded. "How about you?"

"Not so much."

Shadows eclipsed Jett's sharply etched features, and Tristan imagined the story wasn't a happy one. Jett's gaze had drifted to some distant point in the yard, and her body had become unnaturally still—almost frozen. Tristan felt as if Jett was behind a wall of invisible glass, and if she tried to touch her, she would not be able to. That feeling of being locked outside made her want to touch her all the more.

With a shake of her head, dispelling the irrational urge, Tristan said, "Can I get you more coffee, or are you going to be too wired to sleep?"

Jett tilted her head back to look up into Tristan's face. "I'll sleep. How about you?"

If Jett had been any other woman, Tristan would have tried out a line. *I'll sleep better if you're with me. I won't have any trouble falling asleep if you join me for a little workout first. I'm sure you can think of a way to put me to sleep.* Practiced lines designed to let a woman know she was interested. The kind of line that suggested an isolated encounter, a mutually enjoyable diversion, perhaps even the first of a few hot sweaty afternoons stolen from the relentless demands of work that were constant reminders of the fragility and, at times, the inhumanity of life.

"Coffee never keeps me awake," Tristan said instead. She thought Jett was a lesbian, but she'd guessed wrong before. That wasn't what kept her from making a suggestive response, however. And it certainly wasn't because she didn't find Jett attractive. A few days before, she would have sworn she knew exactly what she liked in bed, and the kind of woman she wanted. Those brief few hours of submitting to another woman's desire had taught her that there was more than one way to give pleasure. Or to receive it. When Tristan looked at Jett, she imagined herself beneath that lean, strong body, with Jett inside her. Silently groaning, Tristan forced the image from her mind. She was just exhausted after two nights without sleep, which was why her bodily urges seemed to be running rampant. Jett gave off very clear unavailable vibes, that was easy to see. Why, Tristan wasn't sure, but she'd like to find out.

"I'm not in any hurry to go to bed," Tristan said. "So you're more than welcome to stay."

"I shouldn't." Jett stood.

"Do you need a ride?"

"No, I'm not that far. Thanks for the coffee." She hesitated. "And for the company."

"Any time," Tristan said as she walked Jett to the door. As she said it, she realized she meant it. But she doubted she'd have another opportunity.

Jett was gone before she even left the apartment.

❖

"I heard it was bad out there tonight. Are you okay?"

"Fine." Jett braced one arm against the side of the supply shed. Even with the non-reflective paint, the metal was burning hot to the touch. Registering the discomfort through a haze of mental and physical exhaustion, she jerked her hand away.

Gail murmured in concern and grasped Jett's arm, turning her hand over and cradling it in her palm. "That's going to blister if we don't put some ointment on it. Let's go to the med tent."

"It's okay."

"No," Gail said slowly. "It's not." She stepped closer, brushing the hair from Jett's forehead as she continued to hold her hand. She rubbed her thumb lightly over Jett's cheekbone. "And neither are you. Are you sleeping?"

Jett barked out a laugh. "Is anyone?"

The bombing had picked up, and the noise and ever-present specter of death made sleeping more than an hour or two at a time impossible. Worse, the casualty rate had risen and more and more of the injured she transported were critical. Even those who were likely to recover would never be the same. Life as they knew it, as *she* knew it, was forever changed.

"Come on," Gail said. "Let's go to my tent."

Jett glanced around quickly, concerned that someone might have heard them. Even though the conversation was completely innocent, as was the invitation, she wasn't so certain about her feelings.

Jett woke up with the sun in her eyes, and for a few seconds, she didn't know where she was. She jerked upright, sweeping her surroundings, reaching for the weapon that was no longer there. She was in her room. In her apartment. Safe. She gulped in a lungful of air and let it out more slowly, assessing her situation. She was naked. The cheap plastic clock-radio on the narrow, plain pine dresser said 4:30 p.m. Monday afternoon. She was due back on shift in two and a half hours. Wondering how to fill the time, she stretched out on top of her bed again. A faint breeze came through the partially open window, cooling the sweat on her skin. Absently, she rubbed her hand over her chest and down her abdomen. The breeze and the thought of coffee made her think of the morning, and of Tristan stretched out beside her on the porch, relaxing with a mug balanced on her thigh.

That hour with Tristan was the most time she had spent alone with anyone in months, and to her surprise, she'd been comfortable. Tristan had a way of drawing her out, with her easy smile and her understated confidence. Somehow, Tristan had gotten her to talk about one of the few good things in her childhood. She hadn't thought about flying with Elenor in years and years.

Maybe opening up to Tristan had been easy because they were both tired. Or maybe it was easy because there was nothing to explain. Medicine and war weren't all that far apart. Tristan had seen tragedy and defeat up close too. So maybe Tristan knew that at the end of the day, a lounge chair on a tiny porch beneath a leafy tree, quiet words wafting away on a breeze, was as close to peace as she could get.

Jett replayed the conversation and wondered what the three beautiful sisters looked like, that Tristan would somehow distinguish herself from them. Because Tristan was gorgeous. Smiling at the memory of Tristan and the lazy morning, Jett turned on her side and closed her eyes. She didn't expect to sleep, but she was wrong.

CHAPTER SIX

After the fourth turn around her living room, Tristan grabbed her ID from the small table inside her door, stuffed her keys in the pocket of her jeans, and took to the streets. She wouldn't be on call again until the following night. Twenty-four hours with nothing to do. She had plenty to do, actually, but grocery shopping, laundry, or even an evening round of golf with her father were not on her list. What *was* on her list—right up there at the top, as usual—was a good meal, a bottle of vintage wine, and a passionate woman.

She had choices there. She could call Candace, or Darla, or Sue. All bright, engaging women who knew how to have a good time. None of them asked where she went or who she saw when she wasn't with them. If they already had dates, they just said so along with "maybe next time." The same worked in reverse. She had no hold on them, and wanted none. When they were apart, she didn't think about them, except now and then in the midst of an enjoyable fantasy.

Tristan checked her watch. Hell. Six p.m. Too late to call now with a dinner invitation. Even she couldn't pass that off as anything other than an excuse for sex. She might be casual about her relationships, but she genuinely liked the women she dated too much to treat them like coin-operated vibrating beds. She stopped on the sidewalk by her car, considering alternatives. She could drive to Belmont Plateau, a huge grassy expanse in the center of Fairmont Park where the women's summer softball league played three nights a week and practically all weekend from March until August. She enjoyed watching the games, but she liked watching the women even more. And she could almost always find company for the rest of the night, if she still needed to unwind.

She dug out her keys and tossed them in the air a few times, staring moodily at her twelve-year-old Saab. After four years of medical school, four years of residency, and one year of critical care fellowship, she ought to be able to sleep any time of the day or night. Usually she could, but not today. She'd been restless from the time she lay down shortly after Jett left. She'd tossed, she'd turned, she'd fallen into an uneasy sleep only to awaken every hour. Jittery and wired, she couldn't relax. She thought about sex, but she didn't feel like doing anything about it herself. She was *still* thinking about sex, but she didn't feel like pursuing the usual avenues. She was not herself.

Leaning against the fender, she stared at her running shoes and fondled her keys. Try as she might, she couldn't figure out what the hell was wrong with her. Jesus, she was really slipping. Why the hell hadn't she asked Jett for her number?

"Like that would've done me any good," she muttered. She pushed off from her car and started to walk. With the setting sun at her back and the neighborhood sounds surrounding her, the stretch of her muscles quelled the jangling of her nerves and she finally started to feel settled. When she reached her destination, she laughed and shook her head. Nothing had been quite right since she'd walked into the parking garage that morning and seen Jett McNally's ass.

Now here she was back at the hospital. With a shrug she headed inside. So what if it didn't make sense. This felt right.

❖

Tristan knocked on the hospital room door, pushed it open an inch, and peeked inside. "Anybody home?"

"Just everybody," Honor called back. "Tristan? Come on in."

"Hi." Tristan stepped inside and quickly averted her gaze. Honor held a bundle of what must be Jack, but all Tristan had seen was a snow white blanket covered with small blue flowers and a tuft of light brown, fluffy stuff that must be baby hair. And something pale and creamy that might have been a breast. "Oh, hey. Sorry. I just came to say hi. I'll come back la—"

"No." Honor nodded toward Quinn, who sprawled in a chair by the bed, looking supremely content as she stroked the hair of a gorgeous child sitting beside her on a footstool. "Stay. We're all just hanging out."

Tristan felt a surge of jealousy and couldn't figure out why. She didn't have the slightest desire to have children. She wasn't looking for a wife. So there was absolutely nothing in the room she coveted, unless it was the overpowering sense of belonging that warmed the very air. Belonging. What she'd never felt. Pushing that thought quickly away, she nodded to Quinn and tilted her chin in the direction of Honor and the baby. "Everybody good?"

"Great," Quinn said. "You remember Arly, don't you?"

"Yes. Hi, I'm Tristan." Tristan smiled at the girl who looked like she'd been cloned from Honor. Her hair had that yellow shine of youth that would darken to gold with maturity, but like Honor's, her eyes were already melted-chocolate brown, so unusual in blondes. Dressed in soccer shorts and a loose T-shirt, she leaned with her back against Quinn's knee.

"I remember," Arly said. "But you don't see me, okay? Because I'm not really here." She gazed at Quinn, adoration in her eyes. "Quinn snuck me in early to see Mom and Jack."

"Gotcha." Tristan rubbed her ear. "I'm not even sure I can hear you."

Arly grinned. "Quinn said you're going to help coach soccer. We have our first practice next weekend. Are you coming?"

Tristan glanced at Quinn, feeling slightly panicked. In a moment of weakness, she'd said yes to Quinn's invitation to help coach, but she didn't know a damn thing about soccer. Other than the fact someone kicked the ball. Somewhere.

Honor must have caught her look, because she started to laugh. "You'd better be careful. This is how it started with Quinn."

"What started?" Arly asked.

"Quinn coaching. First soccer," Honor said teasingly, "then field hockey, then volleyball. This year it's softball."

"In a few years I'll be tall enough for basketball," Arly said eagerly.

Quinn groaned. "Hey, Tris, you play basketball?"

Shaking her head, Tristan leaned against the door, enjoying herself immensely. She'd seen Quinn in a lot of different situations, but she'd never seen her look quite this happy—as if everything that mattered in the world was right in this room. For just a second, Tristan wondered what that would feel like.

"I'll be there," Tristan said. "But you'll have to help me, Arly. I'm not very good."

"That's okay." Arly tossed her a grin that was pure Quinn. "I am."

Jett carried the plastic hospital tray to a table in the far corner of the cafeteria. She had a half hour before her tour officially started, and as she did every night she was on call, she had dinner and then went up to check her aircraft. Visiting hours didn't start at the hospital until seven p.m., so the cafeteria was almost empty except for scattered groups of house staff congregated around tables, discussing patients and signing out for the night. It wasn't all that much different from a mess tent filled with soldiers, except none of this group had to worry about being blown to pieces before dessert.

She wondered how long it would be before she didn't think about where she'd been and the things she'd seen every waking moment. Actually, that wasn't true. With a start, she realized she hadn't thought about any of those things—the war or death or even Gail—while sitting with Tristan this morning. Tristan. Jett couldn't figure her out. She'd never been certain of Gail either, but that had been her own misjudgment. Maybe if she hadn't woken up in hell every morning, knowing that she might not live through the day, she would have been more careful. She wasn't going to make that mistake again.

People usually wanted something, and she'd learned long ago if she made it difficult to get close to her or to get anything from her, they quickly turned their attention somewhere else. Then she could decide who to let close, although she never felt the need. When she wanted something other than flying to satisfy her, or when she needed a way to burn off the adrenaline rush or the fear or the anger, she used sex. She could lose herself in sex, wear herself out with sex, as long as she was careful to be sure that what she needed also worked for whoever she was with. She'd gotten good at choosing the right women, and the system of sex without intimacy had worked pretty well her entire adult life. Until Gail.

Tristan was very different from Gail. She didn't seem to hide much, but Jett had no idea why Tristan wasn't put off by her *stay away* signals. That alone was enough to make her wary. She couldn't figure out her own response either. She hadn't had sex in longer than she was used to, as her sleeplessness and constant unrest proved, and Tristan had a great body. But Jett didn't have coffee and conversation with women she had sex with. She had sex with as little personal exchange as possible, other than what needed to be done to pleasure them both. More often than not, bringing a woman to orgasm settled her enough that she didn't need to come right away herself. She could wait until she was alone, replaying the sights and sounds and sensations, until she came in the solitary safety of the night. Thinking about Tristan jogging across the rooftop, dark hair whipping around her bold features and her powerful body covering the distance in commanding strides, or lazing beside her in the sunlight, full lips parted in a teasing smile, Jett had a feeling her imagination might be enough to hold her for quite a while.

As if conjured by Jett's thoughts, Tristan appeared across the room, a cup of coffee in her hand. Dressed in street clothes—jeans, a white open-collared shirt, and sneakers—she looked like an ad in some trendy magazine. And just about as foreign. Tristan halted a few tables away when she saw Jett, a question in her eyes. She waited, as if signaling Jett the next move was hers.

Jett didn't move, her gaze steady on Tristan's. The choice was hers. The choice was easy. No attachments, no involvement. Being alone was safe. She'd learned that lesson a long time ago, and when she'd forgotten, she'd paid. She looked away, then back. Tristan still watched her, unwavering.

Why? What was Tristan offering, and why did she care? Why did the empty chairs at her table suddenly seem to take on life, mocking her for being a coward? Jett leaned over and pushed one of the chairs away from the table, making room for Tristan.

Seconds later, Tristan settled beside her. "I hope you're working tonight."

"I am," Jett said. "Why?"

"Because there's something seriously wrong if you came all the way to the hospital to eat this food for dinner."

Jett looked down at her plate, realizing she hadn't even noticed what she was eating. She always ordered the dinner special, no matter what it was. Tonight it was lasagna. "It's not that bad. I think the law requires that cafeterias like this provide nutritionally balanced meals."

Tristan stared. "Dog food is nutritionally balanced."

Jett smiled. "You should try K-rations."

"That bad?"

"Unimaginative."

Tristan laughed.

"What about you?" Jett asked. "Come for the coffee?"

"No," Tristan said, sounding perplexed. "I didn't know what to do with myself, and I ended up here."

"Not on call?"

"Not until tomorrow night. Usually every fourth or fifth, but we're short right now. You work what, twelve-hour shifts?"

"Technically twelve on, twelve off for a week, then off for seven days and we start the rotation again. But sometimes we get called in or work longer if things are busy."

Tristan sipped her coffee. "Always nights?"

"Technically I should alternate between days and nights, but I like nights, and I never have any problem switching for them."

"Why nights?"

Jett shrugged. "More action."

"That's for sure." Tristan grimaced. "You can pretty much figure after midnight the gates of hell are open."

"There's that," Jett said. "Besides, I like to fly at night."

"Why?"

Jett almost asked why she was asking, but when she searched Tristan's face, all she saw was genuine interest. Like earlier.

"It's more challenging," Jett replied. "When you can't see very far ahead of you, there's always the chance you'll run into trouble."

"Or something good," Tristan murmured.

"That hasn't been my experience," Jett said tightly.

"Things could always change."

Before Jett could disagree, Tristan pushed her coffee cup away.

"So, do you have time to show me your aircraft? I didn't get much of a chance to take a look last night."

Jett didn't need to look at the clock on the far wall to know what time it was. She always knew what time it was. Just the same, she checked it, because just being around Tristan threw her off. Besides not being able to get a handle on why Tristan sought her company, she couldn't understand why she liked the fact that Tristan did. "I was about to go up and do my preflight check. You're welcome to come along."

"Okay." Tristan stood.

"I don't think you'll find it very exciting."

Tristan smiled. "You might be surprised."

❖

"Hi, Jett," a surfer-boy-handsome blond in cargo pants and a tight white T-shirt, carrying a clipboard, called from beside the bright red helicopter with a white cross painted on its side.

"Hi, Mike." Jett gestured to Tristan. "This is Dr. Holmes."

"Hi," Tristan said, extending her hand. Off to the west, the sun was just about to set, and the purple glow of the night sky and the warm wind on the rooftop made her wish that Jett weren't working the rest of the night. It was a night made for walking along the river or through the park. As soon as she thought it, she knew why she'd come to the hospital. She'd been looking for Jett. With a start, she dropped Mike's hand and put both of hers in her pockets. She'd been looking for a woman after all, she just hadn't realized it. Her instincts had taken her where she needed to go.

The idea of being unknowingly drawn to Jett made her uneasy, and she quickly reminded herself that Jett just happened to be the woman she'd spent time with most recently and her subconscious naturally prodded her to reconnect. No mystery. Nothing had changed. Everything was just as it should be. Except when she looked at Jett, standing beside her with her legs slightly spread, her arms clasped behind her back, Tristan didn't get the same urge for a quick, easy tumble. She wanted the hard weight of Jett's body holding her down, and all that pent-up energy she sensed to be unleashed on her. Jett reminded her of storm clouds gathering on a still, heavy summer night and she wanted to be deluged by the ferocity of that storm.

Tristan eased away. She wasn't herself. Sleep deprived, maybe. Or maybe the encounter in Las Vegas when she'd been neatly flipped and ended up loving it had thrown her equilibrium off a little. She'd get herself together soon.

"Mike is one of the other pilots," Jett said.

"How many of you are there?" Tristan said, not really caring, but not wanting to think any more about romantic strolls or summer storms or mind-numbing sex with Jett doing things to her she never knew she wanted.

"Four," Jett said. "That way, we always have a backup pilot."

Tristan laughed. "Kind of like being on second call. Which most of the time means first call."

Both pilots laughed with her. Then Mike handed the clipboard to Jett. "Three routine runs so far today. The mechanic finished all the maintenance this morning. I'll brief you inside whenever you're ready."

"I'll be right there," Jett said.

"No rush." Mike gave a wave and walked away.

"I don't want to keep you," Tristan said, even though it wasn't true. She was looking at a long night alone and right now, standing around on a rooftop with Jett felt just fine as long as she didn't think about anything except how good Jett looked in black military-style pants and a black T-shirt. The contrast with her fair coloring was striking.

"I've got a few minutes before I officially relieve Mike." Jett gestured to the aircraft. "This is a Eurocopter EC-145—the elite model in its class."

"Is this what you flew in the Army?"

Jett stiffened. "No. Black Hawks. The medevac versions mostly. Every once in a while I'd fly a UH 60L, a troop transport aircraft."

"Are there a lot of women flying over there?" Tristan asked.

"Most of the medevac pilots are women. A lot of the troop transport pilots too." Jett glanced past the aircraft toward downtown, where lights in the taller buildings were beginning to flicker on the horizon, and her features settled into an inscrutable expression.

Tristan recognized the look from earlier that morning. When the conversation got too close to whatever it was Jett didn't want to talk about, she walked away. Metaphorically, at least. Tristan knew one way to get her back from wherever she had gone. "So this helicopter's—what—a civilian version of what you flew?"

Jett refocused on Tristan. "Not exactly, but it's easy to make the transition to one of these when you've been flying Black Hawks." She opened the door of the aircraft and gestured for Tristan to climb inside.

"You sure?"

Jett grinned. "You can't break it. Go ahead."

Tristan climbed inside and turned around to take in the main part of the cabin where all the medical equipment and medications she'd used the night before were neatly stowed away. There was no hint of the controlled chaos. "It looks pretty much like any EMS vehicle."

"It is, except for the rotors."

"Oh yeah. That small detail." Tristan grinned. "How fast does it go?"

"Maximum speed is about two hundred eighty kph, but cruising speed is considerably less."

The more they talked about the aircraft, the more relaxed Jett seemed to become. As she described the helicopter's capabilities, Tristan, while interested, found herself focused more on Jett than on what she was saying. The big square halogen lights ringing the helipad came on automatically, backlighting Jett as she sat in the pilot's seat. The lines of her face were normally as sharp as if they'd been etched in precious metal, but as she described what she so obviously loved, her expression softened. For a fleeting second, Tristan had a glimpse of another woman behind Jett's fierce façade. Tristan was reminded of the way she'd felt when she first discovered women, as if every one was a wonderful mystery just waiting to be explored. She hadn't felt that way in so long, she'd forgotten how good it was. Her easy relationships were fun and physically satisfying, but they didn't touch her deep inside. Most of the time that was fine, except on nights like tonight when she wanted something she couldn't quite name. Something more.

"Sorry I can't take you up," Jett said. "Against regulations."

Tristan tried to focus. "That's okay. I know this is serious stuff."

"Well," Jett said, "I hope I didn't bore you."

"You don't bore me." Tristan felt the pressure of time bearing down on her. Jett was going to disappear any second. "I was wondering—"

Linda appeared around the front of the helicopter and peered in. "Hey! You two aren't going anywhere without me, are you?"

"Did we get a request?" Jett asked, instantly serious. She climbed out of the helicopter and Tristan followed.

"No," Linda said. "Mike said you were out here, so I figured it was a good time to catch you before the night got too crazy. Hello, Dr. Holmes."

"Hi." Tristan felt Linda's curious scrutiny as she gazed from Jett to Tristan.

"I'm having a party at the house next Saturday night," Linda said, "and I wanted to invite you before you made plans to take any extra shifts, Cap. You too, Dr. Holmes. Pretty much the whole neighborhood is coming. We hope Honor will be able to make it too."

"That's great," Tristan said. "I'll be there. And call me Tristan."

When Jett said nothing, Linda added, "Most of the flight crew is coming. It's casual. Some beer and burgers. That kind of thing."

"If I don't need to work, I'll try to make it." Jett glanced at Tristan. "I better get inside. Good night."

"Hope it's quiet," Tristan called after her.

"We live around the corner from Quinn and Honor." Linda gave Tristan the address. "I'm sorry we haven't invited you over sooner. It's been a little crazy with me switching from the ER to the medevac crew this spring."

"That's okay. I'm just getting settled myself."

"You're welcome to bring a date," Linda said with a playful smile.

"Thanks." Tristan eyed the stairwell where Jett had disappeared. She'd been about to impetuously ask Jett out when Linda had interrupted her, but she wasn't at all sure that was such a good idea. Jett really wasn't her type, and it was never smart to change a winning game plan. Evie or Darla would be a much better choice. "I just might do that."

CHAPTER SEVEN

N ice flying, Jett!" Linda held open the door to the stairwell as sheets of rain lashed the rooftop. "The ride was so smooth I wouldn't have even known we were in the middle of a thunderstorm if it hadn't been for the lightning."

"Thanks." Jett finger-combed the water from her hair as she and Linda started down the stairwell toward the crew quarters. The storm front had blown up out of nowhere while they were transporting a patient to the burn unit in Hershey, seventy miles away. The eleven-year-old boy had been the sole survivor of a house fire that had claimed the rest of his family. The weather had been clear when they'd picked him up. Jett had put the helicopter down in the twisting two-lane road adjacent to the still-flaming house as fire rescue worked to quench the blaze and locate victims. Jett watched, feeling as if she'd viewed the scene a thousand times before, as first one body and then another had been brought from the smoldering structure. As each casualty emerged, draped in black plastic, she wondered if she would return to base with an empty aircraft. Already, the medical examiner's van stood waiting with doors open twenty yards in front of her. Finally a shout went up and she could feel the excitement all the way into the cockpit. Someone had been found alive. Linda and Juan and the fire rescue personnel swarmed the stretcher, performed the initial resuscitation, and had the boy in the aircraft within minutes.

"Good save out there," Jett said, pausing in the hallway outside the flight crew lounge.

Linda smiled wearily. "I hope so. He's got a long road ahead of him." She touched Jett's bare arm. "He wouldn't have had any chance at all if you hadn't gotten us to Hershey. I was afraid for a few minutes there you were going to have to abort the flight."

Jett shrugged. Flying in electrical storms was hazardous. A lightning strike would fry the radio at the very least, and worst-case scenario, the gears would mesh or the rotors debond and come apart. She'd considered detouring to another hospital away from the storm path, but that would have delayed the boy's essential care for too long. Any hospital could handle most noncritical burns, but with the degree of injuries he had, even a few hours' delay might have meant the onset of fatal respiratory or infectious complications. She'd seen enough burns to know. So she'd set a course around the worst of it and made it to the burn center. She'd pushed to the limits, but she'd still been in her safety zone. Other pilots might've felt differently, but other pilots hadn't flown in the conditions she'd flown under every day for months. "We've got the best aircraft going. It will take us through anything."

Linda laughed. "I think it's the pilot I trust the most."

"Thanks," Jett said again, drawing her arm away. Linda was a vibrant, sensual woman who touched easily, laughed easily, and exuded compassion. Jett knew there was nothing special about Linda's attention, or even out of the ordinary, but she was in that place where the brush of a woman's skin against hers could twist her insides until she couldn't think.

"I'm going to make some fresh coffee." Linda pushed the door to the lounge open and shot Jett a questioning look. "Coming in?"

"I was downwind most of the time out there, and the cockpit took a lot of smoke from the fire. I need to shower and change my clothes."

"Mmm, me too." Linda smiled. "Well, you know where it will be."

Jett nodded and made her way to her room alone.

"The weapons fire was heavy out there tonight," Gail said *breathlessly.* "They must have gotten a new shipment of ammunition from somewhere."

Jett grimaced. "Kept our gunners busy." She rolled her shoulders, trying to work loose some of the stiffness. She'd had a death grip on the stick, trying to maneuver her Black Hawk away from the small arms fire that hammered the air around her aircraft with lethal projectiles. The dense black sky would have been beautiful, bursting with streaks of color, if every one of those pyrotechnic displays hadn't been so deadly. Since the insurgents rarely had sophisticated weaponry, they blanketed the sky with as much small arms fire as possible, hoping for a random hit. Her only choice was to fly as straight and fast as possible while hoping a round didn't hit her fuel tank or her passengers. Or her.

"You've been flying for eight days straight in terrible conditions. You've got to be pretty beat up."

"No more than usual," Jett said.

"Come on, I've got just the thing."

When Gail headed toward her tent, Jett hesitated. It was the middle of the night, and there wasn't much activity in camp, so no one was likely to see them. Nevertheless, going into Gail's tent made her uneasy. Gail was just being friendly, but Jett didn't think spending time alone with her was a good idea. She'd been in the desert for months, and although she was certain she wasn't the only lesbian, she restricted her sexual forays to when she was on leave. As time passed and her sense of futility and anger over the tragic waste of life escalated, her control wavered. She was edgy all the time, and nothing she managed on her own eased the relentless tension. She should go back to her own tent.

But she knew she wouldn't sleep. A drink might help her relax, because that was surely what Gail was offering. One quick drink couldn't hurt. She hurried to catch up. Gail's rank afforded her semiprivate accommodations, and the other bunk in the sparse tent was empty. Gail lit a small battery-operated lamp and set it on the floor where it wouldn't cast shadows for anyone passing by outside to see and gestured to one of the narrow beds.

"Take your shirt off and lie down."

Jett's whole body jerked as if she'd stepped on a high-voltage line. Gail had already turned away and was rummaging in a locker. When she looked over her shoulder and saw Jett standing dumbfounded a few feet away, she smiled and held up a shampoo-sized bottle of gold liquid. It wasn't booze.

"Go ahead. Strip and stretch out." Gail unbuttoned her shirt and took it off, revealing a tight dark T-shirt underneath. Her breasts were larger than Jett had thought, broad full ovals underneath the thin cotton.

Jett needed to decide before her hesitation became awkward. Go or stay. Gail's face was soft in the muted lamplight, her gaze welcoming. The night was very dark and death was everywhere. Jett unbuttoned her shirt. Gail didn't look away when Jett pulled off her T-shirt, baring herself to the waist. Her nipples tightened and she turned to the bunk, hoping to hide them. She lay face down and put her head on her arms. The springs gave slightly as Gail sat next to her, her hip pressed to Jett's.

"I'm sorry it's not warm," Gail murmured, bracing herself with one hand on Jett's left shoulder.

When a stream of thick liquid coursed down the center of Jett's back, she stiffened. Then Gail's hands were on her, spreading oil from the base of her neck to the hollow above her buttocks. In her mind's eye, she saw Gail leaning over her, and the press of Gail's hands transformed into a caress. The muscles in her ass clenched as her clitoris swelled and she fought not to gasp.

"Your shoulders are so tight." Gail brushed the hair away from the back of Jett's neck and leaned closer, working her fingers into the knots along Jett's spine. Her stomach pressed against Jett's back and Jett groaned before she could stop herself. "Too hard?"

"No," Jett rasped. "It's fine. Good. But you must be tired. You don't have to—"

"I want to. It relaxes me."

Gail swept her hands up and down Jett's back, heating her skin, inflaming her deep inside. When Gail's fingers skimmed the outside of her breasts, Jett unconsciously tilted her pelvis into the hard mattress, as if it were a lover.

"Unbuckle your pants so I can pull them down," Gail said.

Jett murmured a protest and tried to turn over, but Gail stopped her with a hand between her shoulder blades.

"Go ahead. I want to get to your lower back. You've got to be sore, strapped in that cockpit for hours."

Jett knew she should stop what was happening, but she didn't. She didn't want Gail to stop either. She wanted Gail to keep touching her. She wanted the heat of Gail's body close to hers and the soft sigh of Gail's exhalation teasing over her skin. She wanted her clitoris to twitch and pulse to the rhythm of Gail's fingers until it exploded. She reached under her hips with one hand, unbuckled her belt, opened her fly, and tugged down her zipper. For one insane second she contemplated pushing her hand inside her fatigues and stroking herself. She knew even without checking that she was swollen and wet and fully aroused. She imagined squeezing her clitoris while Gail worked the muscles in her ass until she came. Seconds, it would only take seconds. Jett jerked her hand from beneath her body and gripped the rough cotton sheets.

"Lift your hips." Gail tugged at the waistband of Jett's pants. Then she palmed the small, firm mounds of Jett's ass and massaged them in firm circles. Jett moaned. "You see. You need this, I can tell."

Gail leaned away for a second, and then Jett felt a trickle of oil run into the cleft between her buttocks. Gail's thumbs followed, digging into the muscles on either side. Jett was so hard the pressure was painful and she desperately wanted to masturbate.

"Turn over. I should do your chest too."

Jett's brain was too muddled for her to do anything except obey. With her pants pushed almost below her pelvis, she turned awkwardly, exposing the triangle of blond hair between her legs. She thought she saw Gail glance down, but her vision was hazy and she wasn't sure. She bunched the sheets in her fists on either side of her body as Gail pressed both hands to her chest. Gail's face was very close, leaning over her, as she smoothed her palms in circles from Jett's breastbone out to her shoulders. Jett's breasts ached and her nipples throbbed.

"I told you you needed this," Gail whispered, her lips moist and full. "Aren't I right?"

"I need…" Jett whispered.

"What? What do you need?"

Viciously, Jett twisted the shower dial to cold, gasping in shock as the frigid stream pounded against her head and shoulders. She braced one arm against the slick wall, panting as she fought to escape from the memories. She needed to come. Her legs shook and she locked her knees to stay upright. With a groan, she slid one hand between her legs and gripped her clitoris. She kept her eyes open as she squeezed and tugged, not wanting to come with Gail's face dancing on the inside of her eyelids. She was close, so close. She leaned her forehead against the wall, fingers circling frantically. She heard Gail's voice.

You see. You needed this.

"No." Jett groaned, yanking her hand away. But it was too late and she was coming. She sank to her knees, closing her eyes in surrender.

❖

"Jett?" Linda called, knocking on Jett's door.

Jett sat on the side of her bed, dressed in clean black pants and T-shirt. She'd been sitting there for a long time, her mind mercifully blank. The second time Linda called her name, she rubbed her face and took a deep breath. Squaring her shoulders, she prepared herself to get on with business. She still had a while to go on her shift, and even if they got called with five minutes left, they'd go out.

"Come on in." When Linda entered, Jett asked, "Another flight request?"

Linda shook her head. "We just got a call from risk management. They want flight records from one of our runs."

"The boy with the burns?" Risk management pulled records when a case was under review or someone lodged a complaint. Jett searched her memory for anything unusual about the recovery or transport. True, she'd flown during the electrical storm, but she couldn't imagine who would have complained about that. And certainly not so soon.

"No, sorry," Linda said, sounding rattled. Jett could never remember her being the slightest bit off balance. "Not this shift, but one from last week."

"Which one?"

"The multivehicle accident—the one with the governor's daughter-in-law."

The flight where she'd first met Tristan. Jett hadn't seen her recently, but then she wouldn't. They worked in different parts of the hospital. She might never see her again. When her stomach tightened, she ignored it and asked sharply, "Why? What's going on?"

Linda's expression was grim. "I made a few calls to the nurses in the TICU right after I got off the phone with the admin from risk management. The patient arrested last night."

"She died?" Jett wasn't surprised, but she hated to hear it. A trauma victim who made it to the hospital alive, especially a young patient, had a very good chance of survival. Sometimes, though, even the best chance wasn't enough.

"No, they got her back, but she's in a coma and they're not sure about brain function."

"I don't get it," Jett said. "What does it have to do with us?"

"I'm not sure, but they want flight logs and our scene reports."

"Okay. I'll get my records together. You and Juan do the same. Just make sure everything you documented is accurate and complete. It was a clean run."

"I wonder if Tristan knows." Linda bit her lip absently. "I'm not sure if she's working today. Maybe I should call her."

"Risk management must have contacted her too."

"You're probably right." Linda sighed. "I'll go get started on the paperwork."

Alone again, Jett thought back to the morning she'd spent stretched out beside Tristan in the sun. She'd never done anything like that with anyone. Just talked. There had never been anyone to talk to when she was growing up, and she'd gone right into the service after high school. It was the quickest way she knew to get to fly. She'd made friends, of a sort. Mostly men and some women who shared the Army experience and the love of flying. No one asked about *her*. Where she came from or what mattered to her. Or maybe they had, and she'd shut them out. She was good at that and it always worked. Except it hadn't worked with Tristan.

For a second, she wished she had another hour in the shade of that oak tree to look forward to. Then she shook her head, having learned once already not to give in to wishes. She grabbed her overnight bag and headed toward the small office on the other side of the lounge where they kept their paperwork. She had a report to review, and then another twelve hours until she could return.

CHAPTER EIGHT

I'm going to take an early dinner break," Tristan told the nurse anesthetist on call with her, a burly guy who had been a medic in the Navy before going to nursing school.

"Sure." He grabbed the sports section from a pile of eviscerated newspapers on the table in the OR lounge and headed toward the men's locker room. "It'll be an hour before they get that femur washout over here anyhow."

"Page me when the family shows up so I can get the consent."

"No problem."

Alone, Tristan surveyed the stark lounge and the detritus of the day's activities. Crumpled newspapers, empty fast-food bags, coffee cups upside down by the sink. A scrub shirt rolled into a ball and tossed into a corner of the couch. A haphazardly folded blanket that before morning would cover someone—surgeon, nurse, OR tech—as they slept on the sofa waiting for the next patient to arrive. When the routine cases of the day were finished and the day shift went home, Tristan always felt a little bit marooned, as if she were completely cut off from the rest of the world, disconnected even from her own life. The handful of staff left behind to cover emergencies during the night assumed the attitude of front-line soldiers, resigned to hold on until reinforcements returned in the morning. Until the sun came up, no matter what came through the door—multiple traumas, gunshot wounds, burns, exsanguinating postoperative patients, obstetrical catastrophes—the team taking night call had to be up to the task. Because no one stood behind them.

Tristan pulled on one of the shapeless green OR cover gowns and took the stairs down to the cafeteria on the second floor. She ordered the special and carried her tray into the dining area, checking out the occupants. When she saw Jett at the table where she'd been sitting the week before, she sighed inwardly, admitting she'd been hoping to see her. She'd had a lousy day and the worst was yet to come. The prospect of a few minutes talking to Jett inexplicably cut through the gloom. When she raised her tray in a questioning gesture to Jett, she held her breath. She'd looked for Jett every night since that night in the helicopter on the roof, but she hadn't seen her. Maybe Jett had been avoiding her. A long minute passed, and Tristan forced a smile before starting to turn away. Then Jett beckoned her over, and a bit of the unfamiliar abandoned feeling disappeared.

"How's the chicken à la king?" Tristan asked, setting down her tray.

"Is that what this is?" Jett's voice rose in surprise.

"That good, huh?" Tristan laughed. "I *am* capable of talking about more than hospital food, but I figured since you already taste-tested it…"

"It's hot. I recognize pretty much everything that's in it." Jett grinned. "That makes it close to gourmet food."

"Is military food really that bad?"

"Not stateside. But you can't expect much when you're deployed."

Busy sprinkling pepper over her meal, Tristan asked offhandedly, "You miss it at all?" When Jett didn't answer, she looked up. Jett's face had gone completely blank. "Sorry. Someday if you ever want to talk about it…" She let the words trail off because she realized she was being presumptuous. Whatever secrets Jett harbored were clearly not happy ones. "You know what. I'm a jerk. Just forget I said that."

"Why did you?" Jett pushed her tray aside and focused on Tristan. Maybe Tristan was just one of those curious people who befriended everyone casually. She'd known plenty of people like that in the Army, men and women alike. People who would talk to anyone about anything because they enjoyed social interaction, or they just liked the sound of their own voices. Jett had never been like that. She didn't share what was important to her with anyone, because she didn't trust anyone that much. She'd learned that lesson at a young age after her brothers scoffed at her dreams and her father tried to beat her into the shape he thought a woman should assume.

"I don't know," Tristan replied. "I mean, I want to know. I'm interested in you."

Jett pushed her chair away from the table, gripped her tray, and stood up to leave. "I'm not that interesting."

"You're wrong about that, but I won't argue," Tristan said calmly. "I'm glad you know what's in this stuff, because I'm not sure."

Jett stopped and looked back. Tristan was pushing the food around on her plate with her fork. Her hand was shaking. Jett slid her tray onto an empty table nearby and sat back down across from Tristan. "I liked the Army because it gave me the one thing I wanted, and all I had to do in return was the job I signed up to do."

"Just one thing?" Tristan regarded Jett intently. "All you wanted was one thing?"

Jett nodded.

"You love it, don't you. Flying."

Jett was so used to keeping what mattered to her to herself, she almost didn't answer. But Tristan's words echoed in her mind. *I want to know you.* She wasn't certain that anyone had ever really wanted to know her before. "If I couldn't fly I don't think I'd want to do anything at all."

"Yeah. I get that." Tristan wondered if Jett had a woman in her life who she wanted with that much fervor. She tried to imagine what it would be like to be the focus of that kind of passion, to have all of someone's energy poured into her. She'd had women want her because she was fun or sexy or wealthy. She'd had women beg her or tease her to touch them, to take them, to push them beyond their limits. But she couldn't remember a single one who had begged to touch her. Hunger like she'd never known rose up inside her.

"You make me wish I were a helicopter."

Jett laughed and after a few seconds Tristan joined her.

"Why?" Jett asked.

"You make flying sound like a love affair."

"It's nothing like that," Jett said.

Tristan couldn't miss the bitterness in Jett's voice. Someone had hurt her, and the realization made her angry. In fact, so angry she was frightened by her own response. In defense, she intentionally changed the subject. "I guess you heard about the patient from last week. The governor's daughter-in-law."

"We got a call asking for records first thing this morning. I know she had some kind of problem." Jett was relieved to get away from personal topics. Some things about civilian life were going to take some getting used to, and hearing lesbians talk openly about their love lives was one of them. Talking about romance with Tristan was way outside her comfort zone.

"I doubt it's a secret. At least it won't be for long." Tristan leaned back in her chair and sighed. "A tooth turned up in her right mainstem bronchus. They saw it on the x-ray after she had a respiratory arrest last night. It didn't show up on earlier films because that part of the lung was collapsed."

Jett hadn't had any formal medical training, but she'd spent enough time with medics in and out of field hospitals to have picked up a lot of the terminology. "She swallowed…no, she aspirated a tooth in the accident?"

"That's one explanation. The other popular theory is that I pushed it down into her lung when I intubated her in the field."

"I imagine if you had, you'd have said so at the time."

The iron band of tension that had been constricting Tristan's head for the last eight hours dissipated as if someone had unlocked it with a key. She'd been reeling all day long from the thinly veiled accusation that she'd been hasty and reckless when she'd decided to intubate the patient at the scene under less than controlled conditions. Having her professional competence called into question hurt. "Thanks. Unfortunately, not everyone agrees."

Jett frowned. "Is it going to be a problem for you?"

"I don't know. Maybe."

"Is it okay for me to ask you that? I don't want to compromise you."

"So far, nothing official has happened," Tristan said. "I don't plan to discuss it with the other members of the medical team, because they'll have to testify if it comes to legal action. You might be questioned too, but not about the medical circumstances."

"She looked like she was in pretty bad shape when you brought her on board."

"Major facial fractures and a lot of bleeding. Anyone familiar with that type of trauma knows you've got loose teeth all over the place. There was just so damn much blood." Tristan grimaced. "I was worried she was going to choke to death on all that blood. Hell, sometimes it's just a judgment call."

"That's why no one should question your actions without a damn good reason," Jett said vehemently. "You're the one on the line. You're the one making the hard call. It has to be that way, and you should have the support of the hospital behind you."

"You want to stand up in court and say that?" Tristan joked.

"I would if it would make any difference," Jett said seriously.

"How do you know I'm worth taking a chance on?"

"You wouldn't be here if you didn't know what you were doing. And I think if you had a problem out there, you'd say so." Jett shrugged.

"Is it me," Tristan dared to ask, "or do you just believe in the system that much?" She wanted to believe it was her Jett believed in, wanted it so much it scared her. Her parents hadn't believed her, or believed in her. And her sisters said they loved her but they didn't want to love her the way she was—they wanted to change her into a person they understood. She'd stood up to them, but it had cost her. She hadn't wished for anyone to really see her, to believe in her, in a very long time.

Jett collected her tray and stood up. Not that long ago she had believed that the chain of command was sacrosanct. Without order there was anarchy. And in the heat of battle, chaos meant death. She didn't believe that any longer. She looked down into Tristan's questioning eyes and saw vulnerability as well as pain. She didn't even hesitate. "It's you."

"Thanks," Tristan whispered.

"Don't mention it." Jett started away, then turned back. Tristan was hurting, and she wanted to give her just a little of the comfort Tristan had unwittingly given her. "I never said thanks for coffee the other day. I—"

Jett's beeper went off and a second later, so did Tristan's.

"Shit," they both said simultaneously.

"Take it easy tonight," Tristan called after Jett, who had left her tray on the table and sprinted away. She caught Jett's brief wave before she took off in the same direction, wondering what Jett might have said.

❖

When Tristan arrived in the emergency room she discovered Quinn and the other trauma personnel resuscitating two young men, both of whom appeared to have multiple gunshot wounds. Penetrating chest and abdominal injuries. Even as she called, "What do we have," she saw the long night ahead of her in the operating room.

"This one," Quinn said, indicating a patient in whom she had just finished inserting a chest tube, "needs to go upstairs right away. Probable punctured lung. Maybe great vessel injury."

Tristan hurriedly assessed the breath sounds. "Portable chest x-ray?"

"It's hanging."

Quickly surveying the radiograph, she saw that the right lung was nearly white. Most likely filled with blood. "O2 SATs?"

"Just getting them," one of the nurses called. "Seventy on sixty percent O2 and a rebreathing mask."

"Hell," Tristan muttered. "Let's get a tube in him."

Another one of the nurses grabbed a suction catheter and cleared blood and fluid from the patient's mouth. For just a second, Tristan hesitated, thinking of the governor's daughter-in-law. So much blood. Maybe she should have waited. Maybe she *had* been hasty.

"His pressure's dropping," a nurse reported.

Tristan glanced at the oxygen readout. Sixty-five. She pushed her way around to the head of the table and grabbed a laryngoscope. "Give me a number eight tube."

In less than a minute she had inserted the tube into the trachea and was pumping in a hundred percent oxygen. The patient's blood pressure stabilized immediately.

"His SATs are coming up," the nurse said.

"Nice, Tris," Quinn said.

Tristan lifted her shoulder. She had only done her job, just like everyone else in the room. With the patient secured, the tension level in the room plummeted. "So, Quinn, they finally made you come back to work, huh?"

"Honor went home today. I don't have any more excuses."

"How's she doing?" Tristan taped the endotracheal tube to the patient's face to prevent it from being dislodged during transport.

Quinn nodded, a fleeting expression of discomfort crossing her face. "Honor insisted she was ready days ago, but with the blood loss… she's still pretty weak."

"Jack go home too?"

"Everybody."

"No wonder you wanted to work."

One of the nurses poked Tristan in the arm. "Some people actually like family life."

Tristan rolled her eyes. "Sorry."

Quinn slid her a grin as she secured the dressing around the chest tube. "Don't forget practice this weekend."

"I'll be there."

"Coming to the party at Linda's?" another nurse asked. "Linda invited all of us."

"Planning on it," Tristan muttered. She hadn't called anyone for a date yet, although she'd thought of it several times. She wasn't sure why she was waiting.

"Okay, that's it," Quinn said, stepping away from the table, all business again. "Let's get him upstairs. The other one is waiting on vascular unless something changes. Any problems, call me."

Tristan secured her tubes and the oxygen tank, one hand stabilizing the patient's head as she pushed the stretcher toward the elevator. Just as she, Quinn, and a nurse crowded on, the trauma beeper went off again.

The second-call anesthesiologist was waiting in front of the elevators opposite the OR when the doors opened. "Healthstar's on its way in with a level one," he said to Tristan. "You want me to take it?"

"No. You take this one. I'll get the incoming." Tristan handed off the patient and caught the elevator doors just as they were closing. She jumped in.

When she reached the roof, the helicopter hadn't yet landed, but several nurses and the trauma fellow were already there. Tristan stepped a little bit away from them as they chatted while waiting and watching the sky. As the helicopter settled onto the landing pad, the turbulence from the rotors and the glare of the bright landing lights brought tears to her eyes, but she stared through the sheen of moisture, hoping for a glimpse of Jett at the controls. As soon as the skids touched down, the trauma team rushed forward and she went with them.

Tristan was almost to the aircraft when the cockpit door swung open and Jett jumped out. She had a brief glimpse of Jett pulling off her helmet and rifling a hand through her hair. Their eyes met and Jett smiled. Tristan had only a second before the medevac crew delivered the patient. Even though her attention was elsewhere, she held on to the smile as if it were a gift. Just before she stepped into the elevator, she looked back. Jett still stood on the rooftop, a solitary figure backlit against the night sky, watching her.

Even though Tristan knew it was crazy, she felt as if Jett had reached out and touched her. Hell, she definitely needed a date, because she was starting to imagine things. Jett hadn't shown any indication of interest, and even if she had, she definitely wasn't Tristan's type. Nothing about her suggested she did anything casually. Of course, that was exactly what made her so intriguing. Despite the almost overwhelming urge to stop and look back again, Tristan forced herself into the elevator. She had a patient to take care of, and she didn't need any complications in her life. Everything was going along exactly the way she wanted it to go. Smooth, easy, and no strings attached. Just the way she wanted.

CHAPTER NINE

When Quinn let herself into the house shortly after eight the next morning, she was greeted by silence. She was used to coming home after twenty-four hours on call to find Arly's grandmother, Phyllis, busy in the kitchen making breakfast or getting Arly ready for school. In the summer when there was no school, Phyllis supervised Arly after Honor left for her shift in the ER until Quinn returned home from night call. And since Quinn would usually have been up all night operating, Phyllis often took Arly out somewhere while Quinn slept. They never left *this* early, however.

Quinn checked the kitchen. A full pot of coffee sat on the warming plate of the coffeemaker. There was no sign of breakfast dishes, and the smell of pancakes or muffins was absent. Nothing felt quite right, and a wave of completely irrational panic swept through her. She shook it off quickly, knowing that if anything had happened to Honor or Arly or Jack, someone would have called her. Still, she wanted to see her family. For all of the excitement of the last week and a half, and the amazing joy of bringing Jack home, she hadn't been able to forget or shake off those few minutes in the delivery room when she'd feared she would lose Honor. Nothing in her life had ever been as terrifying as imagining a future without her.

Telling herself there was nothing to worry about, Quinn climbed the stairs as quickly as she could while trying to be quiet. The master bedroom was situated diagonally across the hall from Arly's room, and she passed her partially open door to peek in Arly's open door. Arly sat cross-legged on the bed in her pajamas, a book open in her lap.

When she saw Quinn, she touched her finger to her lips and shook her head with a warning look. Instantly, Quinn's anxiety dissipated and she crossed to the bed.

"What's going on?" she asked in a whisper.

"Mommy and Jack are sleeping."

"Where's Phyllis?"

"She went home. She said we could call her when everyone got up and she'd fix breakfast."

"Didn't you want to go with her?" Considering that home for Phyllis was the other half of the duplex and that Honor was just across the hall, there was no reason Arly couldn't stay on her own in her room. After all, she slept in her room alone every night too. Still, it was a change. Everyone's routine was disrupted.

Arly shook her head. "I wanted to stay here."

"Are you okay?"

"Yes." But she didn't look at Quinn when she answered.

Quinn sat on the bed and leaned back against the pillows. Arly curled up against her side. "What are you reading?"

"*The Golden Compass.*"

"Do you like it?"

Arly nodded. "It's like Harry Potter for grown-up kids."

Quinn smiled. She'd read some of the book. The story of a young girl in an alternate universe was wildly imaginative and beautiful at times, but darker than Harry Potter. The series was supposed to be for young readers, but some of the events were pretty sophisticated, nonetheless. "Not scary or anything?"

"It's just make-believe, Quinn."

"That's right." Quinn kissed the top of Arly's head. "I forgot that part."

Arly giggled. Then she slid her arm around Quinn's middle and became quiet. After a few seconds, Quinn said, "What are you thinking?"

"Is Mom really going to be okay?"

Quinn was careful to stay relaxed because she didn't want any of her secret fears bleeding over to her child. "Yes, she's going to be fine. Are you worried?"

"She looks kind of sick."

"She's not sick, honey." Quinn pulled Arly close. "She's pretty tired. Mom explained about the operation that she needed so Jack could come out, right?" Arly nodded. "Well, it takes a while to get back to normal after that."

"And then everything will be like before?"

"Things will be a little different because now instead of you and me and Mom and Phyllis being a family, there will be you and me and Mom and Phyllis and Jack."

Arly sat up and regarded Quinn intently. "Is Jack really my brother?"

"What?" Quinn was so surprised she forgot she was supposed to be the all-knowing, rational adult. "Sure he is. How come you're asking?"

"Tommy said that Jack can't be my brother unless we have a father too. And we don't have one."

"There's lots of ways to make families, remember, we talked about that? Families are people who live together because they love each other and want to take care of each other. Like we do."

Arly nodded.

Quinn hugged her hard. "So now we have Jack, and your mother and I love you both and we're all going to live together until you're grown up. So that makes us your parents and Jack your brother."

"So the father part doesn't count?"

"Well, he counts if you have one, but you don't need one." Quinn wondered if they were going to have the birds and the bees talk now. She glanced through the open door to the bedroom across the hall. The door was ajar an inch or two, but Honor was probably asleep. She wished Honor would come to her rescue, but at least now she didn't break into a cold sweat every time she had one of these conversations with Arly. She only wished she had more time to prepare for topics like this one. Someday she was probably going to say something wrong and cause permanent psychological damage.

"Quinn?"

"Yes, honey?"

"Can I call Grandma now so we can have breakfast?"

"Yes. Go call her. I'm starving." As Arly climbed over her, Quinn swatted her on the butt. "I'm going to go check on your mother. If she's still sleeping, we need to still be quiet."

"Okay."

Arly disappeared on her way downstairs to use the phone, and Quinn stood and stretched. Her lower back ached from standing most of the night repairing a torn pulmonary artery in the boy with the gunshot wound. Her eyes were gritty from lack of sleep, and she felt just a little bit fuzzy. Still, all that mattered was that she was home. She walked to her bedroom, cautiously opened the door wide, and paused inside the door to take in the scene.

Honor lay sleeping, Jack cradled in the curve of her arm. She appeared very pale, but incredibly peaceful. Even in her sleep, she looked happy. Quinn drank her in, still amazed that this was her life. This woman, these children, this home. More than she had ever dreamed.

Honor shifted and opened her eyes. Used to waking completely in a heartbeat, she focused on Quinn instantly. "You're home. I thought I heard you talking a few minutes ago. Did I dream that?"

"No." Quinn stretched out on the bed and kissed Honor's cheek. "I was talking to Arly."

"Mmm." Honor looped an arm around Quinn's neck and pulled her closer until she could kiss her on the mouth. "Missed you."

"Missed you too."

"Are you tired?"

"Not so much." Quinn reached across Honor's body and stroked the baby's head. His hair was so soft, like nothing she'd ever felt before. He scrunched up his face and made a tiny mewling sound. "Uh-oh. Sorry."

Honor laughed. "It's okay if he wakes up. He's going to soon anyhow. It's about time for another feeding."

"Should I do anything with him?"

"He's good for a little while. Phyllis changed him earlier, right after he ate." Honor caught Quinn's hand and held their joined hands between her breasts. "Did you eat yet?"

"I was just about to go downstairs. Arly's calling Phyllis for breakfast."

"Phyllis isn't here?" Honor frowned. "What was Arly doing here by herself?"

"She was reading in her room. I think she's a little bit worried about you."

Honor passed the baby to Quinn. "Here, take him. I need to get up so she can see that I'm all right."

"I thought we agreed on bed rest until you get another transfusion tomorrow." Quinn tucked the baby against her shoulder.

"I feel fine. I'm not an invalid."

Quinn wrapped her arm around Honor's shoulders as Honor threw back the covers and sat up. "It will only scare her if you overdo too soon and she sees you not looking good. I've got a better idea. Give me one minute, okay?"

"I just don't want her—"

"One minute." Quinn put Jack back in his bassinet by the bed, pleased when he didn't wake up. Then she ducked out into the hallway and called softly, "Arly? Come on upstairs."

A few seconds later Arly appeared at the foot of the stairs. "Grandma is on her way over."

"Perfect timing." When Arly reached the top of the stairs, Quinn took her hand. "Let's go see Mom for a minute."

Quinn led Arly to the bed and patted a spot next to Honor's hip. "Climb up here." Then she sat down on the far side of Arly and rested her chin on the top of Arly's head. "So what do you think," she whispered to Arly, "about you and me fixing Mom breakfast and bringing it up here. Then she can eat and we'll watch Jack."

"Yeah," Arly said with enthusiasm. "We can make pancakes."

Laughing, Honor extended her arms. "Come here and give me a hug first." When Arly hesitated, she said, "It's okay, honey. I'm a little sore but I'll be much better in a day or two. Especially if you and Quinn are going to spoil me."

"We can spoil you plenty."

"I'm counting on it." Honor met Quinn's gaze over the top of Arly's head as she held her. *I love you*, she mouthed silently.

Quinn caressed Honor's calf beneath the sheets and whispered, "Me too."

She drew a breath of contentment and felt her fatigue drop away. For most of the last twenty-four hours she'd been too busy to think about anything except the work she had to do. But in the brief respite between surgeries, after checking the postoperative patients, or while stealing a moment for a bite to eat, she thought about her family. She knew that however hard the night might be, when morning came, she'd be going home to those who gave her strength and healed her. Life was good.

❖

Tristan headed to the locker room, finally finished making post-op rounds in the recovery room, checking on the patients in the surgical intensive care unit she'd taken care of during the night, and writing follow-up notes. She was done for the day. In fact, she was off for two days, until Sunday. Considering she'd been busy covering extra shifts with people away, first at the meeting and then on vacation, she was ready for a break. She was ready for more than that.

Anesthesia, as she and her colleagues liked to say, was a specialty marked by long periods of boredom interspersed with moments of sheer panic. Most cases were fairly routine once the patient was anesthetized and the procedure was underway. During surgery she spent her time monitoring vital signs and ensuring that the various drugs were at the appropriate levels to keep the patient unaware but not so high as to become dangerous. Induction—putting the patient to sleep—and emergence—waking them up—were the tense times for her and could be pretty challenging when complications arose. And of course, there were the heart-pounding, gut-clenching moments during a trauma resuscitation when she had to make snap judgments and perform difficult technical procedures with only seconds to spare.

She'd spent the last few hours giving anesthesia to an otherwise healthy twenty-year-old woman who'd had a few drinks too many, fallen asleep at the wheel, and driven her car into the Schuylkill River. In addition to almost drowning, she'd broken her neck and the orthopedic surgeons decided to do immediate bone grafts to stabilize her cervical spine. Once Tristan positioned her face down on the table, secured her airway, and anesthetized her, she didn't have all that much to do. So between recording vital signs and checking on the progress of surgery, her mind drifted.

She wondered how the governor's daughter-in-law was doing. She wanted to stop by and check her status but had resisted, fearing it would seem inappropriate. No one had actually said she couldn't review the chart, but she didn't think it was a good idea. Not knowing what was going on with the patient *or* the medical inquiry only made her more agitated, and she wasn't sure what to do with her uneasiness. She didn't want to talk about it with her colleagues. She was mildly embarrassed and figured everyone had a similar story, so what was the point. Still, she'd told Jett, and it felt good. Good to tell her. Good to hear the sympathy in her voice and see the trusting certainty in her eyes.

She'd thought a lot about Jett during the long hours of the night, snippets of conversation coming back to her along with the flash of her eyes or the lightning-quick grin that rarely lingered. Now that she was done for the day, she was still thinking about Jett, and that probably wasn't the best idea. Jett reminded her of a skittish thoroughbred. Not the kind of animal to take out for a casual ride, and too fine to risk breaking with a heavy hand. No, Jett was most definitely not her usual fare. But thinking about her wound her up just the same. A heavy pulse in the pit of her stomach demanded attention.

What she needed was a diversion. Something to help her relax and take her mind off work and the accusation that she was incompetent, and to help her ignore the stirring in her depths whenever she thought about Jett's low, calm voice and intense eyes. While she waited for the elevator to the parking garage, she scrolled through the familiar numbers on her cell phone until she found one that she thought would work. She hit speed dial and waited.

"Darla? It's Tristan." The elevator doors opened, she stepped on and pushed the button for her floor. "Any chance you can be late for work? I was thinking you might like some breakfast in bed. Where are you?" She got off at her floor and strode rapidly toward her car, shedding the skin of one life for another with every step away from the hospital. "I'll pick you up right outside, then. Be there in a minute."

She closed her phone and jumped in her car. She'd been seeing Darla, a statuesque redhead who worked in the accounting department at the medical school, fairly regularly. Darla had been in a long-term relationship that had ended messily, and she wasn't in the mood for another commitment anytime soon. She was, however, usually in the mood for a few laughs and demanding sex. Tristan had soon discovered that Darla especially got off on sex in public places. Since it amused her to amuse Darla, she usually went along with it.

Gunning the engine, she sped down the ramp toward the exit. A little dose of Darla in the morning was just what she needed to diffuse the cloud of disquiet that hung heavy in her mind.

❖

Jett slammed the hood of her Jeep and rocked back on her heels, resigned. After fiddling with her battery, the ignition, and the engine for an hour, Jett finally admitted she wasn't going to get the damn thing to start. It had finally died. Since she wasn't in the mood to hang around waiting for a tow, she'd call when she got home and make arrangements to meet someone before her shift later that night. Besides, walking two miles home would be a good way to unwind. Maybe when she got there, she'd be tired in a good way. Tired enough to sleep without dreaming.

She hustled down the stairwell to the street, blinking when she emerged from semidarkness into the bright sunlight. Hospital staffers hurried toward the main entrance and food vendors jostled for position along the curb. As she waited to cross at the corner, a familiar car slowed for the light. Tristan's car. Jett felt a surge of unfamiliar pleasure. Maybe she could repay her for breakfast.

She leaned down to the open passenger window, about to call out a greeting and an invitation, when she realized Tristan wasn't alone. A very attractive redhead crowded close to Tristan, her hand in Tristan's lap as she nuzzled her neck. Tristan stared straight ahead, her hands clenched on the wheel.

Jett straightened and hurriedly stepped away. Tristan obviously already had plans for the day.

CHAPTER TEN

A re you avoiding me?" Gail slid onto the bench in the mess tent next to Jett.

"No, why would I?" Jett sipped her coffee and hoped she sounded normal. In fact, she'd been all twisted around since the night she ended up in Gail's tent. When her mind wasn't totally consumed with staying alive, and keeping her fellow soldiers the same way, she thought about that night. About how good it felt to have someone else take charge, to have someone else take responsibility, to have someone else blot out the horrors that she could never quite erase from her mind. None of those feelings were normal for her, but then nothing here was normal and the longer she stayed, the more lost she felt. Even flying, her one true pleasure, was slowly becoming associated with tragedy and loss. And because she wasn't really herself, and because she'd almost let Gail do all those things she ordinarily wouldn't want, she'd gotten as far away from her as fast as she could.

But when she closed her eyes, she thought about her.

Gail moved closer and lowered her voice. "You were upset when you left the other night. I was having such a good time, just relaxing with you, I didn't realize you weren't enjoying yourself."

"That's not true," Jett said quickly, not all of it. She'd enjoyed it, and wished she hadn't. And she *had* been avoiding Gail. She didn't have casual friendships with women, although she was perfectly comfortable having casual sex. Gail seemed to want something else— something she didn't know how to give. Gail wanted intimacy, and Jett wasn't certain if that included physical intimacy or not. And that was the problem. Even though Gail outranked her, they were close enough that they wouldn't be crossing any significant lines. Those lines were crossed every day between male and female officers, and people looked the other way. But they were both women, and that was a big line, especially with them working together. Gail wasn't a one-night stand in some liberty town, never to be seen again. Gail was a career officer she'd see every day.

"Then where have you been?" Gail asked. "I've missed you."

"It's just been crazy around here. I haven't been out of the aircraft for more than a few hours at a time in a couple of days." Jett knew the excuse was feeble, but part of her didn't want to say no. And she could hardly tell Gail she didn't trust herself around her.

"I know. Whatever's going on, it's heating up. The casualty count is higher than I can ever remember it."

Jett felt a surge of relief, glad that Gail had accepted her excuse. She'd learned fairly early in life that on those rare occasions when she connected with someone, she connected on every level. When she let herself care about a woman, she wanted her, and more often than not that got her into trouble. So now she stopped it before it even started. Since she was incapable of doing things by degrees, she chose not to let any relationship go too far. Fortunately military life, especially for a lesbian, wasn't conducive to anything long-term or even short-term serious.

But things had already gone too far with Gail. Somehow, Gail had gotten past her normal defenses, and now Jett was powerless to keep her out. Just the same, she didn't think she could offer Gail the kind of close physical contact that came naturally to Gail. Not without wanting, needing, to share everything. And there were a million reasons why that was a bad idea. No, the best course was to just stay away from her.

"I'm not going to let you get away, you know," Gail whispered, shifting almost imperceptibly until their shoulders touched. "I never got a chance to finish with you the other night."

Arousal punched through Jett, and if she hadn't been sitting, she might have doubled over. She took a shaky breath, praying for the strength to resist.

"Hey, Cap! Jett!"

At the sound of her name, Jett stopped walking and stared around her in confusion. Where she expected to see an endless stretch of desert sand, she saw lush grass and thick leafy trees. The bright sun was hot but carried no hint of deadly intent. The morning was beautiful. Linda waved to her from the front seat of a dark blue convertible that idled at the curb, its top down and all the windows open.

"Do you need a ride?" Linda asked.

"No, thanks," Jett said, still reeling from the too-fresh memories. She hadn't been this bad since she'd first left the service. Now she could barely keep the images at bay even when awake, and she couldn't figure out what was triggering them. Linda regarded her expectantly, and she wondered if she'd actually answered out loud. She repeated, "No, thanks. I don't live that far away. Just up on Lincoln Drive."

"I'm going that way. I don't live that far, either, but I'm glad I'm not walking after the night we had. I've just got to stop and pick up my daughter for a dentist appointment. She's right on the way." Linda waited a few seconds. "Come on, get in. It's a beautiful morning for a ride."

Jett was about to refuse again and then realized she didn't really want to. She didn't want be left alone with the recurring images of those barren, arid months when nothing was truly as it seemed except the certainty that no one could outrun death. She walked over to the car, braced her hands on the frame, and vaulted the door into the passenger seat.

"Thanks," Jett said. "A ride would be nice."

Linda gave her an appreciative glance before pulling away from the curb. "Nice move."

Jett frowned. "Sorry?"

"That little show of muscle getting into the car."

"I didn't realize that sort of thing qualified as a move," Jett said with a laugh.

"You're kidding." Linda raised an eyebrow. "You fly a helicopter and you haven't figured out that girls love macho studs?"

"Can't say as I have." Jett tilted her head back and watched the clouds skim by overhead. The wind rushing by the car and the streaming clouds made her feel as if she were flying. Pleasantly relaxed, she answered without thinking. "Probably because I don't qualify as either macho or studly."

"Where exactly did you grow up?" Linda signaled and turned left. "Somewhere the women were blind, obviously."

Ordinarily Jett would have been on edge with the direction of the conversation, but Linda wasn't saying anything Jett hadn't heard her say in one form or another to every other member of the team. Linda was easy to be around. She played at flirting, but Jett had the clear sense it was all in fun. The undercurrent of heat was missing. "On a farm where the nearest girl my age was twenty miles away and engaged by the time she was fifteen. And she wasn't all that unusual."

Linda groaned. "No baby dykes?"

"If there were, we didn't recognize each other."

"Well, I'm here to tell you, we girls love handsome girls like you who handle big equipment with finesse."

Jett laughed. "I never realized my aircraft would be so useful."

"Oh yeah, that helicopter is so sexy."

Tristan's voice came back to her, along with the image of the mesmerizing light in her eyes when she said, *You make me wish I were a helicopter.* A wave of longing broke over Jett and for a second she was breathless. Then she pictured Tristan in the car with the redhead who seemed very very glad to see Tristan. Tristan obviously had her pick of women, and probably said something similar to all of them. She definitely wasn't saying no to what the redhead was offering.

"The next time we're headed into a thunderstorm," Jett said, forcing a smile, "I'll try sweet-talking my aircraft if things get bumpy."

"Never underestimate the power of sex appeal, Captain."

"I wasn't a captain."

"What were you?"

"Chief Warrant Officer."

"Oh, I like that." Linda gave Jett a sultry look. "Chief."

Jett groaned and Linda laughed.

"I'll just be a minute." Linda slowed and stopped on the shoulder in front of a wide expanse of immaculately groomed grass where several groups of youths in various uniforms ran up and down the field.

"Take your time. I'm good."

Jett closed her eyes, determined not to think about Tristan or Gail or feelings she couldn't understand and didn't want. When the car rocked a little bit and a female voice very close to her ear murmured, "Hi. Who are you?" she opened her eyes. A blonde bent over her, her arms folded on the top of the door, her mouth inches from Jett's. The position afforded Jett an unimpeded view down the blonde's scoop-necked top, making it abundantly clear that she wore nothing underneath the tight white ribbed cotton. Her breasts were full and pale and, if the hint of pink was any indication, rose-tipped.

"Jett McNally," Jett said, straightening in her seat and glancing toward the field. Linda was on the far side, her hand on the shoulder of a young child, talking to another adult. "I'm a friend of Linda's."

"Oh, goody. I was afraid for a moment you might be taken." The blonde extended her hand, leaning even further into the passenger seat. Her breast brushed Jett's shoulder. "I'm Mandy. I'm available."

"Nice to meet you." Jett shook her hand and couldn't help but smile. Mandy's eyes danced with unabashed invitation. The total lack of subterfuge was oddly appealing.

"So you work at the hospital?" When Jett nodded, Mandy snaked her fingers up Jett's bare arm and underneath the sleeve of her tight black T-shirt. "I like this new look. So much better than those ugly green scrub shirts."

"I don't wear scrubs. I'm a pilot," Jett replied, shivering involuntarily as Mandy played her nails over her biceps.

"Ooh. Really?" Mandy's mouth curved into a smile, as if she had just tasted something particularly delicious. "That's very interesting. What else can you drive?"

"Almost anything." Jett hadn't sought anyone out for pleasure in a very long time, and her body was telling her loud and clear the absence had been noted. Her unwanted dreams of Gail were becoming more and more frequent, and whether she welcomed it or not, her need spiraled higher every day. She was going to have to do something soon, and this woman, a very attractive ruby-lipped, full-bodied, ripe and luscious woman, was offering.

As if reading her mind, Mandy slowly trailed the tip of her tongue over the surface of her lower lip. "I'm volunteering to navigate."

Linda pulled open the driver's door and pushed the bucket seat forward so a young girl could climb into the backseat. "Hi, Mandy. Out hunting?"

Mandy slowly danced her fingertips up the side of Jett's neck and ran them sensuously through Jett's hair. "Not anymore."

"Jett, this is Kim," Linda said as she helped the child with her seat belt. "Jett's a friend of Mommy's from work, honey."

"Hi," Jett said, turning in her seat to greet the child.

The little girl responded with a shy smile as Linda started the car. Mandy still clung to Jett's arm, and Jett eased away as much as she could in the cramped quarters. "Nice meeting you, Mandy."

"Don't say good-bye." Mandy stepped an inch or two away from the car. "Say you'll call me." She rattled off a telephone number. "I'm sure anyone who can fly an airplane—"

"Helicopter," Jett interjected.

"Even better. A helicopter." Mandy drew out the word with a breathy sigh. "I'm sure you can remember seven little numbers."

Linda eased the car forward. "Bye, Mandy."

"I am invited Saturday, aren't I?" Mandy called.

"Of course," Linda called back, pulling out into the street and accelerating. She glanced at Jett. "So that's Mandy. She owns one of the local gyms and volunteers at the rec center in the summer."

"Uh-huh." Jett suspected there was quite a lot more to Mandy than Linda was saying, although she didn't get the sense that Linda actively disliked her. Their interaction had a teasing, mock-challenging quality to it.

Linda glanced at the backseat, then lowered her voice. "So are you going to call her?"

Jett shrugged. She really didn't know, because calling meant reaching out. Making an effort. Admitting to herself that she wanted contact, closeness, even if it was false. And she still carried too much anger to allow herself that little bit of comfort. "I think she's out of my league."

"Ah," Linda crooned. "I do love a woman with a sense of humor."

"Then I'm glad you put up with me."

"You are coming Saturday, right? Mandy or not?"

"I'll be there," Jett said, surprising herself. Saturday began her week down between flight rotations, and usually she spent her time holed up in her apartment working on her watches and clocks, trying to sleep, and occasionally venturing out for long, solitary walks in the middle of the night. Seven days without flying, without work to distract her, often felt like seven months.

She didn't have a lot of experience with parties, but she imagined they were a lot like bars, filled with superficial interactions that allowed her to circle the edges of real connection. Once in a while, when the urge was strong, she'd find someone willing to take what she could offer for a few hours.

"Good. It'll be fun," Linda said.

"Great. That sounds great."

❖

"Oh baby, yeah, yeah," Darla panted. "God, you're gonna make me come again. God, God that's good."

Tristan knelt between Darla's spread thighs, sweat dripping from her forehead onto Darla's long, taut belly. She had four fingers inside her, pushing deep with each hard thrust, her thumb banging against Darla's clit each time she plunged. She'd already made her come three times and Darla gave no indication of quitting anytime soon. Tristan was fine with that. Darla liked it hard, and she needed the workout. She needed to burn her mind clean. So even though her arm was shaking and her vision blurring with a combination of sweat and fatigue, she kept pumping.

Darla undulated mindlessly, her legs thrashing, her neck arched, her mouth open as she implored and exhorted and exalted. At one point she reared up and clamped onto the arm Tristan was fucking her with so hard her nails broke Tristan's skin. Tristan almost came from the unexpected surge of pain. Instead, she gripped Darla's nipple with her free hand and twisted, and Darla gushed with another orgasm. Eventually, Darla sagged back, moaning quietly. Tristan leaned over her, supporting herself on one arm, and kept going. Darla's internal muscles clutched weakly at her fingers, and Darla finally pushed Tristan away.

"I'm done, baby," Darla said drowsily. "That was fantastic."

Tristan rolled over onto her back. Completely whipped, she closed her eyes.

"I'll take care of you in a minute." Darla sounded practically drunk with satisfaction.

"Don't worry about it." Tristan couldn't feel anything below her aching shoulders. "I'm great."

❖

An hour later, Tristan drove Darla back to the medical school.

"You're going to get me fired, you know that, baby," Darla accused, sounding not the least bit concerned.

"You're too good at what you do for them to fire you. Besides, don't you get sick time?"

Darla inched close and bit Tristan's neck while squeezing her crotch. "But I'm not sick. I might have a thing for you, but it's a healthy addiction."

Tristan groaned and pushed back in her seat. She was still pumped and swollen from their frantic sex, even after a shower. She hadn't come other than a fast explosion in the car on the way to her apartment, and that had been more a nervous discharge than a full-bodied orgasm. "Don't get me started again. That's cruel and unusual punishment."

"I don't want you to think I'm selfish," Darla whispered, rimming Tristan's ear with her tongue.

"I don't think that." Tristan grasped Darla's wrist and eased her hand away. "I think I've mentioned I love fucking you."

"Well, good, then. When can we do it again?"

Tristan hesitated. Darla was exactly the kind of woman she liked to date. Darla knew what she wanted, she asked for it, and when she got it, it was enough. Ordinarily, Tristan would be ready for a repeat with her as soon as possible. Sex with Darla that morning had been just like it had been half a dozen times before. Fast and furious—a flash fire decimating everything in its path. Unlike all the other times, though, she was vaguely unsatisfied. Before she could think too much about why, she said, "How does Saturday sound? There's a bit of a neighborhood gathering and then later, we could sneak away for our own special dessert."

"Why sneak anywhere?" Darla nipped Tristan's earlobe. "I bet I can find a quiet corner somewhere and you can do me right there."

"I work with these people. Think of my reputation."

"I am." Darla patted Tristan's crotch and eased back over into the passenger seat as Tristan pulled up in front of the medical school. "I guarantee after that kind of demonstration, every girl there will want you."

"That's the last thing I need." Tristan laughed. She doubted someone like Jett would be impressed, and just as quickly wondered why she had immediately thought of her. She leaned over and kissed Darla. "I'll pick you up around seven."

"I'll see you then." Darla stepped out of the car, then leaned down and blew Tristan a kiss. "Thanks, baby. You're the best."

Tristan waited until Darla disappeared into the building, then drove toward home. She was tired. Tired and disquieted. Nothing had changed, but nothing felt quite right.

CHAPTER ELEVEN

Jett heard the music and the hum of voices before she even reached the gate in the white picket fence that fronted Linda and her partner Robin's house in a neighborhood of Victorian twins. Linda's home was a brilliant robin's egg blue with darker blue and pale yellow on the detailing along the eaves, windows, and porch. The party was apparently in full swing, which Jett had expected since she was intentionally an hour late. This way she could slip in unnoticed, and leave just as invisibly, if she wanted.

She'd debated for the last day and a half as to whether she was actually going to come to the softball party at all. She'd heard about the huge city women's league—Linda declared it fertile ground for girl-watching and general socializing—but she'd never gone to any games. When she sought female company, she preferred the clubs. The rules were much clearer there, and almost everyone had a similar agenda. Even though Linda had invited a lot of the hospital staff, so Jett was certain she would know people, she doubted she'd fit in very well. She just hadn't developed an easy way of talking to people whose lives were so very different from hers. After spending all her adult life in the military with others whose experiences were almost exactly the same as hers, and having endured eighteen of the last twenty-four months in a combat zone, she didn't know what to talk about with people whose lives revolved around things as simple and uncomplicated as mutual friends, children, and harmless hospital intrigue.

She stared at the warm, friendly-looking house, her hand on the gate latch, and asked herself why she had come. An answer formed in the back of her mind, one that left her even less willing to step through the gate. Tristan would be there. Tristan would be there and she wanted to see her. They'd had a few easy conversations, a rarity for Jett, and Tristan had somehow gotten her to talk about herself. That event was so unusual, Jett still sensed the inner click of connection whenever she replayed the encounter, which was often. But judging from what she'd seen outside the hospital the other day, Jett was certain Tristan would be with a woman. She'd probably already forgotten their conversation.

"If you're looking for the party, you're in the right place."

A woman approached juggling a case of beer and a grocery bag overflowing with chips and other snacks. Her solid build and bold blue eyes were familiar. Jett only caught glimpses of the trauma team as they huddled on the roof, waiting for the medcrew to off-load patients from the helicopter, and she was usually busy securing her aircraft and not watching what was happening outside. Still, she'd seen this woman enough times to recognize her as one of the trauma surgeons.

"Let me give you a hand," Jett said, reaching for the shopping bag.

"Thanks. I'm Quinn Maguire." Quinn handed over the sack.

"Jett McNally. I fly for Healthstar."

"Oh, so you're responsible for stealing Linda away from us. You'd better not advertise that too loudly. My partner is the ER chief and she hasn't gotten over Linda's defection yet."

"Sorry." Jett grinned. "Actually, I don't think I'm responsible. I think it's the helicopter."

Quinn laughed and pushed open the gate, motioning Jett to go ahead. "I can see Linda being into that. Seriously, you guys make a huge difference. Since the hospital got flight approval, I've seen a real decline in our mortality stats."

"That's good to know." Since the choice had been made for her, Jett stepped into the yard and followed a stone pathway around the side of the house. The wood-fenced backyard was bigger than she expected and crowded with women and men and children.

"I've got to dump this stuff inside and find Honor," Quinn said. "We've got a new baby and Honor is probably due for a little break about now."

"Here," Jett said, shifting the groceries to one arm and reaching for the beer with the other. "Where do you need this?"

"Thanks. In the kitchen, I guess." Quinn pointed to the back porch and the open back door. "Straight through there."

"I've got it."

"Appreciate it. Nice talking to you."

Quinn sauntered off into the crowd, and Jett went in search of the kitchen. Having something to do made her feel slightly more comfortable. She nodded to women she didn't know who smiled as she passed, said hi to Juan, who leaned against the railing with a pretty woman she assumed was his wife, and edged open the back door with her shoulder. The kitchen was as crowded as the yard, filled with people replenishing drinks, exchanging empty bowls of food for full ones, and standing in groups talking. To her relief, Jett saw Linda immediately and headed for her.

"I ran into Quinn. Special delivery."

"Hey," Linda said with a big smile. "You made it. That's great. Oh good, more beer. I should've remembered that softball players aren't big on wine. They're going through the beer like mad. The backup coolers are in the dining room. Would you mind putting these on ice in there for now?"

"Sure. Where's the dining room?"

Linda squeezed Jett's arm. "Sorry. Through that door and to the right. Did you get something to eat?"

"Not yet. I'm good."

"Well, don't wait if you get hungry. Soon there won't be anything left but the carcasses."

"Got it." Jett hefted the case of beer and worked her way through the crowd into the relative peace and quiet of the dining room. The table was covered with a paper tablecloth and platters, mostly empty, of the usual summer party fare—salads, burgers, chicken, and pasta dishes. Four coolers sat on plastic sheets against one wall. She set down the case of beer and checked the coolers. When she found one with only a few cans of beer remaining, she squatted to transfer the beer into it.

"Need help with that?"

At the sound of Tristan's voice, Jett's pulse jumped a little and she took a couple of seconds to steady herself. Then she looked up. From her position, she was just about at eye level with the fly of Tristan's low-slung jeans. Tristan wore a white cotton shirt with the sleeves rolled up. Her dark hair was tousled, the way it had been that morning out on her porch, and her lips curved into a smile that Jett could have interpreted as pleasure, if she'd wanted to. She didn't. She rose quickly, needing the advantage of being eye to eye. Actually, she was just a little taller than Tristan, which helped when she was so off balance around her.

"All taken care of. Are you running low outside?" Jett asked.

Tristan slowly shook her head. "I don't think so. I saw you come in with Quinn. I was wondering if you were going to show."

"Linda is hard to say no to."

"I'm glad you made it."

Jett didn't know what to say to that, because she didn't know how to interpret it. Tristan didn't seem to do small talk, but Jett might be imagining the connection she felt. Fortunately, she was saved from replying when several people wandered in, chatting as they began gathering the empty dishes from the table. Jett moved out of their path and Tristan followed her. Jett backed up, aware of Tristan inches away, until she turned the corner into the living room, which was empty. Somehow they ended up standing in the far corner next to an entertainment center.

"When I first saw you out there, I thought for a second you were going to dump that beer and leave." Tristan leaned against the wall, her right hand in her front pocket. Her pose was casual but her eyes were hot and hard as they roamed over Jett's face. "You don't like crowds much, do you?"

Jett laughed. "I've spent the last thirteen years living in other people's pockets. Sleeping in barracks, riding in troop trucks, eating in mess halls—this is nothing." When Tristan only stared, Jett contemplated walking away. Tristan saw things she didn't want seen. And she asked questions that Jett didn't want to answer.

"But you really don't want to be here, do you?" Tristan said.

"I'm not much for socializing."

Tristan laughed softly. "How about dating? Are you much for that?"

Jett's stomach tightened. The sun had been setting when she'd walked over, and now it was nearly dark outside. No one had turned the room lights on, and she and Tristan stood in shadow. A hot breeze blew through the window, and she pictured them in her tent on a still, sultry night, skins wet with sweat, blood pounding as their arms and legs tangled. She shook her head, as much to dispel the image as to back Tristan off. "I don't date."

"But you *do* like women."

"I think you know that," Jett murmured.

"Hoped." Tristan ran her finger inside the open collar of Jett's short-sleeve cotton shirt, along Jett's collarbone.

Jett tensed. Tristan's touch drew a line of fire over her skin. This was nothing like Gail. She hadn't known what Gail wanted and wasn't sure of Tristan either, but Tristan at least was honest about this much. Tristan's message was clear and Jett's body responded to the invitation. A throb of arousal beat hard between her thighs. "What do you want from me?"

"I want you…" Tristan's voice was hoarse and she swallowed. "I want you to go out with me."

"Why?"

"Because you don't go out with just anybody, and I want it to be me when you do."

"Maybe I just don't like people," Jett said lightly, trying to break the spell of Tristan's gaze. Tristan had dropped her hand, but they'd both shifted so their bodies very nearly touched. Jett's nipples were tight and aching. She wanted to capture the pulse dancing at the base of Tristan's throat in her teeth.

"You must care about people, or you wouldn't do the work you do." Tristan eased one leg forward until her thigh grazed Jett's. "So that's pretty much bullshit."

"I do what I do because I love to fly." Jett's temper flared. Tristan pissed her off, pushing and probing, wanting to get inside her. The anger fused with her arousal until her whole body trembled with the need to put her hands on Tristan. She wanted to strip her bare, the way Tristan was slicing away her defenses. She wanted to be inside her, buried in her, the way Tristan was penetrating her. She wanted to make her cry out, with shock and pleasure, the way Tristan was forcing her to feel her own needs and desires.

"Uh-huh." Tristan's breath shuddered out and she tilted her head, her eyes on Jett's as she inched closer. Another fraction and they'd be kissing, if Jett didn't move. "You don't trust people very much, do you?"

"I haven't had much reason to."

"Why? Who hurt you?"

"That's enough," Jett whispered.

Tristan blinked, gasping suddenly as if she'd been held underwater until she was almost drowning and had just struggled to the surface. She clasped Jett's waist with both hands and leaned in for the kiss. "I'm sorry. You do things to me. You make me want—"

"Tristan, don't." Jett saw the redhead coming and backed away.

"There you are," Darla said brightly as she wrapped her arms around Tristan from behind. She kissed the side of her neck. "I thought I'd lost you."

Tristan stiffened and her face went blank. Still watching Jett, she said casually, "Shop talk."

"God, don't you doctors ever get enough." She kissed Tristan again, then leaned around her and held out her hand to Jett. "Hi, I'm Darla."

"Jett. Nice to meet you." Jett edged past Tristan toward the door. "Have a nice night."

Jett hadn't made it out of the room before she heard Darla say, "You owe me dessert."

Out of the corner of her eye she saw Darla wrap her arms around Tristan's neck and press her back against the wall, kissing her hungrily. As Jett escaped, she felt no anger or disappointment, only relief. She'd wanted that kiss, she'd wanted more than that. And now she could stop wanting.

❖

"Uh-oh," Linda murmured.

"What?" Honor had almost fallen asleep stretched out in a lounge chair on the lawn. Robin had hung candle lights from the fence and several trees, drenching the wide yard with a warm, yellow glow. Honor felt the warmth inside, supremely content and satisfied.

"Nothing."

Honor sat up, instantly alert to the oh-so-casual note in Linda's voice. She scanned the yard and in less than a second found the source of Linda's remark. Mandy had cornered Quinn at one of the picnic tables and was practically straddling her lap. Probably the only reason she wasn't actually *in* Quinn's lap was that Quinn had Jack in a baby carrier across her chest.

"Okay," Honor said lightly, pushing herself upright with one arm. "Time to kill her."

"Wait," Linda said, grabbing Honor's arm.

"Nope. No more waiting. I've been patient for almost two years. Enough is enough."

Linda was laughing.

"I'm serious," Honor said calmly.

"I know. I know. But look at her face."

Honor was afraid that one more look at Mandy sniffing around Quinn was really going to make her lose her temper. She didn't actually plan on creating a scene, but she did intend to make it clear that Quinn was off-limits, once and for all. Nevertheless, she checked Mandy out again. After a second, she laughed too. Quinn sprawled back against the picnic table, relaxed and sexy as all get-out. Just the sight of her made Honor want to drag her away somewhere and get her naked. As Quinn grinned up at Mandy, she absently patted Jack's back.

Mandy stared at Jack with undisguised horror, as if he were an alien creature that had somehow landed on Quinn's chest. Ever so slowly, she backed up.

"I guess she's not one of those women who gets teary-eyed at the sight of a baby," Honor said.

"Honey, she looks like Quinn has a contagious disease."

"Quinn looks unbelievably *hot* holding that baby."

"Well, it's a good thing you think so, since she's probably going to be doing that a lot for the next couple of years."

"Look," Honor said, "Mandy is practically running away."

"I think Jack has finally accomplished what even the wedding ring couldn't do. Mandy acts like Jack is a no-trespassing sign hanging around Quinn's neck. Hands off. Private property of Honor Blake."

"Good. I trust Quinn." Honor eased back down into the chair. "That still doesn't mean I like some harlot looking at her like she's a side of beef."

"Harlot?" Linda lowered her voice when several people looked in their direction. "*Harlot?*"

Honor shrugged. "That seemed more polite than some of the other things I was thinking."

"Well, I'd say your beefcake is safe now." Linda followed Mandy's retreat, then muttered again. "Uh-oh."

"What now?"

"I think Mandy's just found fresh meat."

Honor turned to look. "Isn't that your pilot?"

Linda nodded as Mandy honed in on Jett, who leaned against one of the big oak trees, nursing a beer. "I hope Chief McNally can maneuver as well on the ground as she does in the air."

❖

"You promised you'd call me," Mandy said, tapping Jett in the center of her chest with a perfectly sculpted nail.

"Did I?" Jett shook her head, smiling slightly. "Then I should apologize for being so forgetful."

"You can make it up to me." Mandy draped both arms on Jett's shoulders and leaned against her, nestling her pelvis in Jett's crotch. Her breasts were heavy and warm against Jett's chest. Jett wasn't used to public displays of affection and glanced quickly around. No one was paying any attention to them, and more than one couple had cozied up on a lounge chair or sprawled on a blanket. Apparently everyone with children had taken them inside or gone home.

"I think you'd be disappointed." Jett palmed Mandy's hip and tried to put some space between them. Instead, Mandy rocked between Jett's legs.

"You don't know what I want." Mandy ran her tongue along the edge of Jett's jaw.

"More than I've got to offer."

Mandy's breath was hot against Jett's neck as she undulated against her. "I want you to make me feel good. Really good. And I know you know how."

Jett had been aroused since Tristan had touched her, and her body had been simmering for weeks with dream memories and daytime fantasies. Having Mandy climbing all over her was like tossing a match on gasoline. She kissed Mandy's neck.

"I just might."

"Show me," Mandy whispered hotly in her ear.

Jett looped an arm around Mandy's waist and pulled her around the other side of the tree into the shadows. Then she pushed her against the rough bark, wedged her thigh between her legs, and kissed her. Mandy moaned low in her throat and grabbed Jett's ass, grinding into her. Every single thought, image, memory fled from Jett's mind and all she felt were hot ripples of pleasure and merciful oblivion. She wanted more. She needed to find the knife edge of pleasure and slice through the hard heart of her pain until she bled to empty.

"Let's get out of here," Jett rasped, dragging her mouth over Mandy's neck.

"Mmm, yeah," Mandy moaned.

Jett opened her eyes and through the haze saw Tristan staring at her from across the yard. She couldn't read what was in Tristan's face, and she didn't want to know what was in her mind. What she wanted was right in her hands. She grabbed Mandy's arm and dragged her away.

Chapter Twelve

L ook, Rick," Tristan snapped, "if you want the patient to wake up as soon as you finish the case, you need to start estimating your time better. Don't tell me it's going to take three hours and then decide to quit after two."

"If you were watching the case instead of reading the newspaper," the trauma fellow shouted, his face contorted with contempt, "you'd *know* when we were finishing up. I don't have time to do my job and yours too."

Tristan yanked off her surgical mask, not even bothering to untie it, and threw it into the trash can outside the surgical intensive care unit where they had just delivered a forty-nine-year-old construction worker who'd fallen off a scaffold and broken his back. He'd probably never walk again. It wasn't the kind of case that made anyone feel good, and Tristan wasn't in the mood to take any crap from a resident. She got up in his face, and a look of surprise flashed across his as he backed up. When she had him up against the wall, she said tightly, "I'm not a mind reader, even if that is irrelevant in your case, you brainless dipshit—"

"Your job is to make mine easier." Rick's chin shot out. "You're nothing more than a glorified technician, and not a very good one at tha—"

"You're a good one to talk. If you actually had a clue what you were doing—"

"Fuck you, you—"

Quinn barreled around the corner and headed for them. "Whoa. Whoa. Cool off, you two, I can hear you all the way down the hall."

She surveyed first Tristan, then her trauma fellow, and finally fixed on Tristan. "What's going on?"

"We just spent an extra thirty-five minutes with the patient on the table because your trauma fellow *forgot* to tell me he wasn't doing the feeding tubes today and ended the case early."

Quinn gave Rick a questioning look. He glanced away, his jaw muscles working silently. Finally, he said, "Ortho wants to bring him back in three days for a washout of his tibia, so I figured we could do it then if he needs it."

"Sounds reasonable. Did you tell Tris?"

"Well, I, uh—"

Quinn blew out a breath. "Okay. Rick, I'll meet you for rounds in thirty. We'll start in the SICU."

"Right," Rick mumbled, and hurried into the surgical intensive care unit.

"Jerk," Tristan muttered.

"I'll teach him the error of his ways later. So, what's going on with you?" Quinn slung an arm around Tristan's shoulders and walked her down the hall away from the surgical waiting room filled with families and visitors huddled in uneasy knots, alternately terrified and anxious. They stopped at the far end of the corridor where a bank of windows overlooked the expressway and the river beyond. "Rick fucked up, but it wasn't that big of a deal. I've never seen you go off like that before."

"He's a pain in the ass. He thinks he's a goddamned king and treats everyone else like peasants."

"Sure he does," Quinn said easily. "He's a surgeon, after all."

"Bunch of assholes, all of you."

"But we're so good, you have to love us."

Tristan laughed despite the press of anger in her chest. She wanted to lash out at someone, for something, even now. She braced both hands on the windowsill, her forehead nearly touching the glass. Outside the sun shone brightly beneath a crystal clear blue sky dabbed with white clouds. It was so beautiful, it was painful. "Sorry. Bad day."

"You sick?"

"No. I'm fine."

"Family?" Quinn asked gently.

Tristan shook her head. "It's nothing."

"Something's got you twisted around."

"Nah. I'm okay." Tristan lied because she had no explanation that made sense. Even to her. She'd been twisted around for two weeks, ever since the party. She'd made good on her promise to Darla and given her the semipublic thrill she'd wanted, fucking her in the bathroom next to the kitchen while a dozen people talked and laughed a few feet away. She'd even managed to keep her head in the game and not think about Jett while she'd been inside Darla, but she'd lost the battle after that. Darla had wanted to go down on her in the tiny, cramped room, and she'd resisted at first. But making Darla come hadn't blunted her arousal the way it usually did, and Darla kept teasing her, sucking her tongue while she squeezed her crotch, promising to do all kinds of things to her clit. Finally, when Tristan couldn't take it anymore, she'd ripped open her fly, shoved her pants halfway down her thighs, and pushed Darla down to her knees. Darla moved in, and she kept her promises. Tristan lasted twenty seconds before she'd flashed on the fierce expression on Jett's face when she plunged her tongue into Mandy's mouth, and she exploded into Darla's, barely managing not to shout, she came so hard. Darla loved it, laughing as they pulled their clothes on. Tristan had been confused and humiliated and embarrassed, even though she was willing to bet Darla wouldn't care who she was thinking about while she was coming. But Tristan cared. She didn't think about one woman while she was coming with another, but she couldn't keep Jett out of her head. And she still couldn't.

Morning, noon, and night, waking or sleeping, she kept seeing Jett drag Mandy behind the tree in a move so explosive Tristan was breathless just remembering. She could only imagine how it would feel to have Jett take her that way. She was certain no one ever had, and she wanted it. Wanted Jett to be the one making her explode. God damn it, this didn't happen to her.

"Tris."

The kindness in Quinn's voice broke her. She leaned her forehead against the window and closed her eyes. "I'm sort of fucked up over a woman."

"Well, that could definitely make it easy to lose your cool."

Tristan grimaced. "I'll say. In more ways than one."

"Anything you want to talk about?"

"Not really." Tristan spun around and tilted her head back, staring at the ceiling. "I don't usually get into women enough to get fucked up. Not since I was too young to know better."

"But now you have?"

Tristan shrugged. "Not exactly. I'm not sure what's going on, really. Nothing, actually."

"But you want there to be something."

Tristan thought about that, trying to sort through her tangled emotions. She went out with women all the time who were smart and capable and interesting and sexy, all the things she sensed Jett was. But Jett was something else too. She held herself back, away from other people. Tristan had watched Jett talk to Quinn at the party, seen her acknowledge people as she moved through the crowd, had caught glimpses of her chatting with Linda. Despite the interactions, Jett still seemed alone—until she'd kissed Mandy with such force and fury Tristan had felt the passion yards away. She could only imagine what might follow a kiss like that, and that was her problem. Imagining wasn't enough. She hungered to be the one who held the key to all that restless, seething energy, and the need went beyond simple desire. She wanted to know Jett's secrets.

"Fuck," Tristan muttered. "I don't know what I want. You know that old saying 'be careful what you wish for'?"

Quinn nodded.

"I think I should listen to that."

"Are you going to?"

"I don't think so."

❖

Jett cradled the delicate inner workings of the hundred-year-old timepiece in the palm of her hand and studied the mainspring through her loupes. At some point someone had replaced the original mainspring with the current one, which was slightly wider and thicker. As a result, the barrel cap would not seat evenly and the watch could not function properly. Finding the appropriate mainspring might be a challenge, but she was patient.

She set the watch aside and straightened, grimacing at the cramps in her shoulders and lower back. When she glanced at the wall clock, she realized she'd been working for four hours. Four hours when she'd thought of nothing at all. She closed her eyes and sighed. Two more days until the next rotation would start. A little more than forty-eight hours to fill.

For the last four days she'd read and worked on her timepieces and taken long walks at night. Sometimes she'd slept. On one late-night stroll in a fine misty rain, with all the houses along her way dark for the night, she'd walked down Tristan's street, her hands in the pocket of her jeans, her head bare and water streaming down her face. She'd stopped for a few seconds across the street and glanced up. Tristan's apartment was dark like all the others. When she started to wonder if Tristan was alone, possibly awake like she was, she walked on, faster, until thoughts of Tristan fled.

When her doorbell buzzed, she almost didn't recognize the sound. It was the first time anyone had come to her door, at least while she was home. The apartment complex was equipped with an intercom system, and she flipped the switch on the speaker next to her door.

"Yes?"

"Jett? It's Mandy."

Mandy. Forty-eight hours to fill and Mandy at her door. Jett glanced around her apartment—at the smooth white paper spread out on the table in the center of the room, covered with tiny watch workings, her screwdrivers and pin pusher and polishing bits arranged in a precise row. Her life was neat and orderly and controlled. Mandy was not. Jett grabbed her keys off the small table by the door and punched the intercom button. "I'll be right there."

When she got downstairs, Jett opened the inside door and stepped into the foyer where Mandy waited by the rows of mailboxes. The overhead light was out and the small space was dense with shadows. "Hi."

"Hi." Mandy smiled and looked her over in a way that told Jett she was thinking of them in bed. "Would you believe I was in the neighborhood?"

"No."

"Okay." Mandy hooked a finger over the waistband of Jett's jeans and pulled her close. "Would you believe I've been thinking about you and I'm horny?"

Jett laughed. "Yes."

"Do you have any suggestions?" Mandy tugged Jett's T-shirt from her jeans and slid her hand underneath, swirling her fingertips over Jett's stomach in slow circles. When Jett's muscles tightened, she said, "Mmm. Nice."

Jett's clitoris grew stiffer by the second as Mandy toyed with her, but she had a firm rein on her body. Unlike the last time Mandy had taken her by surprise. That time she'd been primed—halfway there from Tristan's touch. Now she was prepared. "I don't think this is a good idea."

"Why not?" Mandy sounded unperturbed. She popped the snap on Jett's fly with a practiced flick of her wrist and eased the zipper down. "I seem to remember there were a few things I wanted to do we never managed."

"We managed fine." Jett trapped Mandy's hand flat against her stomach. "Sometimes one night is perfect. Let's leave it that way."

Mandy studied Jett for a long moment. "I'm not looking for a girlfriend."

"Neither am I."

"Then we're perfect for one another. You're great in bed and I like sex." Mandy kissed her lightly. "You seriously fuck like a dream."

"Thank you."

"And you don't quit." Mandy laughed. "Most girls back off when it gets that intense. You don't."

Jett had lost it a little bit Saturday night. That hadn't happened since Gail. Fortunately Mandy had driven to the party Saturday night, because Jett wouldn't have been able to wait if they'd had to walk all the way to her apartment. She would have pulled Mandy into some dark alley before they'd gone six blocks. She often went months without sex and then spent two or three days doing nothing but exorcising the images of too much human misery with wild, relentless, continuous sex. She'd felt that way Saturday night, and Mandy had been the perfect partner, urging Jett to take her harder, harder, *harder* until both of them were too exhausted to move. In the morning, Jett had awakened in a tangle of sheets surrounded by the smell of sex and sweat and desperation, and when Mandy wanted more, *again, baby, come on*, she'd put Mandy off by saying she had to go to work. Then she'd walked Mandy down to her car and avoided promising to call. Because she knew she wasn't going to.

"You were amazing," Jett said, because it was true and she was going to disappoint her.

"But you're not going to fuck me again, are you?" Before Jett could answer, Mandy pressed her fingers to Jett's mouth. "No, don't answer that. Then you won't have to take it back when you get hungry again. Because you will. You can't keep that inside of you forever." She slid her fingers deeper into Jett's jeans until she brushed the base of Jett's clitoris. "Say no now."

"No."

Mandy laughed easily and removed her hand. "God, I really hope I'm around when you get the urge next time." She kissed Jett and backed away. "Still remember my number?"

Jett nodded.

"Use it when you can't wait any more. 'Night."

"Good night," Jett said softly as Mandy let herself out. She waited a minute or two for her breathing to settle, wondering why she hadn't just taken Mandy to bed. Mandy understood her in a lot of ways—and wasn't frightened or put off by her needs.

Jett slowly climbed the stairs to her apartment. She returned alone because it wasn't about what she needed, it was about what she wanted. And she didn't want Mandy.

She hadn't wanted anyone, in any way, for a long time. She stood in her quiet apartment and refused to lie to herself. She had wanted to kiss Tristan. She'd wanted a lot more than that.

When the phone rang, she almost didn't answer, thinking it might be Mandy. Then she realized it wouldn't be. Mandy would wait for her to call, because if Jett gave in and called, *Mandy* would be calling all the rest of the shots. Jett grabbed the phone on the fifth ring.

"McNally."

"Oh good," Linda said. "I was afraid for a minute you weren't there. Mike just went home sick with some kind of stomach bug. Can you take his shif—"

"I'll be there. Give me twenty minutes."

Jett hung up and hurried to shower. Twelve hours of work ahead. Then there would only be thirty-six until she was up again. As she stepped under the hot spray, she wondered who else might be on call tonight.

Chapter Thirteen

The first person Jett saw when she walked into the flight crew lounge was Tristan, leaning against the counter next to the refrigerator, laughing at something Linda had just said. She had a cup of coffee in her hand, and her maroon scrubs signaled she was on call. To a casual observer Tristan probably appeared totally relaxed, but Jett picked up the wariness in her gaze when their eyes met.

"Hi," Jett said.

"How you doing." Tristan's eyes drifted down the length of Jett's body and back again.

"Hey, Chief," Linda said. "I'm glad you could come in. Without a pilot we'd all be sitting here listening to Tristan's bad jokes for hours."

"No problem. Anything happening?" Jett walked to the rack against the far wall and grabbed one of the clipboards holding the preflight checklists. She was probably imagining that Tristan watched her as she moved. Probably. She'd worn black cargo pants and a dark gray T-shirt, and the way Tristan looked at her wasn't all that much different from the way Mandy had earlier—like she was sizing her up for bed. But this time, heat skittered along her skin. Of course, she probably imagined that look too.

"We were just about to go out on a call to pick up a preemie from Atlantic City Hospital. Necrotizing enterocolitis." Linda dropped into one of the seventies-style blocky tan vinyl-covered chairs, kicked off her clogs, and curled her legs under her. "The baby's pretty rocky and they requested a physician on board, which is how we lucked out and got Tristan. Then Mike got sick and we've been holding for you."

"Let me take a look at the aircraft," Jett said. "You can put us back on active status now."

"Okay."

"Mind if I tag along?" Tristan fell into step with Jett as she headed for the stairwell to the roof.

"No. Come on up."

Once outside, Jett walked to the waist-high concrete wall on the far side of the aircraft and breathed in the night. The air lay motionless, a heavy blanket of deep August heat beneath thick, unbroken clouds.

"Feels like a swamp out here," Tristan said from beside her.

"Rain's coming."

"You can tell?"

Jett hunched a shoulder. "You get a feel for it after a while."

"No wind." Tristan braced her arms on the wall and leaned out, craning her neck to see the river and the ribbon of cars that flowed along beside it like pearls on a string. "Funny how everything looks so much more beautiful at night."

Not everything, Jett thought to herself, studying Tristan's profile in the muted moonlight. Her dark hair blended with the sky, the slivers of pale light etching her features against the black backdrop in delicate relief. She was beautiful, hauntingly so. But Jett had seen her in bright sunlight too, and knew the shades of blue that swirled in her eyes. Just remembering, she experienced the same dizzying sensation as flying above crystal-clear water, drowning in the splendor.

"What are you thinking about?" Tristan murmured, aware that Jett had drifted away.

"The ocean," Jett answered as truthfully as she could.

"No, you weren't." Tristan leaned closer. "You were thinking about flying, weren't you?"

Tristan was inches away. Jett tried not to look at her mouth, and failed. The last time they'd been this close, they'd nearly kissed. Two weeks and an exhausting night with another woman hadn't diminished the memory. Or the desire. "How could you tell?"

"Because you looked happy." Tristan remained completely still, afraid to break their tenuous connection. She doubted that Jett had any idea how revealing her expression was when she wasn't carefully guarding her feelings. Right now, her lips were parted slightly, her lids heavy and shuttered. She looked completely desirable and completely unaware of the naked need in her eyes. Tristan sensed that if Jett realized how much she was revealing, she would instantly retreat. Tristan wanted to kiss her and knew that she couldn't. Because if she kissed her, Jett would know what Tristan had seen in her face. That need was part of Jett's secret, and one did not steal secrets from a woman like Jett. "Am I right?"

"About what?" Jett asked, sounding confused.

Tristan laughed. "About flying."

"No. Well, partly." Jett wanted to tell her, because Tristan so carefully hadn't asked. Unlike the last time they'd been together, when Tristan had pushed and needled her into nearly succumbing to Tristan's charm and her own hungers, tonight Tristan held back. Waiting, maybe. Waiting for Jett to own what pulsed and breathed between them. Jett never shied away from taking calculated risks when she was flying, but she'd learned her lesson with Gail. She couldn't trust herself with women. If she'd been thinking, if she'd been in control of herself, she never would have touched her. Next to her, Tristan waited. Maybe, maybe she could risk a little of the truth. "I was thinking that your eyes are the color of the Mediterranean at dawn."

"Jesus," Tristan whispered, completely blindsided. She was instantly, totally, mind-dazzlingly turned on. "This is the first time in a couple of weeks I haven't felt completely nuts. It would be good if you don't make me crazy now. Not when we're standing on a rooftop, and any moment we have to go to work."

"Bad week?" Jett eased back, giving herself space. Giving Tristan space. She needed it, and she had a feeling Tristan did too. Desire she understood. Sex she understood. These tentative touches to places far deeper she didn't, and wasn't at all sure she wanted to. When she was in control, she was safe.

"You could say that."

"Work?" Jett asked.

"Partly. The governor's son is understandably upset about his wife. Unfortunately, he's also a Class-A asshole."

Jett frowned. "He's still making trouble about the loose tooth in the airway?"

"Maybe not lawsuit kind of trouble, but he's been vocal about his unhappiness. She's out of the ICU but still on a respirator." Tristan turned her back to the sky and canted her hips against the wall. "The people in risk management don't think anything is going to come of it, because the media fallout would be bad. The governor isn't going to want an immediate family member suing one of the state medical school hospitals. But the son has everyone walking on eggshells just the same."

"Sorry. You don't deserve to be in the middle of that."

"Ah, hell," Tristan sighed. "It comes with the territory."

"It shouldn't," Jett said vehemently. "You do a job that not many can, and you deserve to be supported for doing it."

"Sounds like you have some experience with that."

"No system is perfect," Jett said evasively. "I should check out the aircraft."

"You never answered my question," Tristan called as Jett started away.

Jett looked back. "What question?"

"About women. Do you date women?"

"No. Not really." Jett grinned ruefully. "The military wasn't exactly a great place for it."

"I'll bet." Tristan stayed where she was because Jett looked like she was about to flee. Just like she always did when the conversation veered into the personal. Trying to get close to her was like trying to sneak up on a wild animal. Jett's senses were sharp and completely honed to guard against being taken by surprise. She expected Tristan to put some kind of move on her. To kiss her maybe, the way Tristan almost had at the party when she'd stopped thinking and given in to the crushing urge to touch her. But Tristan was thinking now, and she had a good hard hold on the desire that had her aching inside. She wasn't making any kind of move, sudden or otherwise, because she'd decided the only way she was ever going to get close to Jett was to keep surprising her. "You're not in the military now. So what do you say we get out of the city on Saturday. Take a ride up into the mountains. Hike a little bit."

"And that would be a date?" Jett bounced the clipboard against her thigh.

"Well, I figured we've already done the dinner date routine. Twice." When Jett frowned, Tristan added, "Hospital cafeteria."

Jett laughed. "Sorry. And they were memorable moments too." She was suddenly serious. "What about the redhead?"

Tristan tried not to let her discomfort show. She hadn't been certain if Jett had seen Darla move in on her, but now she knew. She wasn't about to apologize for something there was no need to apologize for, but she also wanted Jett to know…what? That her interest in Jett wasn't the same as it was with Darla? Was that really the truth? She'd been fascinated by Jett from the moment she'd seen her, even though Jett was nothing like the women she usually went out with. She thought about her. Dreamed about her. Christ, she fantasized about her. Fantasized about her taking her the way women never did, hard and fast and in charge. Okay, so *that* was different. But it wasn't like she was looking for a relationship with anyone. Still, it felt important to clear the record. "Darla is a friend."

"No promises there?"

Tristan shook her head.

"All right. Saturday." Jett nodded, turning the idea around in her mind. "Let's do that."

"Yeah," Tristan said, letting out a sigh and trying to ignore the way her heart jumped around in her chest. "Let's."

When they arrived at Atlantic City Medical Center to pick up the baby, the neonatal intensivists informed them that the surgeons had gone back in to stop some unexpected bleeding. The last update from the OR nurses was that the surgeons were closing. Linda checked with PMC for clearance to wait. With luck, they'd be airborne within the hour.

In the meantime, the flight team hung out in the lounge, picking at food left on a tray from someone's abandoned dinner, watching an old Vincent Price movie on the TV affixed high in one corner, and leafing through three-month-old magazines. It was Tristan, Linda, and Jett, and the conversation ranged from hospital gossip to politics and back to the casually personal.

"So, Jett," Linda said, "what made you decide to leave the military?"

Tristan stiffened and glanced quickly at Jett, who slouched on a sofa. Tristan didn't think this was a casual question for Jett. Seeing Jett's expression shutter closed, Tristan had a completely foreign urge to protect her, to prevent whatever bad memories the question stirred from hurting her.

"Probably the same reason you left the ER," Jett said smoothly. "It was time. I liked the Army. I always liked it. But…" She shrugged. "I wanted something else. Different experiences, I guess."

"Makes sense," Linda said, appearing not to have noticed the cool, detached tone of Jett's voice.

But Tristan noticed. Before she could change the subject, Linda continued on in her usual indomitable fashion.

"It must have been hard having a personal life. Did you worry much about it—you know, the 'don't ask, don't tell' thing?"

Tristan's insides quivered, and she wanted to jump up and wave her arms, as if warding off a freight train barreling down on a car stuck on the tracks at a railroad crossing. She felt about as helpless to stop the conversation as she would have been to divert the locomotive.

Jett rose suddenly and walked to the soda machine. As she dropped change into the slot, she said with her back to the room, "I didn't have much reason to worry about it. A lot of other people did." She popped the top on the soda as she turned, the fine lines around her eyes deeper than they had been. "They had reason to worry. Even over there, where everybody was needed and people tended to look the other way when rules got broken, that one could still take you down." She lifted the can and sipped, then headed toward the door. "It's hot in here. I think I'll be hot outside where there might be a breeze. Page me when I need to warm up the bird."

In the next instant she was gone. Linda stared after her. "Uh-oh. I stepped in something, didn't I?"

"I don't know. She doesn't say much about over there."

Linda rested her head on her hand and regarded Tristan contemplatively. "She is interesting. I like women with a lot of passion."

"Is that what you think it is?" Tristan asked, drumming her fingers on the tabletop.

"What do you think it is?"

"Pain. I think it's pain." Tristan stood abruptly and went after her.

❖

The landing pad at ACMC was not on the roof, like at PMC, but adjacent to the emergency room. Several emergency vehicles, angled to disgorge passengers, crowded around the emergency bay on the far side of Jett's chopper. Otherwise, the area was deserted. At three in the morning, only the dead and the dying and those who stood as the last barrier to inevitable fate moved through the silent hallways inside. Jett leaned against a pole beneath the short overhang in front of the ER entrance and smoked a cigarette she'd scored from a police officer as he'd been climbing into his patrol car.

"Got another one of those?" Tristan asked as she crossed the silent lot toward her.

"No, sorry," Jett said, holding it out to her. "Be my guest."

Tristan carefully took the half-smoked cigarette and drew deeply before handing it back. She coughed and shook her head. "I smoked for a year in college and then quit. Every time I bum a smoke, I remember why."

Jett smiled, took one last drag, and stubbed the butt out against the concrete pillar. Then she slid it into the outside pocket of her cargo pants. "I won't contribute to your delinquency."

"I didn't see you smoke at the party," Tristan said. "Most smokers do when they're drinking."

"I'm lucky. I can smoke or not smoke. I don't crave it."

Tristan thought about cravings. She liked women and she liked sex, but she rarely craved either. She wanted the pleasure sometimes, replayed moments with a woman she'd enjoyed on occasion, but only recently had being with a woman begun to feel like an obsession. Since Jett. "So you're basically a nonsmoker who indulges occasionally."

"Pretty much." Jett bent one leg and braced her foot against the pillar. "There's not much to do in the desert except smoke, toss a football if it's not too hot, and write letters home or wait for letters to come."

"I'd be thinking about sex a lot," Tristan said lightly.

Jett smiled a crooked smile. "Yeah, that too, I guess."

"Maybe it's that old adage about needing to feel alive when you're surrounded by death." Tristan spoke quietly, carefully, uncertain of her ground. But Jett had opened the door ever so slightly by mentioning her service, and Tristan desperately wanted to walk through. She wanted to be on the other side of the wall Jett erected between herself and everyone else.

"You must feel the same way," Jett said, neatly turning the tables. "You've probably seen more deaths than me."

"I don't think it's the same. I see violent death. I see senseless death." Tristan watched Jett's face in the slanting red light cast by the emergency sign over the double doors behind them, searching for guideposts. She couldn't find any so she followed her instincts. "I haven't watched my friends die—maybe for no reason that made sense to me. I don't think I could take that for very long."

"You lose your sense of time," Jett said as if talking to herself. "One day, two days, ten. Three months, six months, it all becomes just one long endless day and night, always the same." She looked at Tristan, her expression confused. "If you really think about it, really let yourself think about what's happening, you'd go crazy."

"I'm sorry." Tristan didn't want to say the wrong thing, do the wrong thing, but she ached for her. Gently, she cupped Jett's jaw, tracing her thumb along the sharp angle.

For a few seconds, Jett leaned into Tristan's hand, then slowly drew away. "Not your fault. Besides, I signed up for it, right?"

"I don't think anyone signs up for that kind of madness, do you?"

Jett shoved her balled hands into the pockets of her pants. "Some do, I think. The engagement is what it's all about for them. Others just love the service, being part of something bigger, grander than themselves. Gail was…"

The sudden silence in the hot still night was nearly suffocating. Tristan took a deep breath and still felt as if she were drowning. "Gail. A…friend?"

"Not exactly." Jett pulled her beeper off her waistband and peered at the readout. "They should be ready for us pretty soon, don't you think?"

"Babies are tricky," Tristan said, taking her cue from Jett and letting the subject drop. Part of her wanted the story on this woman who was obviously more than a friend, but part of her didn't want to hear there was someone special somewhere. That was different for her too. Very different. "None of their systems are mature, so they don't quite respond to anything the way you expect."

"Sounds like a real challenge." Jett strode toward the emergency room doors, all business again.

Tristan kept pace with her. "I don't mind. I thrive on challenges."

CHAPTER FOURTEEN

"What's our ETA?" Linda shouted, leaning around the Plexiglas shield that separated Jett from the treatment bay in the helicopter. She clamped a hand on Jett's shoulder to get her attention.

Jett pulled her headset away from her ear so she could hear and checked beside her. Linda, Tristan, and the patient were crowded into the space just to her right and behind her. When she was transporting an adult, usually all she could see were their legs. "About fifteen minutes. Problem?"

"The baby's looking bad. Bleeding again, Tris thinks."

"Roger. Tell her to hold on. I'll push it."

Linda nodded and scrambled back to inform Tristan "Another fifteen minutes max. How's it going?"

Tristan knelt on the deck next to the incubator, sweating under the heat lamps that kept the 2800-gram preemie warm. She shook her head grimly. "O2 SATs are falling and her pressure's bottoming out. God damn it, they never should have transferred her when she was this unstable."

"Is it her lungs?" Linda squatted next to Tristan and rehooked her safety harness. The ride was smooth—it always was with Jett flying—but she didn't want to get tossed around if they hit unexpected turbulence.

"I don't think so. She's either septic or bleeding again." Tristan raced through a mental checklist of therapies she needed to institute and the signs and symptoms of further decomposition she couldn't afford to miss. Linda was experienced and a great medic, but Tristan alone could make the decisions that might mean life or death for the neonate. "I think they'll need to go back in to be sure."

"I'll radio ahead to tell them we have a full alert."

"Better give the OR a heads-up too."

"Will do."

"How much blood did they send with us?" Tristan asked, watching the BP tail downward. Either the baby was bleeding or her heart was quitting on them.

"Just the one unit."

"Is it all in?"

Linda tilted the small plastic bag and squinted at it. "Just about. Do you want me to start some saline?"

"Yes, but keep it slow. We don't need to add fluid overload to her problems." Tristan gently probed the abdomen. "Tight as a drum. There's so much pressure below the diaphragm, I'm having trouble ventilating. Another couple of minutes and I'm going to have to open that incision. Jesus. Call the surgeons again and see what they say."

A minute later, Linda pulled off her headset. "I talked to Quinn. She says if we release the sutures, the sudden drop in intra-abdominal pressure will probably make her blood pressure fall too. She might arrest. Last resort only, she said."

"She's going to arrest if I can't get some oxygen into her." Tristan checked all the monitors again. "Tell Jett to find someplace closer. We're not going to make it like this."

"All right." Linda scooted forward and got Jett's attention. "We're in trouble back here. Is there anyplace else?"

Jett shook her head. "It's too late to turn back to Atlantic City, we're more than halfway to PMC. We might try Cooper in Jersey, if they can take us. Hold on, I'll get them for you."

When Linda got one of the ER nurses on the Technisonic radio, she quickly relayed the situation. After listening for a few seconds, she disconnected. "They just closed to emergencies. Their OR is backed up with victims from a five-car crash on the New Jersey Turnpike."

"Then we head for PMC. Tell Tristan I'll have her down in five minutes." Jett spared a quick glance behind her and saw Tristan working feverishly over the tiny form that was nearly invisible beneath the array of tubes, wires, monitors, and IV bags. It was always a shock to look back and not see the deck awash in blood or to hear the screams of the wounded.

Jett pushed the throttle to the max and as they streaked above the expressway, the flashing headlights below them came at her in the dark like tracer fire. The first time she'd taken a helicopter up after coming home, she'd seen the lights and thought she was under attack. Even now when caught unawares, she braced for bullets to pierce the cockpit and hit her. Tonight the enemy was time. She tried not to think about Tristan and the war she waged behind her, but she couldn't help it. She wanted to help her. So often she'd felt helpless to help, to stop the waste. Now as then, her impotence fueled her anger. Quickly, she shook her head to clear her mind of the past and the things she could not change. She pushed her aircraft, because that was all she could do. It didn't feel like enough, but then it rarely had.

"How long?" Tristan shouted. She hand-bagged the baby, hoping to get enough oxygen into her to keep her heart and brain working. Every breath was harder to deliver than the last. The infant's lungs just didn't have enough room to inflate with her intestines pushing up against her diaphragm.

"Three, four minutes." Linda took in the numbers on the portable O2 monitor. "God, Tristan, this is bad…"

"I can't push in any more air. If I increase the inspiratory pressure much more, I'm going to blow a lung." Tristan flicked the thin blanket away and exposed the distended abdomen. So much blood had accumulated beneath the surface, the thin skin appeared purple. "Give me a pair of scissors."

Without hesitation, Linda handed the instruments to Tristan. "I'll get wet packing ready."

Tristan clipped the first few sutures holding the abdominal incision together and loops of small intestine and bloody fluid immediately poured out. She caught the thin, delicate ribbons of bowel in her palm and protected them until Linda could wrap them in sterile saline-soaked gauze. Immediately, she was able to ventilate more easily. And just as quickly, the blood pressure fell. Sixty. Forty. Twenty. Nothing

"She's arresting!" As Tristan began closed cardiac compression, she realized the engine sounds were fading. They'd landed.

The doors flew open and Quinn jumped in. "What have you got?"

"Twenty-nine-week-old preemie," Linda announced. "Dead bowel resected at ACMC, prolonged intra-abdominal bleeding. We think she's still bleeding."

"I had to open the incision," Tristan told Quinn as the rest of the OR team sorted the monitors and lines to offload the patient to the waiting gurney. She jumped out and grabbed the stretcher across from Quinn. "I lost her pressure right away."

"Are we ventilating now?" Quinn asked tersely as they raced across the rooftop toward the elevators.

"Better. O2 SATs are coming up."

"Good." Quinn pressed a finger to the baby's groin. "I've got a pulse. Linda, can you run downstairs to the blood bank and get two units. I don't want to wait for a courier to bring it up. And call and see if the peds surgeon is here yet."

"You got it."

Linda disappeared down the stairs while everyone crowded into the elevator. The doors closed, and silence descended on the rooftop, broken only by the faint ping of the cooling helicopter engine and Jett's quiet footsteps as she secured her aircraft.

Gail pushed Jett toward the cockpit after they lifted the injured soldier inside. "We have to go! There's too many of them."

"Not yet!" Jett ran a few steps back toward the bodies still lying in the smoldering, twisted wreckage amidst mounds of rubble thrown up from the roadway when the transport vehicle had run over the IED.

"They're dead," Gail shouted.

Jett kept going until a hail of bullets stopped her. They'd just begun the evacuation when insurgents had poured out of several nearby buildings, opening fire on them. One of their medics had been hit, and for a heart-stopping moment she'd thought it had been Gail. They'd managed to get most of the wounded into the aircraft, but steady small arms fire made it impossible for them to get to the last few casualties.

"Jett," Gail screamed. "Go. We've got wounded on board. Go. Go."

Still, Jett hesitated. Her aircraft was filled with badly injured men and women, but leaving anyone behind, even the dead, violated everything she believed in. A bullet pinged off a nearby rock, and a shard of stone tore a hole in the shoulder of Jett's flight jacket. Another few inches and it would have hit her in the neck. The sharp pain and warm gush of blood down her arm sharpened her focus. She twisted and dove into the pilot's seat. Then she took the Black Hawk up and out of harm's way.

When Jett landed at the field hospital, Gail disappeared with the wounded and Jett staggered wearily to the showers. Almost too tired to think, she stripped and examined the gash in her shoulder in the wavy metal mirror above the sinks. It was long, but not deep. A little blood seeped from under the edges of the dark crust that had formed over it already. She turned the shower on as hot as it would go and stood under the water, her arms braced against the wall, her head down. She didn't know how long she'd been there, but the water had begun to cool when she heard movement behind her. Then a hand grasped her uninjured shoulder and spun her around.

"What the hell were you doing out there?" Gail shouted. She seemed oblivious to the fact that she was standing under the spray, still in her uniform, or that Jett was naked. "Were you trying to get killed?"

"I didn't want to leave them," Jett yelled back.

"Do you think I did?" Gail grabbed Jett's shoulders and shook her. "Do you think I wanted to see you blown apart?"

Jett winced and blood trickled down her shoulder.

Gail's eyes widened. "Oh my God. You're hurt. Why didn't you say something?"

"I'm all right."

"No, you're not." Gail's voice was tight. "I have to be able to trust you out there. I can't worry about you when I'm—"

Jett jerked away, heedless of the blood still seeping down her chest and over her breast. "Just worry about the wounded. I don't need you to worry about me."

"I worry!" Gail skimmed her fingers over Jett's chest and stared at the drops of blood on her fingers. "Don't you understand?" She cradled the back of Jett's neck with her other hand. "I don't know what I'd do if anything happened to you."

Gail hadn't touched her since the night of the aborted massage. Her fingers trembled over Jett's skin, softly caressing her. The pain from Jett's injury and the agony of leaving the wounded behind and the adrenaline coursing through her blood from the near-death experience stripped away the last of Jett's restraint. With a groan, she grasped Gail's arms and pushed her against the shower wall. Then she pinned her there with her body while she drove her hands into Gail's hair and her tongue into her mouth.

For an instant, Gail's arms came around her and her tongue swept over hers, hot and demanding.

A wave of hunger rose from Jett's depths, so primal, so powerful, all she knew was need. Gail was warm and alive and hers.

Jett came out of her half-doze with a start and looked around the lounge. Six forty-five a.m. She was alone, but the day shift would show up at any moment. She rubbed her face, stood, and shook the stiffness out of her shoulders. She hadn't really been asleep, just drifting in that disengaged state where she was aware of her surroundings but her mind was free to wander. Unlike so many other times before when she'd traveled back to her time with Gail, she came back to herself neither aroused nor angry. If she had to put her finger on exactly what she was feeling, she would have named it resigned.

She wandered over to the coffeepot, sniffed the few inches of black liquid in the pot, and grimaced. Then she emptied the dregs into the sink, rinsed the carafe, and poured a fresh pot of water into the coffeemaker. While she was digging around in the drawer for a packet of coffee, she heard footsteps behind her.

"If you're making coffee, I might have to marry you," Linda said.

"Is that legal in this state?"

"What? Gay marriage?"

Jett hesitated for a second, then laughed. It was getting easier to talk about what had always been forbidden. "I meant polygamy."

"No to both," Linda sighed. "God, what a night."

"Did you get any sleep?"

"No." Linda searched through the cabinets above the sink and found a clean coffee cup that she didn't think belonged to anyone. Even if it did, they probably wouldn't mind if she used it. "I had my beeper, so I knew you could reach me if there was another flight request. I stayed in the OR with Tris and Quinn."

Jett poured them both coffee. She didn't really have an excuse to go to the operating room, but she'd wanted to. She wanted to find out what happened to the patient, and she wanted to see Tristan. While she was flying, she couldn't pay much attention to what was going on with the patient, but enough had come through to her for her to understand how difficult the situation had been and how much pressure Tristan had been under. Since she couldn't go searching for her, she'd waited in the lounge, hoping for word.

"How did it go?" Jett asked.

Linda stared into her coffee cup as if the answer were somehow written inside it. "Sometimes no matter what you do, it's not enough, you know?"

Jett took a slow breath. "Yeah."

"The mortality rate for preemies that size is five times higher than a full-term baby. Add to that the multiple surgeries and the dead bowel and the bleeding…" Linda shook her head. "Just too much."

"I'm sorry." Jett replayed the flight in her head. Maybe if she'd pushed harder, she could have bought a few more minutes. Given Tristan a few more minutes. "Do you think if we'd been able to divert to Cooper—"

"I asked the same thing. Quinn didn't think so. Neither did Harry Noone, the pediatric surgeon."

"I guess that's something."

"It helps a little." Linda set her coffee aside. "Tristan doesn't believe it, though."

"Where is she?" Jett asked as casually as she could.

"I think she left. She was pretty strung out over the whole thing."

"She blames herself?" Jett wasn't surprised, not after listening to Tristan talk about the governor's daughter-in-law and her feelings of responsibility. Tristan took a lot on herself.

"I don't think anyone was able to convince her that opening up the abdominal incision isn't what tipped things over the edge." Linda smiled ruefully. "The good ones like Tristan and Honor and Quinn always blame themselves."

"And like you," Jett said gently. "But you shouldn't. You and Tristan and the others—you're good at your jobs, and you care. That's what counts."

Linda brushed her fingers over Jett's arm. "Thanks." She glanced toward the clock. "Hey. We're off duty. I'm going to go home and seduce my wife into making mad passionate love to me. Then I'm going to sleep for ten hours—or at least until the kids get home from day camp."

"I'll see you this weekend."

"Do you want to come over for breakfast?"

"Before or after you have sex?"

Linda gave her a little shove. "I could wait for that."

Jett shook her head. "Thanks, but I think your first plan is probably a better one."

"All right, but if you change your mind, you probably have a twenty-minute window of opportunity. Need a ride?"

"I'm good. I drove in."

"I'm out of here, then."

Linda disappeared into her on-call room and Jett headed for hers to collect her gear. When she pulled out of the hospital parking lot, she still hadn't shed the sadness over the night's events, and she could only imagine how Tristan must feel. Knowing Tristan hurt bothered her more than she wanted to admit.

Chapter Fifteen

Honor rolled over and listened for the sounds of her family. Jack slept peacefully beside the bed in his bassinet, his breathing gentle and sweet. Arly's laughter and Phyllis's mellifluous tones floated up to her through her open bedroom door. The shower ran in the adjoining bathroom. Quinn was home.

She lay still for a few more moments, appreciating the joy in her life. Then, moving carefully so as not to wake the baby, she got out of bed, padded barefoot to the bedroom door, and closed and locked it. On her way to the bathroom, she lifted her nightgown over her head and draped it on a chair in passing. Through the steam and streaks of water on the glass shower door, she could make out Quinn's form inside. Even the distortion of the glass and pounding water could not disguise the tight muscular shape of her athletic body. Honor slid the door open and stepped under the spray.

"Welcome home." Honor wrapped her arms around Quinn's waist and kissed her between the shoulder blades.

"Did I wake you?" Quinn spoke without turning, her voice gruff, as if she'd been shouting for a long time and had gone hoarse.

"You didn't, but I wouldn't care if you did." Honor rested her cheek against Quinn's back, one arm still around her waist. She ran her other hand over Quinn's chest between her breasts, tracing her fingertips over the scar below Quinn's collarbone where her defibrillator had been. "I missed you."

Quinn clasped Honor's hand and leaned back against her. "Missed you too. Missed the kids. How are they?"

"Everyone's fine. Phyllis helped Arly give Jack a bottle yesterday afternoon when I went in to the ER for a few hours to do some paperwork. Arly hasn't stopped talking about it yet."

"You didn't work too hard, did you?"

"I couldn't if I'd wanted to. Everyone treated me like spun glass." Honor shook her head, touched by everyone's concern, but tired of being immobile and basically useless except for providing meals for Jack. As much as she loved everything about her children, she needed a little bit more than twenty-four-hours-a-day motherhood. She needed to work for her own sense of self, and she wanted the kids to grow up seeing that family meant helping everyone else realize their dreams.

Keeping one arm around Quinn, Honor reached for the soap and began lathering Quinn's back. "I scheduled myself for half days starting next week."

"You sure?"

"Really, I'll just supervise. I already talked to Phyllis, and she's good with taking care of both kids. I don't want to go back full time until Jack's a little older anyhow. But I need to get out of the house." She laughed and turned Quinn in the spray. "I need to remind the troops who's in charge in the ER before certain surgeons I know take over."

"Like we'd forget." Quinn smoothed her hands over Honor's shoulders, then cupped her chin, scrutinizing her face. She brushed her thumb along the ridge beneath Honor's eyes. "You're still really pale."

Honor was about to dismiss Quinn's concerns, but when she got a good look at Quinn's face, she forgot all about the ER and working and what she needed. "God, baby, you look absolutely beat." She brushed wet strands of hair back from Quinn's forehead. "You didn't get any sleep at all last night, did you?"

"Not much," Quinn said nonchalantly, averting her gaze.

"Did you operate all night?"

"Most of it." Quinn reached for the shampoo. "Turn around. I'll wash your hair."

Biding her time, waiting for Quinn to elaborate, Honor turned her back to Quinn and let the water soak her hair. "I'm getting spoiled with all this pampering."

"If you're just now getting spoiled, I've been falling down on the job," Quinn murmured as she worked her fingers through Honor's hair.

Honor moaned quietly with pleasure and settled her butt against

Quinn's crotch. "Believe me, you are doing just fine in the pampering department."

"Good." Quinn disconnected the handheld portion of the showerhead and used it to rinse Honor's hair. When she was done, she finger-combed the thick silky strands, then lightly clasped Honor's shoulders, pulled her around, and kissed her. "All done."

Honor snaked her arms around Quinn's waist. "Thank you. Now, tell me about last night."

Quinn's grip on Honor's shoulders tightened. "Later. Let's go to bed."

There was something in the way Quinn looked, the way she sounded, as if she were keeping something painful at bay, that made Honor want to comfort her. Honor grasped Quinn's hand, turned off the shower, and led her out. They quickly dried off, and after a few more seconds were on their way to bed.

Quinn stopped next to Jack and watched him sleep. "He looks good. He's good, right?"

"He's perfect." Honor lifted the covers and slid under them, then held them up. "Come on. Come to bed, Quinn."

Quinn stretched out next to Honor and sighed. When she reached for Honor, Honor propped herself up on one elbow and stroked Quinn's face. Then she kissed her. "You're trying to pretend you're relaxed, but I can tell you're not. Your body is tight as a drum."

"Just tired."

"That's part of it." Honor brushed her hand over Quinn's breasts and Quinn jerked, vibrating at the touch. Her eyes were the deep, deep blue they became when she was troubled or aroused, or both. Quinn didn't want to talk, Honor knew that, and she wouldn't push her. Quinn would tell her what was troubling her when she was ready. In the meantime, Honor would give her what she could. "Close your eyes and let me put you to sleep."

"Honor," Quinn said, her voice dropping low. "It's too soon."

"Not for everything." Honor kissed her. "Close your eyes."

Quinn hesitated for a second longer, and then as if the decision had been made, she circled Honor's shoulders with one arm and pulled her closer. She pressed her mouth to Honor's ear. "I want you. I love you."

"I love you, baby," Honor whispered, cleaving to Quinn's body as she caressed Quinn's face, her neck, her chest, her abdomen. She kept stroking her as she followed the same path with her mouth, bestowing soft kisses across the hard muscles and silky skin. Even though Quinn's breathing quickly grew shallow and uneven, Quinn held Honor ever so carefully, trying not to squeeze too tightly, not to move too much, not to do anything that might hurt her. Honor wanted to break that restraint, but she knew Quinn needed it. Quinn needed not to worry about her right now.

"I'm going to make you come," Honor whispered, her mouth against Quinn's neck. She slipped her fingers between Quinn's legs and continued her caresses, slowly at first, increasing the pressure and speed until Quinn's hips lifted beneath her hand and Quinn groaned, shuddering in her arms.

"That's right, baby," Honor whispered. "Everything is all right."

When Quinn turned her face into Honor's breasts, Honor cradled her head and smoothed her fingers through Quinn's hair. Honor held her until her breathing gentled, easing into the same quiet rhythm as that of their baby sleeping nearby. When she was certain that Quinn was safe from whatever demons had followed her home, Honor closed her eyes and slept.

❖

Tristan poured an inch of scotch into a glass tumbler and swirled the honey-colored liquid until small eddies climbed up the inside of the glass. It might be seven thirty in the morning, but she'd been working for the last twenty-four hours, and it had been a hell of a night. She walked to the door leading out to her small porch and thought about sitting outside, but she was too restless to sit. She sipped the scotch. The burn was familiar as it made its way down. Otherwise, it was tasteless. A waste of good scotch, but safer than some of the other potential remedies for a hyped-up nervous system and the waking nightmares that were guaranteed to follow her into sleep. A morning, better yet, a day of sex might put her right, but she couldn't keep dragging Darla away from work, and now that she thought of it, she hadn't connected with any of her other usual dates for a few weeks. She could hardly invite them over out of the blue to service her needs. She poured another inch of scotch. Thinking about sex made her aware of the edgy energy that thrummed at her center. She remembered coming in Darla's mouth, but as she looked down in her mind's eye into Darla's face, she saw Jett looking up at her. Her body twitched and the pressure between her legs surged.

"Jesus," she muttered. When she lifted her glass, she was surprised to find it empty. With another soft curse, she set the glass aside and strode toward her door. Her head was fuzzy but she still wasn't tired. She needed to do something to unwind, and drinking wasn't going to do it and there was no sex on the horizon. Walking. Maybe walking would wear her out enough so she could sleep without creaming. She yanked open the door and stared. Maybe she'd had more scotch than she thought. The thrum low in her belly became a drum roll.

"Uh…" Tristan said.

"I owe you breakfast," Jett said, indicating a Dunkin' Donuts bag in her hand. "I wasn't sure what you like. I'm a chocolate glazed myself."

"Apple fritter, but I can do chocolate in a pinch," Tristan said, feeling anything but tired now. Jett still wore her black cargo pants and charcoal T-shirt from the night before. Her sandy hair was darker at her temples, damp with sweat and a little bit mussed. Windblown, or maybe disheveled from the helmet she'd worn in the helicopter. Tristan didn't want to think about the helicopter, or the hellacious ride back from Atlantic City, or her futile battle to save the infant. She'd much rather think of how good Jett looked right now, and of how glad she was to see her, and of how very much she'd like to finish their almost-kiss. God, the timing sucked. "I'm not very good company right now. In fact, I think I'm half drunk."

"I didn't come to be entertained." Jett held out the bag. "There's coffee in here too. You can take it and close the door. I won't mind. I know what it's like to need to be alone."

"I don't need to be alone," Tristan said way too fast. "What I need could be a problem, though."

"I don't think so," Jett said softly.

"You don't have any idea what I—"

"Sure I do." Jett stepped forward, forcing Tristan back inside the apartment. Jett caught the edge of the door on her way in and closed it behind her. Without taking her eyes off Tristan, she set the donuts and coffee down, then straightened and took another step. Only an inch or two separated her body from Tristan's. "I know what you need, and it's not a drink. It's not talking about it. It's not even sleep." She slid her hand behind Tristan's neck and gently gripped a fistful of her hair. She pulled Tristan's head toward her until she could skim her lips over Tristan's. It was barely a kiss but Tristan shuddered and grabbed Jett's hips. "You need it now, but tonight or tomorrow you might think differently."

Tristan pressed her forehead to Jett's shoulder. "How do you…"

Jett didn't ask what Tristan meant. She wrapped an arm around her shoulders and held her tightly, caressing the back of her head and massaging her neck. With her lips brushing Tristan's ear, she murmured, "Been there. Lots of times."

"I won't regret it. I'm not that drunk." Tristan ran her hands up and down Jett's back, squeezing the muscles in her shoulders and along her spine. She kissed her neck. "You feel so good."

"So do you." Jett wanted her. Tristan's need was so naked, so raw, she couldn't help but want her. Trouble was, she wanted a lot of things where Tristan was concerned, and not all of them made her happy. She wanted to soothe and protect her, but she also hungered to claim her, hard and fast. She was pretty sure Tristan would let her, right this moment.

Maybe if she hadn't been with Tristan in the helicopter, hadn't seen her desperate fight, hadn't witnessed her anguish, she might have been able to focus only on what they both wanted right now. But Tristan wasn't some anonymous woman in a nameless bar in a soon-to-be-forgotten town. And *she* wasn't the woman she had been, mindlessly seeking solace in the arms of another. She wasn't giving in to that need again.

Jett eased away, her hand in Tristan's hair again, tugging Tristan's head back. She kissed her, not fleetingly this time, but a deep, probing kiss to stamp the taste of her in her memory. To quench the thirst for just an instant, to savor later when she was alone and the need rode her hard.

"Let's lie down on the couch. Let me hold you," Jett said.

"I'm climbing out of my skin," Tristan groaned. "Jesus, I don't need you to hold me. I need you to fuck me."

"Five minutes," Jett said. "Five minutes, and I will."

Tristan grabbed Jett's hand and dragged Jett toward the couch.

When Tristan's knees hit the edge, she kept going, falling back, pulling her legs up, and Jett stretched out beside her. Jett shifted until she was almost on her back and Tristan lay half on top of her, Tristan's head nestled on her shoulder. Jett resumed massaging Tristan's neck and shoulders, using both hands now. Tristan shivered, drawing one leg up until her thigh rode in the vee between Jett's legs. The sudden pressure detonated a shock wave up Jett's spine, but she concentrated on Tristan.

"Close your eyes." Jett kneaded the knotted muscles at the base of Tristan's skull.

"I think about you," Tristan said, her voice soft and slow. "I think about you inside—"

"Shh," Jett whispered. "Tell me later."

After a long moment of silence, Tristan said, "What if there isn't...any later."

Jett remembered not being able to count on another day. When any day, every day, could be the last. How the fear became anger, and the anger need. She kissed Tristan's forehead and continued to stroke her. She didn't say, *there will be time later*, because she didn't know if there would be another day for them. If there was nothing else between them, at least there would be truth.

When all Jett could hear in the quiet room was the steady tick of her watch and Tristan's soft breathing, she gently slipped away.

CHAPTER SIXTEEN

Jett let herself out of Tristan's apartment, half hoping as she made her way down the stairs that the apartment door behind her would open and Tristan would call her back. Leaving her had been hard, but not nearly as hard as not touching her. She wasn't exactly sure why she had held back. Tristan had made it clear what she wanted, and Jett couldn't deny she had too. She'd been drawn to Tristan from the start, and physical attraction she understood. Every time she saw her, the attraction grew. If she went back upstairs, she wouldn't resist again. Which was why she kept walking until she was outside. Sex with Tristan wouldn't be what she was used to—it couldn't be anonymous, and she wasn't even sure it could be casual. She knew Tristan. She liked her. She felt for her, watching her struggle with sadness and pain. She cared. Hell.

When Jett reached the street she found the air already oppressively heavy and hot despite the early hour, but the idea of returning to her apartment to toss and turn held no appeal. For a few seconds she thought about Linda's invitation to breakfast, then dismissed the idea with a mental laugh. Linda was most likely in bed, either sleeping or making good on her earlier promise to seduce her girlfriend. Besides, Jett didn't just drop in on people. Like she'd just dropped in on Tristan. She wondered just exactly what was happening to her, because she was behaving less and less like herself every day.

Disturbed, aroused, she strode rapidly to her Jeep, and then simply walked past. If she got in she'd go home, and that seemed just a little bit like prison today. By the end of the block she was sweating, but she barely noticed the heat. Nothing would ever truly feel hot again after the desert, and working her body was what she needed. Usually she dispelled her mental anxiety and physical tension with aggressive sex, but the fast pace in the broiling sun was almost doing the job—almost. She couldn't quite shake the sensation of holding Tristan. And she couldn't forget Tristan asking her, almost begging her, to take her. The encounter had her needing sex, more than she had in a long time. Sex and something more, and the more part scared her.

Jett's stomach tightened at the thought of having Tristan beneath her, of making her writhe and cry out with pleasure, of letting go of everything except the sight and sound of Tristan. She couldn't pretend it was just sex she wanted. She wanted Tristan. She picked up her pace, hardly registering the presence of anyone else until a woman called to her.

"Hey you," a familiar voice said. "Hungry already?"

Jett slowed and noted exactly where she was for the first time in blocks. To her left lay the playing fields where Linda had brought her the night she'd driven her home from the hospital. And coming across the grass toward her was Mandy, a self-satisfied smile on her face. Jett wondered, as she watched Mandy's breasts rise and fall beneath her tight white T-shirt, if she'd come here with the subconscious intention of finding what she needed. Mandy had said she'd come looking for her when she got needy, and here she was.

"I've got T-ball practice in a few minutes," Mandy said, rising on her tiptoes to kiss Jett quickly. "But after that you could definitely talk me into leaving early."

"Hi." Jett stepped back a pace. "Would you believe *I* was in the neighborhood?"

"Sure I would. I'd also believe you've got an itch that I know just how to scratch."

Jett laughed, because Mandy had her number—as far as Mandy knew. "Several of them, probably. But not today."

"You're kidding."

Jett shook her head.

"You mean you actually *are* just in the neighborhood?"

Jett nodded.

"Well, all right." Mandy traced her fingers down the center of Jett's chest. "Since you're here, we should still make the most of it." She studied Jett through narrowed eyes. "Let me guess. You haven't had any recreation to speak of since the last time we were together." She ran her fingernail along the edge of Jett's jaw and Jett jerked back. Mandy chuckled. "Mmm, yeah, and you are very ready for some fun."

Jett wasn't going to deny it. The lie would show. "I'm still going to pass."

"Why?" Mandy sounded genuinely confused. "You had a good time. I had a good time. We understand each other. That's unusual and not something to just throw away."

"I know." Jett slid her hands into her pockets and watched the children run up and down the field shouting exuberantly. She tried to remember when her life had stopped being simple and spontaneous. When she was their age, maybe, maybe younger. About the time she realized she was different, and others noticed too. "You make it sound simple. I'm not sure why it isn't."

"When sex stops being about sex, it gets complicated." Mandy tapped Jett's chin teasingly. "I'm not interested in complicated. I didn't think you were, either." She leaned close but didn't touch Jett again. "What I'm interested in is you doing what you did to me last time. More than once and in many different ways."

Jett thought about Tristan, about her pain and how much she'd wanted to ease it. She thought about how much she'd wanted *her*, and she couldn't tell if the two were connected. Gail had been one of the few women in her life who she'd had feelings for, and when her feelings got twisted up with her desires, she'd suffered for it. Maybe mixing sex with caring just didn't work for her. Mandy was watching her, waiting. Mandy wanted simple. That she could do.

"You're right," Jett said. "I'm not interested in complicated. I'm just not as ready as you think I am right now."

"You'll call me when you are."

It wasn't a question.

"Maybe. I'm not making any promises."

Mandy smiled and kissed the tip of her finger, then pressed it to Jett's mouth. "I wasn't asking for any."

❖

Tristan sat on the edge of the couch trying to figure out what the hell had just happened. She was so used to being awakened during the night by a phone call informing her of some emergency, and needing to be instantly awake and alert, that even the alcohol she'd consumed couldn't suppress her natural reflexes. The quiet click of her apartment door closing behind Jett had been enough to rouse her. Her first instinct had been to go after her, and then her rational mind caught up to her libido and some sanity returned. She was out of control where Jett was concerned. She needed to get a grip.

Head still fuzzy from lack of sleep and the scotch, Tristan stumbled into the bathroom, turned on the shower, and stepped in after leaving her clothes in a pile on the floor. She twisted the dial to cool and washed her hair and body, waking herself up and clearing the cobwebs from her mind. After briskly toweling off, brushing her teeth, and downing a glass of orange juice, she pulled on nearly threadbare jeans, deck shoes, and a light blue short-sleeved shirt. Feeling more human, if not quite herself, she stepped out onto the back porch and leaned against the railing. Finally, she let herself replay the few minutes with Jett.

She saw herself folding into Jett, letting herself be held, letting herself be soothed when what she wanted—at least, what she'd thought she'd wanted—was a different sort of comfort. From the signals her body was still sending, despite the shower, a big part of her had definitely wanted sex. She was still vibrating from the sexual charge of Jett's hands on her neck, in her hair, coursing over her back. She smelled Jett's skin, tangy and rich, and recalled the long, hard planes of her body and the surprising softness of her breasts when Jett had embraced her.

After the catastrophic night she'd had, her guard might have been down, but she hadn't been lying when she'd said she wanted Jett to fuck her. That was exactly what she'd wanted then, and having a clearer head now didn't change her mind. She couldn't deny it any more than she could quite explain it.

Until the last few weeks, Tristan had been accustomed to being in charge when she was with a woman, and that's how she liked it. No surprises, no disappointments—for anyone. But Jett called to a completely new and different part of her, one she was only beginning to embrace. She craved Jett's solid strength, thrilled to the hardness of her body, and hungered for that intense, dark gaze and all it promised. She wanted, perhaps had *always* wanted, to be the singular focus of that kind of intense passion.

"Why not just admit it," Tristan muttered to herself. "You want her to do to you what she was doing to Mandy." She shook her head. She couldn't see herself as Mandy, but she could see herself opening to Jett, taking her in, taking her deep, and the idea downright terrified her as much as it turned her on.

One thing she was clear about. She needed to see her. Jett had come to her with the offer of friendship, and she'd been too fucked up to appreciate it, or to thank her. She needed to fix that right now.

Tristan was halfway down the stairs before she realized she didn't know where Jett lived. God damn it. She stopped, considering her options. The hospital might page Jett for her, but they wouldn't give Tristan her home number. Neither would the business office. And what if Jett wasn't wearing her beeper or had turned it off? Tristan didn't want to wait. Couldn't wait. She had to see her.

Linda. Linda must know how to reach her. Tristan took the rest of the stairs two at a time and shoved through her front door. She sprinted toward the sidewalk, then slowed when she saw Jett's Jeep parked a few houses away. At least she thought it was Jett's.

If Jett was still around, where was she? Who had she gone to see? Mandy lived in the neighborhood somewhere. The thought of Jett with Mandy, holding her, caressing her, made Tristan's head ache. The idea of Jett going to Mandy for what she hadn't found with Tristan made her half crazy. Tristan forgot all about her destination while she tortured herself with images of Jett backing Mandy up against a tree, kissing her, dominating her, taking her the way Tristan had wanted to be taken. She groaned aloud.

"Tristan?"

The picture of Jett and Mandy dissolved and the world snapped back into Technicolor focus. Tristan turned and Jett was there.

"Hi," Tristan said.

"Hi." Jett shot her a half grin. "Couldn't sleep, huh?"

"I heard you leave."

"Sorry." Jett ran her hand through her hair and sighed. "I probably shouldn't have come over. Company was probably the last thing you nee—"

"Wrong." Tristan kissed her, then moved back quickly before Jett could touch her. She didn't trust herself if Jett touched her. "That's for the coffee and doughnuts. Thanks."

Jett's eyes were hungry as they swept over Tristan's face. "Next time I'll bring sandwiches."

"I've got a better idea," Tristan said, determined not to let her get away. She didn't want her out of her sight. "Let's get out of here." She pulled her keys from her pocket and gestured to her Saab, parked two cars behind Jett's Jeep. "I've got a place an hour from here in the mountains. It will be at least ten degrees cooler up there."

"I don't think so," Jett said, her voice low and gravelly.

"I've got to be back tomorrow for practice at two."

"I'm flying tomorrow night," Jett said.

"I'll have you back by one at the latest."

"I need to shower, change clothes."

"No, you don't. I woke up thinking about the way you smell. The way your skin tastes." Tristan moved into Jett again, sliding her hand over Jett's shoulder and down her arm. "You're just fine the way you are."

Jett grabbed Tristan's hand. "What are you do—"

"Hey, Tristan!" Arly came racing up, nearly colliding with them as she skidded to a stop. "Quinn's sleeping, but my mom is taking me to the park for practice. Are you coming?"

Tristan eased back from Jett and smiled at Arly. "Not today, sport. I'm the Saturday coach, remember?"

"I know," Arly said, "but sometimes Quinn—"

Honor caught up to Arly and put her hand on top of her head. "Honey, Tristan might have other plans for today. Hi, Tris." She held out her hand to Jett. "I saw you at Linda's party, but never got a chance to talk to you. I'm Honor Blake."

"Jett McNally."

"I know. Linda flies with you and can't stop talking about how great it is." Honor frowned. "I'd appreciate it if you stay away from the rest of the ER nurses."

Jett was silent for a second and then laughed when Honor's frown turned into a warm smile. "Quinn already warned me about that. I promise the ER is officially a no-fly zone."

"Oh, I can see exactly why Linda left," Honor said with a shake of her head. "You're slick."

"Yeah, she's got a way about her," Tristan said, grinning at Jett. "How are you feeling, Honor? And how is Jack?"

"He's great. He's with his grandmother right now." Honor took Arly's hand. "We are having a play date while Quinn sleeps in. I needed to get out for a while. If I walk slowly I don't feel a day over eighty."

"Can I drop you somewhere?" Tristan asked.

"You two look like you were headed out. And we're doing fine," Honor said.

"We're headed up to the mountains," Tristan said, casting a sideways glance at Jett.

"Nice. Have a great time." Honor tugged on Arly's hand. "Come on, honey. Let's go to the park."

Arly went with her mother, walking backward a few steps, her gaze riveted to Tristan. "What about Saturday's practice? We have that big game next week and Quinn said she might have to work that day."

"Got you covered, no problem," Tristan called after her. "I'll be there Saturday and I'll give Robin a hand with the game next week too."

Arly grinned back. "Okay. Have fun."

Tristan laughed. "She's got Honor's looks, Quinn's persistence, and probably both their smarts. She's going to give some boy or girl a run for their money one day soon."

"I think she's got a crush on you," Jett said.

"Girls always get crushes on their coaches. It'll pass."

"Not always."

Tristan gave her a look. "You're right." She opened the Saab with the remote. "You ready to get out of here?"

Jett looked at the car, then back to Tristan. "This is crazy."

"No," Tristan said softly. "Pretending we don't want to would be crazy."

Jett didn't say anything, she just got into the car. That was enough for Tristan, for now.

CHAPTER SEVENTEEN

Tristan started the engine and powered down the convertible top. "No pets, right?"

"Pardon?" Jett still didn't entirely believe she was about to go off who-knew-where with a woman who by turns pissed her off and turned her on and made her want things she'd never thought of having. Like quiet moments in the sun and the sound of another heart beating in the dark. When she took in Tristan's bold sharp profile, her dark hair still wet from the shower and gleaming in the sun, she didn't feel as if she were with a stranger. Weathering a crisis together and struggling through the aftermath had a way of stripping away the veneer and letting you see people for who they really were. She'd seen Tristan under fire, more than once, and she knew her to be fearless and brave. She'd seen Tristan blame herself for perceived failures that were not her responsibility, and witnessed her pain. Jett recognized a warrior with a tender heart.

"Dogs? Cats?" Tristan glanced over, blue eyes glittering. "Canary? Anything that needs food in the next twenty-four hours?"

"I've spent my whole life being sent around the world with a few hours' notice. I don't even keep plants."

"Good." Tristan pulled out and gunned the Saab down the street in the direction of the interstate. She didn't plan on giving Jett any time to reconsider because she needed to get away, and she wanted Jett with her. She needed to leave the sadness behind and recharge where there were no schedules and no demands and no tragedies. Just the smell of the pines and the clean mountain air and a woman to share it with. Jett.

Jett to share it with. Tristan hit the on-ramp and glanced at Jett. "Then we don't have any reason to hang around here."

"Guess we don't." Jett was used to being driven to unknown destinations, only usually she was crowded in the belly of a troop transport or bouncing around in the hold of a plane or the back of a Jeep. Speeding out of the city with Tristan at the wheel couldn't have been more different. Or more exciting. She stretched out her legs and tilted her head back. She must have sighed, because Tristan reached across the space between them and rubbed her shoulder for a second.

"Tired? Feel free to take a nap."

"I'm good just like this." Jett rolled her head on the headrest and squinted in the bright sunlight. Tristan glowed, and Jett almost touched her just to be sure she was real. "How about you? I think your night was a lot rougher than mine."

Tristan's jaw tightened. "I'll need a nap later. I'm all right to drive now." She cut another quick look in Jett's direction again before focusing on the road. "I didn't have that much to drink."

"I wasn't worried about that."

"I don't make a habit of—"

"Tristan," Jett said gently. "I get it. Remember? I've had my fair number of shots first thing in the morning. Morning is relative when you've been on duty for God knows how long."

"I don't know why last night got to me more than usual." Tristan spoke slowly, as if the landscape of her own feelings were unfamiliar and dangerous territory. "I've had patients die before. Kids, pregnant mothers, twenty-five-year-old guys who should've lived to be eighty. I don't know." Her hands tightened on the wheel. "I just keep wondering if I did the right thing."

"Was there something else you could have done? Something you missed?"

"Maybe." Tristan laughed shortly. "Aren't you supposed to assure me that of course I did the right thing?"

"I probably would, if I didn't know you." Jett gripped Tristan's forearm, then brushed her fingers over the inside of Tristan's arm below her sleeve, caressing her soft, warm skin. Then she pulled back. "If I didn't like you, I wouldn't mind blowing smoke at you."

Tristan exhaled slowly, trying to dampen her edginess. The barest touch of Jett's fingers had her insides quivering. Her clit strained against the inside of her jeans. She ought to be used to the constant arousal by now—every time she was with Jett her body went in one direction, no matter what her head was doing. She forced herself to think about what Jett was saying, despite the urgent throbbing between her legs. "I'm glad you like me."

"So what do you think you should have done last night?"

"Jesus, don't you ever give up?"

"Sometimes," Jett said quietly. "We're not talking about me."

"We never do," Tristan said mildly.

"There's nothing to talk about. Quit stalling."

Tristan crossed lanes onto the expressway heading north. "Quinn warned us if I opened the incision to relieve the pressure on the baby's chest she'd probably arrest. I did it anyway, and she arrested just like Quinn said. Even though we got a heartbeat back, it was all downhill from there."

"I was flying, but I could still hear what was going on. I'm not a medic, but it was pretty clear that baby was headed downhill a long time before you put her into my aircraft."

"You're right. She was in bad trouble," Tristan said. "And maybe if I'd seen that earlier and refused to transfer her—"

"Oh, now you're responsible for the judgment of the surgeons and neonatologists at the other hospital?" Jett shook her head. "You would have made a crappy soldier."

Tristan glowered at her. "What is that supposed to mean?"

"You can't accept that you are one link in a chain. You might be a vital link, but you're still only responsible for part of what happened last night. Being part of that chain means you do your job and count on others to do theirs."

"I suppose you never took anything extra on yourself, huh? Captain McNally."

"Chief, and we're not talking about me."

"Cut that out," Tristan griped. "Jesus, you sound like a therapist."

"Hey," Jett protested, "no need to get insulting."

Tristan grinned. "Did I mention one of my sisters is a psychiatrist?"

"Sorry."

"No need. She's given up trying to analyze me. Finally."

Jett heard the fondness in Tristan's voice, but there was sadness there too. She suspected Tristan's family had pressured her to change the way she felt about women. As if it was just a simple choice. "You did say your family didn't always understand you."

"They all have the same picture of life. One I never had." Tristan sighed. "Last night I did what I did up there in the helicopter because I believed that infant didn't have four more minutes. Or even two."

"Then you made the right call," Jett said.

"Why are you so sure?"

Tristan's eyes were dark, pain-filled, when she searched Jett's face. Jett leaned across the space between the seats and cupped the back of Tristan's neck. She stroked her slowly, her fingers playing up and down the tight muscles. "I don't have to be sure. You do."

"Usually I am. It's been a rough month." Tristan relaxed against Jett's hand. "Damn, that feels good."

"I'll finish when we get there." Jett sifted Tristan's hair through her fingers, then slid inside Tristan's collar. She squeezed the ridge of muscle between Tristan's neck and shoulder with deep, rhythmic compressions. "Your back could probably use some work."

"That would be great." Tristan tried to sound casual, but her head swam and she had to force herself to watch the road. She didn't want Jett to know that every caress made her blood surge. Darla got a charge out of teasing her while she was driving, playing with her until Tristan couldn't hold back and laughing when Tristan flamed out. But even while Darla was making her come she didn't have this kind of trouble focusing, and Jett was only rubbing her shoulder. She hadn't felt this dizzy with need since she'd first discovered the miracle of girls, and then it was touching *them* that got her off. She didn't think she'd ever wanted anyone to touch her as much as she did Jett. She prayed Jett wouldn't stop.

"There's a lake," Tristan blurted. "We can go swimming first."

"I'd like that," Jett said drowsily. She probably shouldn't keep touching Tristan, but Tristan's skin was so damn soft. She rested her cheek against the seat and watched Tristan's face as the clouds rolled by overhead and the wind sang through the car. She thought of walking barefoot on dusty roads, of lazy summer afternoons and cool shady ponds. "I haven't been swimming in a long time."

"Then it's about time."

"Yeah. Maybe it is."

Tristan drove on as Jett slept beside her, more settled than she had been in days, all from the simple touch of Jett's fingers on her neck.

❖

"We're here," Tristan said, gently shaking Jett's shoulder.

Jett opened her eyes and sat up. "Sorry. I just got too comfortable."

"I think that's the idea."

"I don't fall asleep in front of people."

"Never?"

Jett shook her head. "Not the way I just did. A catnap, maybe. You could've dumped me out by the side of the road and I wouldn't have known it."

Tristan laughed. "Believe me, getting rid of you was the last thing on my mind."

"Oh yeah?" Jett braced an arm on the door and pushed up with her legs, then swiveled and dropped over onto the ground. She put her hands on her hips and grinned. "What was on your mind?"

"Oh, very smooth." Tristan pocketed her keys and got out on the opposite side of the car. No way was she telling Jett she'd been fantasizing for the last twenty-five miles about lying next to Jett again, this time without clothes in the way. "I was thinking a swim, a bottle of wine, and some steaks."

Jett turned in a slow circle, surveying their destination. A one-story wood cabin with a broad front porch stood in a half-acre clearing surrounded by pines. A grassy slope led from the small knoll where they'd parked down to a still mountain lake. A short dock extended into the water. A canvas-covered boat was tethered to the dock. She couldn't see any houses on either side of the cabin, but there were a few on the far side of the lake. It was just about midday, and the surface of the clear water reflected the sunlight like glass.

"This is a great place." Jett looked over her shoulder. Tristan was watching her intently. "Your family's?"

"No. They have a big compound in the Poconos. My sisters have cabins—well, they're not really cabins, more like houses—on the family land. I opted for something smaller."

"And more private?"

Tristan nodded ruefully. "I enjoy socializing with my family, but—"

"Tough to bring dates?"

"Not that so much anymore." Tristan walked around the car and joined Jett. She looked out over the water, her expression brooding. "I might bring a date to dinner at the country club, but extended weekends aren't exactly my style." She met Jett's eyes. "I've never brought anyone here."

"I've never been to a woman's cabin before." Jett shrugged, a dimple appearing to the right of her mouth. "I've never been to the country club, either."

Tristan rested her hand in the middle of Jett's back. Jett's shirt was damp with sweat and she imagined how slick her skin would be underneath it. She could almost taste the salt and feel the heat against her lips. A heavy ache settled in her stomach and her legs trembled. "Some night when you're feeling masochistic, I'll take you."

"How could I refuse an invitation like that?" Jett brushed a lock of hair from Tristan's forehead with her fingertips. "I didn't bring a bathing suit."

"Neither did I."

"How private is private?"

"No motors of any kind on the lake. I suppose we might scare a canoer if one wanders by."

Jett backed away a step and unbuttoned her shirt. She wore nothing underneath it. The dimple deepened as she watched Tristan's eyes grow smoky. "You ready to go swimming?"

"More than ready," Tristan said hoarsely. She started down the gentle slope toward the water, her gaze never leaving Jett as Jett walked beside her, shedding her shirt. Jett was lean, muscle and bone beneath smooth bronze skin. The vee between her breasts was darker than the surrounding skin, left over, Tristan imagined, from the months beneath the broiling sun. A thick pink scar, three or four inches long, stood out on her left shoulder. It was fresh and it wasn't an incision. Her stomach plummeted. It could only be a wound of some kind. While she knew intellectually that Jett had been in combat, she hadn't absorbed the true reality. She wondered if anyone who hadn't been there really could. Jett had not only seen death, she had faced it.

"It wasn't anything serious," Jett said, knowing from Tristan's expression that she had seen the scar. "A little bit of flying debris."

"I'm sorry." Tristan gently touched the scar. Jett's breast, a slightly paler, perfect oval, lay just below her hand, but she didn't stroke downward to caress it. Jett was baring far more than her body, and Tristan knew it. "Is this the only one?"

"Nothing else but bumps and bruises." Jett caught Tristan's hand and held it for a second. "Don't feel bad. I'm one of the lucky ones."

"Okay." Tristan smiled shakily. "I just don't like thinking about you being hurt."

"It's over now." Jett rarely thought about the wound, because everything else about that night had been so much more critical. When Gail's face flashed through her mind, she resolutely put the memory aside. Gail wasn't here now. Gail wasn't anywhere in her life. And Tristan was. "Tristan…"

"What?" Tristan took off her shirt by the water's edge, unzipped her jeans, and pushed them down. Then she kicked off her boat shoes and was naked.

Jett halted with her zipper halfway down, drinking in Tristan's body. Shorter by an inch, Tristan was more muscular, her thighs and chest thicker. Tristan's breasts were broader than hers and Jett imagined the weight of them in her hands. As if she had touched them, the dark nipples tightened and Tristan's breasts rose.

Tristan shuddered in a breath. "I like the way you look at me."

Jett's control slipped a notch. They were already on dangerous ground. If she let go, if she touched her, one touch would never be enough. "I don't know what you're expecting—"

"Nothing," Tristan said quickly. "Nothing. Just for us to be here for a while."

"You're sure."

"Take your clothes off. Come in the water." Tristan turned and dove. She was underwater for a long time, her path marked by faint ripples on the surface.

Jett shed her shoes and the rest of her clothes and waited until Tristan surfaced. Then, marking the spot, she took a breath and followed her. The cool water closed over her, and she swam with her eyes open. After three strong strokes she saw the pale outline of Tristan's body in the water. Tristan's breasts swayed gently, beckoning to her. Jett stroked closer and then surfaced, her body brushing Tristan's. She scissored her legs between Tristan's, cupped the back of her neck, and covered Tristan's mouth with hers. Tristan groaned and wrapped her arms around Jett's shoulders, opening her mouth to draw her in.

The sun beat down on Jett's shoulders, but it was nothing like the desert. Water lapped at her throat and cooled her feverish body. And Tristan was nothing like any woman she had ever touched. Her body was powerful and strong, made stronger by her yielding. Tristan broke the kiss and Jett felt teeth on her neck. She tilted her head back and let Tristan take more. When her control snapped and she was seconds from sliding her hand between Tristan's legs, she grasped Tristan's shoulders and pushed away from her. She kicked back, dunked her head, and came up flinging the hair from her eyes.

"It's not physically possible to do what I want to do to you out here," Jett said.

"How do you know?" Tristan swam toward her, her eyes on fire. "How many women have you fucked in a lake?"

"How do you know that's what I had in mind?" Jett said.

"If it isn't, I'm in trouble." Tristan gripped Jett's shoulder, kicking gently to stay upright in the water. "Are you going to make me beg you?"

"That's not what I want. But you might not want what I—"

"Believe me, I *do*." Tristan let go and drifted back away from Jett. "But I don't want you thinking about what *I* want when you're making love to me. I don't want you thinking about anything."

"I'm not sure that's a good idea."

"Then we should get our clothes on and I'll make something to eat." Tristan stroked swiftly to shore and climbed out of the water.

Jett, treading water slowly, watched her get dressed. Then she made her way in to shore as Tristan climbed the hill toward the cabin. Pulling her clothes over her wet body, she told herself she'd held back because Tristan didn't know what she was asking. But there'd been another reason too. Jett walked up the hill, thinking she'd already come too close to completely losing control, and all she'd done was kiss her.

CHAPTER EIGHTEEN

Quinn parked the Volvo in the shade of the big maples bordering Whitman Park, three blocks from her house. She headed for the largest group of kids she could see, figuring Arly would be in the middle of the pack. A minute later she found Honor on a park bench watching an impromptu soccer game. She sat down next to her, slid an arm behind her shoulders, and kissed her.

"Phyllis told me you and Arly walked over here. How are you feeling?"

Honor sighed and leaned her cheek against Quinn's shoulder. "Truth?"

Quinn brushed her lips over Honor's temple. "No, I prefer you lie to me whenever possible."

"If you didn't bring the car, you're going to have to carry me home."

"Is your incision bothering you?"

"Not really. I'm mostly just out of gas."

"I figured you might be tired. I drove over." Quinn stroked Honor's hair and watched Arly outrun a boy two years older than her, deftly dribbling the soccer ball between her knee and foot. "She's really good."

"Give her a ball and she's in heaven." Honor rested her hand on Quinn's thigh. "What if she's not tall enough for basketball? She's going to be really upset."

"She'll be fine. She can play point guard. That suits her personality better, anyhow."

"Are you any good at basketball?" Honor asked.

Grinning, Quinn shrugged. "I'm going to have to be."

"Was Jack all right when Phyllis gave him the bottle?"

"I fed him." She hugged Honor gently. "Not that I don't think your breasts are a marvelous invention, but I don't think he really cares where dinner comes from. He chowed down, no problems."

Honor laughed. "Good. Because my breasts have other uses, and I'd like to get them back to that sooner rather than later."

Quinn nuzzled Honor's ear. "Oh yeah?"

"Children present," Honor murmured, although she didn't move away.

"They're not watching."

"Behave anyhow. If you tease me and I'm too tired to do anything, I'll just get cranky."

"You don't have to do anything." Quinn kissed Honor's cheek and drew back before she wanted to do more than she could do outside. "I'll do all the heavy lifting."

"Somehow the idea of me lying there like a lump doesn't strike me as sexy."

"You're sexy no matter what you're doing." Quinn held Honor's hand. "Besides, I was pretty much a lump when I got home, and you didn't seem to mind."

"You were a gorgeous sexy lump. How are you feeling?"

"I got five hours of solid sleep. I'm good."

Honor rubbed Quinn's thigh. "I'm glad. Although that wasn't exactly what I meant."

"I'm okay," Quinn said quietly. "Healthstar brought in a preemie with NEC. Things went south pretty fast and we lost her."

"That's rough. I'm sorry." Honor rubbed Quinn's hand against her cheek. "You sure you're okay?"

"Yeah." Quinn sighed. "Better now. Thanks for this morning. It was just what I needed."

"Baby," Honor murmured, "that was for me too."

"Good."

"Was Linda on last night? She hates it when kids are involved."

Quinn nodded. "Tristan and Linda did the transfer."

"I'll call Linda when we get home. Check in on her." Honor paused to wave when Arly shouted across the field that she had just made a goal. "I saw Tristan on the way over here. She and Jett were headed off somewhere together."

"Oh yeah?" Quinn gave Arly a thumbs-up. "Interesting."

"Is it?" Honor studied Quinn's grin. "Oh. Huh. Jett doesn't look like Tristan's usual."

"That's when you have to watch out," Quinn said. "It's the ones you don't expect to get to you who always do."

Honor laughed. "Well that was certainly true for me where you were concerned."

"Really? I understood you went for the handsome, sexy types." Quinn made a move to nuzzle Honor's neck again and Honor pushed her away.

"Oh, your nap definitely got your batteries recharged," Honor said. "What is there about out of shape, recently pregnant women that you find so irresistible, Dr. Maguire?"

"I look at our amazing kids and realize they came from you," Quinn said gently, "and it's like witnessing a miracle. Plus, you're the most exciting, beautiful woman I've ever known."

Honor caught her breath. "You'd better take me home now. I think I'm ready for you to do that heavy lifting you promised."

Quinn jumped up and waved her arms. "Yo, Arly. Wrap it up. Time to go!"

A minute later Arly came running over. "Did you see me score?"

"Sure did," Quinn said. "Nice move getting around that guard too."

Arly grinned. "Kevin is here. Can I stay just a little bit longer? He can walk me home."

Quinn shook her head. "No go, sport. But I'll make a deal with you. We'll come back after supper, okay?"

"When will I be big enough to stay by myself?"

"Soon," Quinn said, slinging an arm around Arly's shoulders while thinking in five or six years she might feel comfortable not knowing where Arly was every minute of the day. Big maybe. "Right now Mom's pretty tired."

Arly grew serious. "Okay. We should take her home."

Honor rose, hiding her stiffness and the brief twinge of pain, and took Arly's hand. "I think if I take a nap this afternoon, I'll be ready to come back over with the two of you tonight. Maybe we can bring Jack. Sound like a plan?"

"Deal."

Arly swung her parents' hands as she walked between them toward the car. Honor smiled over at Quinn, and Quinn let the last remnants of sadness and regret drift away on the wings of children's laughter.

❖

Just as Jett reached the porch, Tristan came out of the cabin, jiggling her keys in her hand. Jett didn't blame her for wanting to leave, but she didn't expect the disappointment to be so sharp. She turned to go back down the steps to the car. Leaving was for the best, she knew that, but the prospect of spending the next day alone, when she'd be thinking of Tristan constantly, saddened her in a way that was completely foreign. After Gail, she'd felt shell-shocked—part angry and part wounded— but the pain had been blunted by her own self-recriminations. This pain was razor-edged and nearly unbearable.

"There's a mom-and-pop store a couple miles up the road," Tristan called from behind her. "I'm heading out to get a few supplies. Unless you trust me to pick out steaks and wine, you'd better come along."

Jett turned back. "You want to stay?"

Tristan came down the stairs and strode along the gravel path, slowing when she reached Jett. "Babe. One of these days you're going to have to tell me why you think the only thing a woman would want from you is sex."

"Maybe that's all I want," Jett said, although even as she spoke she wasn't sure she believed it any longer.

"Things change," Tristan said, almost to herself. She smiled ruefully. "Come on, let's go shopping."

Jett climbed back into the car, acutely aware of Tristan just inches away as they drove along a narrow, twisting dirt road dappled with sunlight filtered through overhanging trees. For moments at a time she felt completely disconnected from anything she'd ever known, her past heartaches and mistakes seeming to exist in another lifetime. The Army, the desert, even the city she'd just left faded away, until all that remained was Tristan and sunshine.

"Pull over for a second," Jett said.

Wordlessly, Tristan eased the Saab onto the shoulder of the road, leaving just enough room for one vehicle to pass. She regarded Jett expectantly.

Jett leaned over, slid her hand behind Tristan's neck, and tugged her close enough to kiss. She kissed her more slowly and more carefully than she'd ever kissed a woman in her life. She traced Tristan's lips with the tip of her tongue, slipped inside to taste her heat, teased her by drawing back when Tristan would have probed more deeply.

"Jesus," Tristan gasped. "What are you trying to do to me?"

"I just wanted to say thanks," Jett said. "For bringing me up here. I thought if I kissed you out here, it wouldn't be about sex."

"Wrong. Very wrong." Tristan's chest heaved. "But you're welcome just the same."

Jett skimmed her fingertips over Tristan's jaw. "I've never kissed a woman in the sunlight before."

"Christ," Tristan whispered. "You kill me, you know that?"

"Is that bad?" Jett asked.

Tristan shook her head, not trusting herself to speak. A dusty red pickup truck piled high with wooden crates filled with chickens rattled by, but Tristan never took her eyes off Jett's face.

"I never kissed anyone until I'd been in the service a couple of years, and then, well..." Jett shrugged. "Everyone pretty much had to hide."

"I hate myself for being a little bit glad that this was a first." Tristan wanted to be Jett's first, because she was coming to realize Jett was *her* first in all the ways that counted. She'd never wanted to give herself to another woman the way she did right now. She'd never hungered to know another woman, heart and soul, as much as she wanted to know Jett. And God help her, she just wanted her. She wanted to climb over the gear shift and into Jett's arms. She wanted her out of those clothes so bad, she thought she might cry.

Jett frowned. "You're shaking."

"It's nothing."

Jett reached for her. "Don't blow smoke at me. Something's—"

Tristan jerked away. "Christ, Jett. I'm not made of stone. You're driving me out of my mind."

"Sorry. I didn't mean—"

"Don't be sorry. God damn it." Tristan threw her head back against the seat and fisted her hands on her thighs. She squinted up at the sky and took a deep breath. "If it weren't so fucking painful, it would be great."

"What?"

Tristan turned her head and grinned at Jett. "Being this turned on."

Jett laughed. "You're a little bit crazy."

"No, I'm a lot crazy." Tristan held out her hand and Jett took it. Tristan rubbed her thumb over the darkly tanned, wind-roughened skin. "This is different, this thing between us."

"Tristan, I don't think—"

"Don't," Tristan said quickly. "Don't tell me there's nothing here, because I know differently." She released Jett's hand, straightened, and started the car. "At least for me."

Jett didn't contradict her, because she didn't understand what was happening, and even more importantly, she had no idea what she wanted to happen. So she didn't say anything, and she didn't touch her again.

❖

Tristan was careful not to push for the rest of the afternoon. She'd gone too far in the car earlier, moved too fast, and Jett had immediately withdrawn. Even so, Tristan had experienced a sense of giddy freedom, almost elation, when she'd voiced her feelings to Jett. Still—too much, too soon. Hell, even *she* didn't know what it meant. All she knew was that she'd never enjoyed shopping for groceries and cooking a meal with anyone quite so much. Come to think of it, she'd never actually done those things with any of her dates. Her dates were just that, appointments for some social function with the unspoken understanding that sex would likely follow. One step up from a business arrangement. The only thing that made those encounters anything more than cold, calculated exchanges was the fact that she and her companions genuinely enjoyed one another. But just the same, those dates were nowhere near as enjoyable as the afternoon she'd spent with Jett doing something as simple as barbecuing steaks. Part of the pleasure had come from Jett finally relaxing enough to tell her a few things about her life. They'd discovered a shared love for baseball. They were both Yankees fans.

When Tristan confessed to having a huge collection of classic sci-fi movies on tape, Jett was eager to see them.

And all the time they'd talked, moving around each other in the small kitchen, carrying plates of food back and forth, opening wine, refilling glasses, Tristan remembered the dark, dusky taste of Jett's mouth and the strength in her hands. A few times, Tristan had had to walk out of the room on the pretext of checking the coals in the grill or opening another bottle of wine, because she couldn't hide how much she wanted her. Because somehow, she had to convince Jett she wasn't with her just for the sex.

Now Jett sat on the top step of the wide wooden front porch, her back braced against the rough-hewn post that supported the slanted metal roof above their heads. The sun rode low across the lake, gilding the treetops and painting long, wavering shadows on the opalescent surface of the water. Jett's profile appeared carved in bronze, and Tristan ached to run her fingers over her cheekbones and along her jaw. She wanted to taste her and lose herself in the hot mystery of her mouth. Tristan shifted in her Adirondack deck chair, her legs tight and her stomach twisting. She needed to think about something else, and quickly, or else she was going to need to excuse herself for a few minutes.

Looking for a diversion, Tristan lifted the bottle of wine from the floor next to her and poured half a glass for herself. "More wine?"

"No. Thanks." Jett indicated the nearly full glass beside her. "I'm good."

"We could have gotten beer," Tristan said.

Jett planted one foot on the porch and draped her arm over her bent knee. "I'll admit, beer is a little more my style, but I enjoyed the wine."

Tristan sat forward on the end of her chair. A foot of space separated them. "I'm really glad you came up here with me."

"I'm glad you invited me." Jett couldn't miss what was so plainly written in Tristan's eyes, and the look had been there all afternoon. She owed Tristan more than a safe, polite response. But she had no idea what to say, how to explain that she had no reference for the afternoon they'd shared. She'd spent all her life with men and women in close quarters—comrades—eating together, sleeping together, living and breathing and dying together. But she couldn't remember a single day that she'd spent in the company of someone by choice, for the pleasure of it. She wanted to tell Tristan how special this day had been, even more because Tristan wasn't asking.

"I don't know how to do this," Jett said.

"Do what?"

"Be with someone—a woman—like this." Jett stood abruptly, frustrated by her inability to express what she felt, especially since she didn't understand most of what was happening. With her back to Tristan, she braced her forearm against the post and leaned out over the railing, watching night fall and the moon ascend. "I've known women I would die for, and those same women I've never touched, never told a secret to. I've made love to women whose names I didn't know, whose names I didn't *need* to know." She rapped her fist sharply on the post. "Nothing about being here fits, Tristan."

Tristan rose. "Was there ever a woman to bridge that gap? A woman you knew, a woman you touched?"

"No." Jett bit out the word, half turning. Tristan was right behind her. So close, so close. "No. There wasn't. There was only my mistake."

"Whatever happened, that doesn't mean things couldn't be different with someone else."

"What if I don't want things to be different?" Jett's back was to the railing and Tristan was almost against her now. She kept her hands clenched at her sides. "I don't like complications. I prefer sex to be simple."

Tristan laughed abruptly and took another step. Jett only wanted what Tristan herself had always been satisfied with. The physical connection had always been enough. It could be enough again. "Hey, I think you know I've never been one to disagree with that. So why do you keep running?"

Jett couldn't answer. Tristan was a breath away, so near Jett could make out flecks of moonlight dancing in her eyes. Her skin shimmered with silver highlights. Jett swore waves of heat swirled and danced around them. She was so beautiful. Still, Jett didn't touch her, because she didn't believe her. Someone would get hurt, and she didn't want it to be Tristan. "Back off, Tristan."

"No."

"Tristan," Jett warned, her voice low and tight.

"Simple." Tristan began to unbutton her shirt. "We'll keep it simple. Just the way you like it."

The white shirt parted, exposing Tristan's breasts. And just that fast, the distant croak of frogs, the mournful cry of a loon, the wind in the trees—all went completely silent. The stars winked out and the sky overhead became an endless void. The world receded until there was only Tristan, living, breathing, offering Jett a gift more precious than the promise of tomorrow.

"Take it," Tristan whispered. "Please, Jett. Take it."

Jett slipped her hands under the edges of the white cotton shirt, sliding her fingertips along Tristan's collarbones until she gripped Tristan's shoulders. She turned her suddenly, forcing Tristan's back against the post, then leaned into her, her mouth against Tristan's ear.

"Are you sure you know what you're asking?" Jett pushed a leg between Tristan's. "Because I'm not going to ask again."

Tristan dug her fingers into Jett's ass, forcing Jett's leg more firmly into the cleft between her thighs. "The answer is yes."

Chapter Nineteen

"Hold on to the railing behind you," Jett said, keeping Tristan pinned to the post with both hands on Tristan's shoulders and one leg between her thighs. She slid her teeth along the edge of Tristan's jaw, then down the center of her throat. When she reached the hollow between Tristan's collarbones she sucked the soft skin between her lips and tugged at it with her teeth.

"What?" Tristan muttered, struggling to find her mental balance. She'd fantasized about Jett doing something just like this so many times that she was halfway to an orgasm already. She swept her hands up and down Jett's back until Jett pushed her shirt down over her upper arms, tethering them close to her sides.

"If I wanted you to touch me I would have said so." Jett worked Tristan's left arm free of her shirt, leaving it dangling from her other arm. "Now grab the railing behind you."

Tristan could barely think clearly enough to understand Jett's words. Her body had been constantly stimulated for hours, and she'd been psychologically aroused for days on end. Every nerve in her body was firing erratically, and all she could think about was Jett touching her. But the second Jett did, she was going to lose it. "I need to slow down."

"No, you don't." Jett angled her thigh higher between Tristan's legs, crushing Tristan's clitoris against her pubic bone. "I know what you need."

Tristan groaned, the pressure nearly unbearable. She desperately needed to explode and she couldn't with her clitoris so compressed. Mindlessly, she clutched Jett's hips and tried to push her away. If she could just catch her breath, just get a little control. But she didn't want to be in control. She thrust down on Jett's leg, poised on a precipice— her head insisting she take charge, her body screaming for her to let go. "Please, I need to come and I—"

"You think I don't know that? You think I couldn't see what you wanted all afternoon?" Jett jammed her leg higher and tighter, and Tristan cried out, more from surprise than pain. "Did you get yourself off while I wasn't looking this afternoon?"

"No," Tristan gasped.

"But you wanted to, didn't you?" Watching Tristan's eyes lose focus, watching her slide toward the edge, Jett punctuated each word with a hard thrust of her leg. "Didn't. You. Tristan."

"Yes. Yes. Jesus. *Yes*."

"Now you'll come when I say you will."

Tristan's head was spinning. Spots danced in front of her eyes. She was right there. Right there. "Jett, I don't think I can hold—"

"When I say, Tristan." Jett grabbed Tristan's wrists and forced them behind her back. "Your hands. On the rail."

When Tristan gripped the wooden banister, her fingernails digging into the unpainted surface, Jett lifted her breasts in the palms of her hands and squeezed them together until the nipples almost touched. Whimpering, Tristan stared down at her stiff nipples as Jett sucked them both into her mouth. Jett's face in the moonlight was stark and feral.

"Bite them," Tristan mumbled feverishly. Almost. Almost there.

Jett sucked harder, working them in and out between her lips until Tristan was panting. Then she closed her teeth on one of the blood-engorged tips, pinched the other, and tugged.

Tristan jerked and threw her head back, writhing in Jett's grip. Her legs trembled wildly and only the weight of Jett's body kept her upright. She drove her fingers into Jett's hair, forcing Jett's mouth harder against her breast. "Please, I can't take—"

Jett wrenched her face away. "You'll take it. As long as I want you to take it. Now move your goddamn hand."

Reaching blindly behind her, Tristan felt the post and wrapped one arm around it. Just as she did, Jett dropped to her knees between Tristan's legs and ripped open her fly. Tristan braced her legs wide apart and watched as Jett yanked her jeans down to her ankles. Her clitoris, released from the agonizing compression, instantly became fully engorged. The cool air streamed between her legs and teased her fevered flesh, the breeze a tantalizing caress over her erect clitoris. She held her breath, the muscles in her stomach like a board as Jett kissed low on her belly, moving languidly toward the tops of her thighs. Jett's lips were wet and hot and Tristan couldn't help thrust her hips. She heard her voice begging, *kiss it, please kiss it, please kiss it,* over and over, but she wasn't aware of speaking. She couldn't make the connection any longer between her mind and her body. All she knew was need.

As if knowing Tristan couldn't control her muscles any longer, Jett steadied Tristan's hips against the railing with a hand on her hipbone and kissed her clitoris.

"Oh fuck, Jett." Tristan lifted her pelvis and Jett sucked her. Watching Jett's lips move on her, Tristan pushed and pulled in and out of Jett's mouth. "Here it comes."

Jett abruptly pressed one hand low on Tristan's belly and grasped the base of her clitoris between her thumb and finger. She squeezed as hard as she could, preventing the nerves from discharging, blocking Tristan's orgasm.

"Please," Tristan whimpered, her belly convulsing futilely. "It hurts."

"Breathe," Jett said sharply, easing up with her fingers until Tristan's clitoris surged outward even harder. Then she sucked the entire length into her mouth.

Tristan felt as if she were turning inside out. Her legs gave way but she didn't fall. Somehow Jett had braced one shoulder beneath her thigh, keeping her standing. She started babbling. "Coming. Coming. Coming in your mouth."

Jett squeezed, holding her off again. Tears ran down Tristan's face and she clutched Jett's head.

"Please."

Jett replaced her fingers with her lips, sucking her while she wrapped both arms around Tristan's hips. She kept up the on-again off-again squeezing and sucking until Tristan doubled over.

"Can't breathe," Tristan gasped. "Need...need you."

Jett held her tightly and finished her.

Tristan broke apart as a million volts of white-hot lightning erupted inside her, scorching her mind and soul. On some distant plane she was aware of her body writhing and jerking, of shouting incoherently, of collapsing into wordless sobbing. The last thing she registered was Jett gripping her fiercely in the curve of her body while the cataclysm raged on.

❖

When Tristan came to, she was in bed and naked. And she was alone. She felt nearly bereft, as if her endless orgasm had hollowed her out and left her empty. The isolation was so devastating she literally sensed her heart about to stop.

"Jett," Tristan whispered brokenly.

"I'm here, Tris," Jett said out of the darkness.

The bed dipped and then Jett was beside her. Desperately, Tristan pressed her face against Jett's neck. "I thought..."

"I know. I know what you thought," Jett murmured, stroking Tristan's hair. Despite Tristan's half-conscious protests when they'd stumbled into the bedroom earlier, Jett wouldn't lie down with Tristan after she'd gotten her undressed and into bed. She knew if she did she would want her again, and Tristan was in no shape for it. They'd both worked all night the night before, and Tristan had been through hell losing that baby. She didn't need Jett making even more demands of her than she already had. But Jett hadn't left her, and wouldn't have, even if she *had* been able to find her way in the dark to some semblance of civilization. She'd left plenty of women in the middle of the night to awaken alone in the morning, but this was Tristan. No matter how Tristan might feel about her after what happened, Jett was going to stay and face her.

So she'd pulled a chair over to the window and watched the night sky. She'd forgotten how pure and unsullied it could be when it wasn't lit up by fire and bombs. With Tristan's soft breathing in the background, she felt unexpectedly content, not the cranked-up, agitated way she often felt when she'd had some sex, but not enough sex. The pulse of arousal was a low-level hum in the background of her body and mind, but she didn't feel the usual frantic need for more. As long as she kept some distance between them, she'd be all right.

"Try to go back to sleep," Jett said.

"What the fuck did you do?" Tristan groaned.

Jett felt just a little bit sick. "I'm sorry. I'm sorr—"

"Sorry?" Tristan laughed weakly. "Jesus. I think I might have crossed over into another dimension."

Jett stilled. Tristan didn't sound upset, but Jett was still prepared for the accusations. She hadn't meant to take her so hard and for so long. She'd just wanted her so badly, she'd lost herself in the powerful currents of Tristan's excitement. She should've known that would happen, because she'd been wanting her more and more every day. "I didn't realize you believed in that out-of-body sort of thing."

"I didn't, before tonight. I didn't even have a clue how much I wanted that." Tristan tried to sit up but found that her arms and legs still weren't working. She slowly began to sort out her surroundings as she got her mind and body back together again. "You still have your clothes on."

"It's cooler up here than in the city, and I couldn't find any wood for the fire."

"I take it I more or less conked out on you."

"You were a little tired."

Tristan snorted. "I can't even remember getting in here, and it wasn't because I was tired. I've never come like that before. I thought my flesh was going to peel off my bones." She frowned. "Fuck. I left you hanging, didn't I? Hell."

Tristan started to sit up and Jett stopped her.

"Believe me," Jett said, "if it was good for you, it was better for me. You didn't leave me hanging."

Tristan didn't look convinced. "Did you...you know? Handle things?"

Jett smiled. Tristan talked so easily about things Jett had always kept secret. "Yeah. I did. It was about a five-second flash bang."

"Then I owe you big."

"No," Jett said softly. "You don't owe me anything at all."

"Why didn't you get under the covers with me?" After a moment of silence, Tristan asked, "Jett?"

"I wasn't sure you'd want me to."

"Turn on the light."

"What?" Jett asked.

"Turn on the light next to you, because I can't reach it. In fact, I still can't move," Tristan said.

Jett rolled over and fumbled on the bedside table until she found the pull chain for the old-fashioned brass lamp. The fabric shade with thin tassels along the edges cast a pale yellow glow over half the room and a portion of the bed. Cautiously, Jett eased back against the pillows, still mostly on top of the covers. She was barefoot but still wore her pants and shirt.

Tristan propped herself up and began to open the buttons on Jett's shirt with one hand. "In case you've forgotten," she said conversationally, "I told you I wanted you to make love to me. If you thought I meant I wanted you to service me and then be on your way, I'm sorry I gave you the wrong impression."

"I didn't think that."

"Then I'm confused as to why you're not in bed with me." Tristan opened Jett's shirt and felt suddenly dizzy again. "Jesus, you have an amazing body." She kissed Jett swiftly, then watched Jett's face as she caressed her breasts. She smiled when Jett trembled. "You like that?"

"Yes," Jett whispered.

Tristan bent her head and licked a nipple. "Just yes?"

"Yes. A lot."

Tristan cupped Jett's breast but no longer caressed her. She searched Jett's eyes. They were murky and dark, troubled. "What do you think you might have done that I wouldn't have wanted?"

"You said I hurt you."

"No. I don't remember exactly what I said, considering that I was losing my mind. But I think I said *it hurts*. It did." Tristan grinned crookedly. "It hurt so fucking good I about came all over your hand a dozen times. Tell me you didn't know that."

"I know what I made you do," Jett said quietly. "That doesn't mean you wanted it."

"Of course I wanted it. Did you hear me say no? Jesus Christ. Who fucked with your head like this?"

Jett stiffened. "No one."

"Bullshit. *Bullshit.*" Tristan shook her head vehemently. "One of these days, one of these days, you'll tell me. But not tonight." She smoothed her hand down the middle of Jett's belly and opened her pants. "Lift up, take these off."

Jett gripped Tristan's wrist. "Tristan, it's late. We should get some sleep."

"You think I'm going to leave it like this?" Tristan said sharply. "Without touching you? Without tasting you? You think all I wanted was to get off?"

Jett knew once they started again she would need more, would end up taking more, and they wouldn't sleep for the rest of the night. She was certain that Tristan would never let her own exhaustion prevent her from satisfying Jett, if she thought Jett needed it. "I've got to fly tomorrow night, Tristan."

"Fuck," Tristan muttered. "I'm not on call again until Monday. I can go the rest of the night without sleep." She brushed her fingers through Jett's hair. "But you can't. You have to be safe." She rested her forehead against Jett's. "Ah but Jesus, I want you so much."

Even in the soft light the deep circles beneath Tristan's eyes were obvious, and despite her protests that she didn't need sleep, her hands were shaking. Jett curled her arm around Tristan's shoulder and pulled her down. "Would you mind if we just held each other?"

"If that's what you need, you got it." Tristan rested her hand on Jett's stomach and settled her head on Jett's shoulder. "Okay?"

"Yeah," Jett said, amazed and perplexed because it was true. "Absolutely okay."

CHAPTER TWENTY

Jett woke with the dawn, as she did every day. This morning was completely different from any she could ever remember, because this morning she held Tristan in her arms. She lay on her side with Tristan curled in the curve of her body, her arm around Tristan's waist and Tristan's ass nestled against her pelvis.

Tristan seemed so vulnerable in her sleep, and Jett wondered how she could be so trusting. She was humbled by Tristan's trust, humbled and in awe. She didn't think she could ever give up that much control, surrender so completely to the care of another. That Tristan did made Jett feel fiercely protective, and she held very still, not wanting to wake her. What she wanted was to absorb the feel of her, the scent of her, the taste of her. Carefully, she moved her lips to the back of Tristan's neck and kissed the skin below her hairline, tasting salt and a surprising sweetness, like sun-warmed strawberries fresh off the vine. When Tristan sighed and caught Jett's hand, drawing it to her breast, a shaft of pleasure hit Jett so hard she groaned. Then Tristan's breathing deepened again, and Jett realized she had made the movement in her sleep.

Nothing about being with Tristan was what she expected. She'd had women tease and taunt her until she made the first move, bearing responsibility for what they both wanted. She'd had women force her hands to the places that craved her touch and had women rake her flesh in the throes of orgasm until they drew blood, but she'd never had a woman reach for her in her sleep. Jett's chest tightened as she softly, cautiously caressed Tristan's breast, feeling Tristan's nipple harden even as Tristan shifted restlessly and murmured under her breath. Jett abruptly stilled.

Tristan turned onto her back, her gaze already eclipsed by desire. She hooked an arm around Jett's neck, pulling her down for a kiss. "Why did you stop?"

"I didn't want to wake you."

Tristan raised an eyebrow. "Why not?"

"You were sleeping," Jett replied.

"There's a non sequitur in there," Tristan muttered, rolling over onto Jett. She slid her leg between Jett's and braced herself on her elbows, a hand on either side of Jett's head. She combed her fingers through Jett's hair. "But I don't feel like figuring it out right now." She kissed her again, longer this time, exploring in a way she hadn't been able to the night before when Jett had taken her so completely. Jett tensed beneath her, hard muscles quivering, and Tristan feasted on the power of exciting her. "You're so fucking sexy."

"Tris," Jett whispered, partly in wonder and partly in need. She'd slept, but restlessly, her body sending mixed signals of satisfaction and lingering arousal. Once she'd touched herself, squeezing her turgid clitoris, and cutting points of pleasure had shot through her. But she hadn't wanted to finish, preferring instead to tease herself while remembering Tristan surrendering in her mouth. Recalling it now, she shuddered.

"Baby," Tristan murmured. "Baby, what do you need?"

"Anything," Jett whispered, reaching for Tristan's hand.

Tristan laced her fingers through Jett's, gripping her fingers tightly. "Tell me what you don't want me to do."

"Nothing," Jett said, arching into her. "There's nothing I don't want you to do."

"That's good." Tristan eased to one side so she could run her fingers down the center of Jett's stomach. "Because I want to do everything."

Jett kept her eyes on Tristan's as Tristan slid her fingers between her legs. Jett's lips parted on a silent moan, and Tristan's eyes shifted from blue to deep purple. Tristan's satisfaction was Jett's greatest pleasure, even now.

"You're so hard," Tristan murmured. "Have you been like this all night?"

"Yes," Jett whispered.

"Baby." Tristan kissed her, harder, catching Jett's lip between her teeth, sucking as she gently rolled Jett's clitoris between her fingers. "You should've let me do this last night."

"You're doing it now." Jett panted, trying and failing to control herself as Tristan's practiced strokes worked her closer and closer to coming. She grabbed Tristan's hand.

"Too hard?"

"No," Jett gasped. "You're going to make me come."

Tristan laughed, picking up speed. "And the problem is?"

Jett groaned, her hips lifting and circling of their own volition, chasing the sweet relief Tristan's caresses promised. "Ruins...my reputation."

"I'll never tell." Tristan watched Jett's eyes roll back. Jett was right on the edge, and Tristan wanted to satisfy her. But she wanted so much more. She wanted to imprint her touch on Jett's mind, on her body, on her soul, and the force of her desire frightened and confused her. She relaxed her grip and slowed her strokes.

"Oh God," Jett moaned. "Tris..."

"I'm here," Tristan whispered. "I want to be inside you. Can I?"

Jett covered Tristan's hand with hers and pushed Tristan's fingers lower, curling her own until Tristan glided inside her. The unfamiliar sensation was at once so exquisite and so intense her muscles spasmed and she had to bite her lip to keep from crying out. A small whimper escaped.

"It's all right," Tristan crooned, holding completely still until Jett relaxed enough for her to move her fingers. Then she thrust, slow and deep, using her thumb to massage Jett's clitoris at the same time. Jett was swollen and hard and Tristan knew she could not hold her off much longer. Still, she wanted more, and she could think of only one thing that might prolong Jett's pleasure. "Jett. Jett, baby, can you touch me?"

Jett traced Tristan's forearm to the curve of her hip, over her thigh, and between her legs. She pressed against the base of Tristan's clitoris, then circled.

Tristan sucked in a breath, instantly on the verge. "Oh yes." She kissed Jett, starting to lose her grip, her mind completely unleashed. She pushed deeper, Jett manipulated her, and she had to pull away before she lost herself entirely. "Slow dow—"

"No," Jett implored. "Come with me. Come with me, Tris, come with me."

Somehow, Tristan sensed Jett waiting, holding back, and knew what Jett needed to trigger her. "Do me hard like you did last night."

Jett's hips jerked, and she squeezed Tristan tightly between her fingers. Squeeze, release, stroke. Squeeze, release, stroke. Once, twice, three times.

"Oh yeah," Tristan cried, the first jolt racing through her. Instantly, Jett surged around her fingers, muscles clamping down, legs rigid as iron. Tristan felt teeth against her upper arm as Jett bit down, jaws working soundlessly as she exploded. Tristan rode the brief spike of pain to another peak, coming so hard she forgot to breathe until spots danced behind her eyelids.

"Tris, Tris," Jett whispered, her face pressed to Tristan's shoulder. "Oh, Jesus. Don't stop."

"Don't worry, baby. I won't. I won't."

Tristan was in trouble, because she never wanted to stop.

❖

Tristan hadn't meant to fall asleep again, but every time Jett made her come, the physical and emotional catharsis was so intense her body just shut down. This time when she woke she was immediately aware of bright sunshine and the utter stillness of being completely alone. Abruptly, she sat up, scanning the room. Jett's clothes were gone. She leapt from bed, crossed the small room in three rapid strides, and yanked open the door to the main room of the cabin. Empty as well. A minute later, she jerked open the front door.

Jett turned at the sound of the door opening, and for a second or two, she thought she might still be in the midst of her daydream. She'd been reliving the moments with Tristan—the heat of her body, the insistent press of her hands, her sharp cries of pleasure. She often replayed her sexual encounters, especially as the weeks between real life experiences stretched on. Faces and places would blur as she spliced highlights together, struggling to call up the perfect combination of sights and sounds to take her over the edge. As she gazed at Tristan's naked body, she knew she would never need to imagine any other image to find satisfaction.

"I thought you were gone," Tristan said, feeling a little foolish and a lot disoriented. She did not get bent out of shape over women. She certainly didn't panic if one of her dates left in the middle of the night. In fact, they often did. Then she realized what was different about Jett. She expected Jett to go because everything she knew about her indicated that Jett did not let people close, anywhere, even in bed. That was nothing different than what Tristan was used to; in fact, it was exactly what she sought in the women she slept with. And while Jett might be behaving exactly as she usually did, Tristan definitely wasn't. Because she did not want Jett to go anywhere.

"I'm not exactly sure where we are," Jett said. "I don't have a car." She eased her wallet from her back pocket and riffled through it. "And I don't think seventeen bucks would get me too far."

Jett replaced her wallet, opened the screen door, and wrapped both arms around Tristan's waist. Then she backed her into the cabin, nudged the door closed, and turned Tristan against the door. She caught Tristan's jaw in the palm of her hand, fingers spread on one side, thumb on the other, holding her head still as she scraped her teeth along the tight muscle in the side of Tristan's neck. She leaned into Tristan, sucking on the buttery skin below Tristan's earlobe, and eased her hand between Tristan's legs. "And I had something else in mind."

"Christ," Tristan gasped, unable to believe she was ready again. She couldn't see Jett's face because Jett kept her head turned away. Jett's shirt and pants felt like sandpaper against her sensitized skin. The metal grommet at the top of Jett's pants was hot against her stomach. Jett's lips as they nibbled and tugged and sucked at her neck had the same effect as if Jett had her mouth between her legs, teasing her there. And then Jett's fingers *were* there, sliding and stroking and slipping into her. She grabbed Jett's ass, digging her fingers into the hard muscles.

"Ah, Jesus, baby," Tristan moaned. "You're making me so hot."

Jett rimmed Tristan's ear, breathing hard as Tristan tilted her pelvis and invited her to take more. She had a hard time focusing on anything except the way Tristan grunted softly each time she touched her clit. "I think you're always hot." She pinched Tristan's clit, then rapidly circled it. Tristan's knees buckled and she sagged. "You like that."

"Yes." Tristan closed her eyes. The pressure was building. She was close. "Yes. Yes."

"Yes what?" Jett lifted her fingers away.

"Oh fuck," Tristan groaned. "I want to come."

"Do you?" Jett licked her way down to Tristan's collarbone, reaching between them to open her own fly. She kept Tristan pinned to the door with her mouth against Tristan's throat while she worked the hand she'd been using to immobilize Tristan's head inside her pants. Then she stroked them both at once.

Through her haze, Tristan heard Jett moan, felt her tremble, and tightened her grip on Jett's hips. Knowing that Jett was getting off getting *her* off did it for her. "Feel me, baby? You're making me come."

As soon as Tristan started to climax, Jett barely had to touch herself to follow her over. Then they were both shivering and groaning and slowly sliding to the floor. Jett ended up on her knees, her forehead pressed to Tristan's shoulder, Tristan's hands rubbing her back and her neck while she whispered softly.

"So good, babe. So so good," Tristan crooned.

"Needed you," Jett gasped, "again. Sorry."

Tristan laughed. "Oh, it was a hardship." She sagged back against the door, stretching her legs out on either side of Jett. With an arm around Jett's shoulders, she cupped Jett's chin and lifted her head, studying her glazed eyes. The worried look was back again. So was the uncertainty. "I happen to like having you hungry for me."

"Sometimes I forget to ask."

"You don't have to. I told you before what I wanted." Tristan found Jett's hand and pressed it between her legs. "And *how* I wanted it."

Jett fondled her, and after a minute, Tristan moved Jett's hand away and sighed. "We're going to have to head back soon. Keep doing that and I'm going to want you to make me come."

"You don't really want me to stop."

Tristan didn't, but she felt the press of time at their backs, and she didn't want this—whatever *this* was—to end right here, right now. She couldn't think when she was this turned on. "I have to stop."

Jett pulled away. She wanted Tristan again right now, would want her for hours, and the need frayed her temper. Her need, always too much. Jett managed to sit up and put some distance between them. One of the nice things about not waking up with a woman was that she didn't have to say good-bye, and neither of them had to pretend that they'd done anything other than use each other for a few hours.

"Wait." Tristan grabbed Jett's hand, not knowing quite what to say, because she didn't have any practice at what they were doing. She didn't even know exactly what she wanted. "Look, about last night…"

"There's nothing to say, Tristan. Last night was what it was." This was a talk Jett didn't want to have, especially not with Tristan. She got to her knees, then unsteadily to her feet, and zipped up her pants. Her hands were shaking and she tried to hide it by jamming in her shirttails. "We've both been here before. Let's not complicate it, okay? I had a great time. I hope you did too."

"You know I did." Still sitting with her back to the door, Tristan studied Jett, trying to read below the surface of her cool, closed gaze. She couldn't, but she sensed yet again that if she pushed, Jett would retreat. "I had a lot more than a good time."

"Yeah." Jett stepped back.

Tristan stood, conscious of being naked with Jett fully clothed. She felt naked in a lot more ways than just being without clothes. Jett was much better at keeping what she was feeling, if she felt anything at all, hidden. Suddenly, Tristan didn't like being the one completely exposed. She might like being controlled in bed, but she didn't like being out of control in any other part of her life. She turned and walked toward the bedroom. "I'm going to grab a quick shower, and then it's all yours if you want it. Then we should go."

"Right," Jett said. "We should go."

❖

"Quinn!" Honor called from the back porch.

"Watch your follow-through, Arly." Quinn crouched to catch Arly's pitch. When the softball landed in her glove with a resounding smack, she nodded in approval and stood, shading her eyes with her gloved hand. "Yeah?"

"Phone. It's the hospital."

"I'm not on call," Quinn replied.

"It's Dave Barnes from emergency management. He said he has to talk to you."

"On my way." Arly stood ten yards away, a worried look on her face, and Quinn walked over to her. "Shoulder feeling okay? You put a lot of speed on that ball, kiddo."

"Feels great. Are you going to have to go to work?"

"I don't know." Quinn cupped the back of Arly's head and stroked her hair. "Let me go find out."

Honor met Quinn on the porch with the portable phone.

"Maguire." Quinn listened for a minute or two, then responded. "Call the OR supervisor next and alert all the backup teams. Then have the head of nursing start calling in the evening shift. I'll be there in fifteen minutes."

As soon as Quinn disconnected, Honor asked, "What is it?"

"A section of the I-95 overpass collapsed. All the hospitals are going to mass casualty alert."

The phone rang again and Honor answered. "Dr. Blake. Yes, I just heard. Get me a status report from the blood bank and round up as many off-duty ER staff as you can. Also, call the chief of medicine and tell them we need to pull residents from the floors down to the ER. What? No, it's covered under the mass casualty protocols. I'll be there soon."

"Honor," Quinn said quietly. "You—"

"I'll supervise. I won't see patients."

"Promise."

"I do." Honor took Arly's hand and carefully bent over. "I'm sorry, honey. There's been a big accident and there might be a lot of people who are hurt. We both need to go."

"When will you be back?"

"Probably not until tomorrow. We'll get Robin to take you to practice, and you and your brother will stay with your grandmom tonight."

"Will you call me?"

Honor smiled and kissed Arly's forehead. "I will."

"Okay."

"Good girl." Honor headed into the house. "I'll call Phyllis."

Quinn wrapped her arm around Arly's shoulder. "I'm sorry, Arly. I wouldn't miss practice if I didn't absolutely have to. I know you're disappointed. Me too."

Arly shrugged and leaned her head against Quinn's side. "I know you'd be there if you could."

"You can count on that." Quinn and Arly followed Honor into the house. Every chief of staff and on-call personnel would be getting the same phone call she just did. Quinn wasn't happy about Honor going to work, but she knew there was no way she could stop her. They were all in for a very long weekend.

CHAPTER TWENTY-ONE

"What's the longest relationship you've ever had?" Tristan said out of the blue, while shifting into fifth to pass an eighteen-wheeler on the Pennsylvania Turnpike. She knew she was headed down a dangerous road, but since the very first instant she'd seen Jett, she hadn't been able to take the safe or smart path. Somehow, she always veered into unknown territory, both in terms of how she felt and what she knew was likely to push Jett away. Just the same, she could tolerate anger a lot better than she could stand the silence. No, it wasn't really the silence that bothered her. It was the distance that separated them at this moment. Even though she could have reached out and touched Jett, the chasm seemed insurmountable. And she knew if she *did* touch her, it would be like touching a marble statue, cold and unyielding. After the consuming heat of what they'd shared, she couldn't bear the cold.

Jett watched the slower traffic flicker by as they flew past. She didn't fear speed, and a big part of her wanted nothing more than to get back to the city so that she could get out of the car and away from Tristan. Tristan held the key to things she preferred to keep locked inside—her physical needs, her emotional uncertainty, her fear. Her fear that she would come to want what until this point in her life she had only needed. Needs were so much easier to control than wants. And when she looked at Tristan, when she *thought* of Tristan, she wanted. She wanted with a hunger that hollowed her out and left her shaking. She wanted to touch her, hold her, be held by her. She wanted to tell her the things she had never even dared to dream of. Wanting was dangerous and only led to disappointment.

"I've never had a relationship," Jett finally said.

Tristan looked over at her, then back at the road. "Never had a girlfriend?"

"No."

"Why not? Because of the military?"

"Mostly." Jett had plenty of practice staying relaxed under fire, and she kept her body still and her voice even, despite the fact that her stomach was in knots. Tristan was upset and she hated that she had been the cause. The night before she had feared hurting her physically, or pushing her to do something she wouldn't enjoy or would later regret. Nothing had been further from the truth. Tristan had not only welcomed her, she'd read her body and mind so clearly she'd been able to give Jett exactly what she craved—passion without restraint. Jett had never once considered that Tristan might be wounded by the emotional gulf that Jett had no idea how to bridge.

"What was the other part of mostly?" Tristan gripped the wheel, not because the vehicle demanded it, but because she wanted to touch Jett so badly she could barely breathe. When they made love, and she realized that's how she thought of it—not had sex, made love—nothing stood between them. She felt stripped bare, exposed to her core, adored and desired. She felt owned in the most fundamental of ways, and she was shocked to discover she liked it. The sense of belonging was more acute than anything she'd ever experienced, and now she felt adrift, disconnected, lost. The sensation was nearly unbearable.

"I never met anyone who I trusted enough, I guess." Jett thought fleetingly of Gail. "Or who trusted me."

Tristan knew she had to be thinking of a woman. "Who was she? What did she do?"

Jett clenched her jaws and turned to look out the open passenger side of the car. Tristan saw too much.

"Did she break your heart?"

"No," Jett said sharply. "I never gave her my heart."

"Why not?"

Jett whipped her head around. "Because she didn't want it."

The pain in Jett's eyes hurt, because Tristan hated to see her hurting and because whoever this woman was, Jett had cared for her. Jett had cared in a way she didn't for her. Even knowing that the answer was going to hurt even more, Tristan whispered, "But you wanted to give it to her, didn't you."

"Like I said," Jett said flatly, her face expressionless again. "My mistake."

"I'm sorry."

Jett shook her head. "Nothing to be sorry about. What about you? You've got at least one girlfriend."

Tristan's heart leapt, then she chided herself for being foolish for the second time that morning. "You mean Darla?"

"That's the redhead, right?"

"Darla is a friend." Tristan laughed. "And before you ask me if I fuck all my friends, the answer's no. She's a special friend."

Jett raised an eyebrow. "Do you have a lot of special friends?"

"Not a lot. Not currently."

"So why friends and not..." Jett wasn't even certain of the term, since such things were beyond her realm of experience.

"Lovers?" Tristan shrugged. "It's weird. My parents love me—I know that in my head. But my sisters were always the perfect ones, and I never measured up. I never felt special. Hell, I never even felt adequate."

"I don't follow."

Tristan grinned wryly. "I'm sure it would take years of intensive therapy to unravel it." Jett laughed, and the sound of her laughter lightened Tristan's heart even as the sadness washed through her. "Somewhere along the way I guess I stopped wanting to be special. To anyone."

Jett couldn't imagine anyone not thinking Tristan was special. She was amazing—bold and brave and honest. Beautiful. Sexy. Remembering the way Tristan felt in her arms that morning, in her mouth the night before, inside her a few hours ago, she was swamped with so many unfamiliar feelings. Tenderness, gratitude, wonder. Her heart ached. Her clit got hard and she wanted to touch Tristan again. She looked out the windshield because she couldn't keep looking at her, not and think. Not and keep her hands off her. "You're special."

"What?" Tristan asked, still thinking about what she'd just said. She'd given up. Given up hoping that she'd ever be more to anyone than a great fuck. Jett's voice had dropped so low she could barely hear her. "What?"

Jett cleared her throat. "I'm sure your special friends think you're special too."

What about you, Tristan wanted to ask, but she'd been asking since the first day they'd met and she wasn't about to beg. Darla thought she was pretty special in bed, she was sure of that. Until Jett, that had been enough. "You start your seven on tonight?"

"Yes," Jett replied, happy to leave the topic of Tristan's girlfriends behind. Then she wondered what Tristan would do with the rest of her weekend off. Saturday night. She probably went out on Saturday night. Last night had been an exception, an anomaly. They'd both needed an escape, and they'd run from the death and destruction into twenty-four hours out of time. Now they were nearly back, and life would get back to normal as well. Jett would fly for her pleasure, and Tristan—Tristan would have her special friends.

"Jesus," Tristan muttered. "Look at the traffic backed up heading east. Glad we're not going that—" She grabbed at her waist as her beeper went off. She'd barely lifted it to eye level to read the number when Jett's went off as well. She glanced at Jett. "Trouble."

Tristan signaled and pulled off the turnpike an exit early so she could park and they both could return their calls. They sat with the engine idling, cell phones to their ears, while they waited to make their way through the labyrinth of hospital operators. Tristan turned slightly away to take her call. When she disconnected she stared at Jett.

"Jesus. They call you in?"

"Yes," Jett said. "You?"

"Yep." Tristan gunned the engine and pulled away from the curb. "We'll take the back roads. I can get us there in ten minutes."

The secondary roads leading to the hospital were crowded too, and it was closer to fifteen minutes before Tristan pulled into the doctors' parking lot. She switched off the engine and turned in her seat, finally doing what she'd wanted to do for the last hour and a half. She slid her hand over Jett's shoulder to the back of her neck and caressed her. "It's going to be crazy. I don't know when I'll see you again."

"Okay." Jett tried to ignore the glide of Tristan's fingers through her hair. She wished Tristan hadn't touched her. She'd been keyed up in the car, and then the adrenaline spurt from hearing about the disaster had put her nerves on high alert. Now the physical stimulation was almost more than she could take. Still, she didn't want to pull away.

"I can see it in your eyes," Tristan whispered, circling her thumb over the base of Jett's skull. God damn it, she wasn't a quitter. "Last night isn't over yet."

"I have to go," Jett said, her throat tight.

"I know. So do I." Tristan yanked Jett toward her and covered her mouth with hers. She needed to be sure Jett didn't forget her, and she needed part of Jett to take with her. Jett grabbed the front of her shirt and kissed her back, hard, their tongues seeking, searching. Tristan groaned. "Jesus. Jett."

Jett pulled away and fumbled behind her for the door handle. "I don't want to go." She pushed the door open and got out, her legs feeling too weak to hold her up. "Okay? I don't want to go."

"Yeah. Okay," Tristan said, her chest heaving. "Be careful."

"Always."

"I mean it."

Jett backed up, shaking her head. "Don't worry. I'm always careful when I fly."

"Remember what I said," Tristan called after her. "Last night isn't over."

Jett turned and jogged away.

❖

"You running the show?" Tristan asked when she saw Quinn changing in the surgical locker room. Quinn was chief of trauma, so the normal protocol would be for her to coordinate the hospital's emergency surgical response.

"Yep. Honor's downstairs in the ER. They'll handle triage at that level."

"Honor?" Tristan banged open her locker, kicked her shoes off, and unbuttoned her shirt. "She okay?"

Quinn shrugged her shoulders. "She's Honor."

"Yeah, I guess that's true." Tristan pulled off her shirt. "What's the word?"

"Conflicting reports. A three-hundred-yard stretch of the overpass collapsed just north of the city. Most of it ended up in the Delaware."

"Jesus. How many cars?"

Quinn shook her head and hooked the trauma and code beepers on the waistband of her scrub pants. "Nobody knows. I've heard anywhere from a dozen up to a couple hundred. There's talk of mobilizing the National Guard."

"How long before we can expect casualties?" Tristan pulled on scrub pants and reached for a shirt from the pile she kept on the top shelf of her locker.

"Anytime. The Coast Guard is working the waters. I just got a call for physicians and medics to triage on shore." Quinn slammed her locker door. "Want to come?"

"Hell yeah." Tristan kneed her locker closed. "I don't want to stay here squeezing a bag all night. Can I take some respiratory techs with me? If many people went into the river, we're going to have a lot of respiratory arrests."

"Just make sure we don't leave the intensive care units uncovered here. We're hitching a ride on Healthstar, so limit it to two. Collect your people and meet me on the helipad. You've got five minutes."

"Right," Tristan called, already sprinting toward the hall and the intensive care units at the other end. Healthstar. Healthstar meant Jett. She was going to see her again a lot sooner than she'd thought. She spared herself twenty seconds to enjoy the anticipation, then she focused all of her attention on what she needed to do.

❖

Jett kept a change of clothes in the closet in her on-call room and had just pulled out a clean shirt when a knock sounded on the door. "Come in."

When Linda entered and shut the door behind her, Jett turned her back and stripped. She hadn't put on any underwear after showering at Tristan's, but she figured Linda had seen more than her fair share of bare butts in her time. "What's up?"

"There's someone here to see you," Linda said.

"If it's another one of those jerks from risk management, tell them I don't have anything else to say."

"Even those anal idiots wouldn't be trying to interview us in the middle of all this." Linda laughed at the absurd image. "Well, maybe they would, but it isn't them."

"Who is it?" Jett zipped her fly and yanked a black T-shirt over her head. She found a pair of socks in the bottom of her flight bag and pulled them on along with her combat boots.

"I think it's a personal visit."

Frowning, Jett straightened. "Hell of a time for it. Tell them to go away." She grabbed her helmet and started out into the hall. "See you upstairs."

"Okay," Linda called after her. "Be there in five."

Jett took the stairs two at a time and pushed through the exit door onto the rooftop. Clear skies, bright midafternoon sunlight. Perfect day for flying. Her aircraft waited within the white lines delineating the landing pad. Just seeing it made her heart beat faster and her mind settle. This was where she belonged. This she understood.

"When I heard what was going on at the waterfront, I knew this was where I'd find you," a voice said from behind her.

Jett stopped, almost believing she was daydreaming again. She pivoted and blinked as a shaft of sunlight struck her eyes. They watered and her vision wavered, and she still thought she might have conjured the slender figure walking toward her.

"I know you've only got a minute," Gail said, and Jett's heart stuttered in her chest.

She was in uniform, but not the desert camo Jett remembered. She looked taut and trim in the crisp Army blue service uniform with navy trousers and gray shirt. The oak leaf insignia of the Nursing Corps shimmered on her shoulder, and Jett barely stopped herself from saluting.

"Major."

Gail smiled faintly. "Chief Warrant Officer McNally."

"I've got a flight check to do."

"I know. Your flight nurse told me." Gail stopped just inches away, her eyes searching Jett's.

"What are you doing here?" Jett's throat hurt. Her heart hurt.

"I came back on a patient transport from Ramstein. I've got two weeks' leave." Gail brushed the tips of her fingers through the hair at Jett's temple. "It's getting long."

Jett forced herself not to flinch at the touch. Instead, she stepped carefully back. "I don't have any time."

"Not now. I know." Gail's hand fell slowly to her side. "But in a day or two. I'm at the Hilton at Thirty-sixth Street. I want to see you."

"Gail…" Jett stopped when the doors bounced open on the far side of the roof and Linda and several others came out. "I don't—"

"Please. Jett, please." Gail's voice broke.

"All right," Jett said hoarsely.

Gail waited another heartbeat, then turned and walked away. Jett watched her for a few more seconds before climbing into the cockpit to prepare for the upcoming battle. She couldn't think about Gail now. Couldn't think about what she saw in her eyes. Regret. Sadness. Desire. She couldn't think about what she'd felt when she'd first seen her face. Recognition. Anticipation. Desire.

CHAPTER TWENTY-TWO

The elevator doors opened and Tristan jumped out, nearly colliding with a good-looking brunette in a snappy uniform. "Oh, sorry." She grabbed the woman by the shoulders to steady her, surprised by the firm muscles in the lithe frame. "You okay?"

"Yes, fine. My fault. I was crowding the door." She smiled at Tristan. "Bad habit I have, always being in a hurry."

"I know what you mean." Tristan stepped around her, then realized there was no parking on the roof. So if the soldier wasn't up there parking a car, where did she come from, and what was she doing? The only thing outside was the flight deck. Suddenly the pieces fell together. The only other soldier, well, ex-soldier but not ex by much, who was likely to be up on the roof was Jett. So this woman—this very attractive, actually pretty hot woman—was there to see Jett. Tristan was two seconds from demanding who she was and what she wanted with Jett before she mentally ordered herself to calm down. She was making some huge leaps of logic, and even if she was right and the brunette *was* there to see Jett, Jett probably had lots of friends from the Army, most of them women. Why shouldn't she have a visitor. Perfectly natural. Tristan narrowed her eyes. "You're not lost by any chance, are you?"

The soldier turned back to Tristan, a curious question in her eyes, and the elevator doors opened and then closed, leaving her still standing in the small foyer. She pushed the down button again. "No."

Well then, why are you here, Tristan wanted to ask, but it wasn't any of her business, and she didn't have any time left. "Enjoy the rest of the day."

"You too, and stay alert out there," the brunette said.

"Thanks," Tristan said, and ran for the helicopter. Linda, with one hand on the handle of the large side sliding door, leaned out of the aircraft, whose rotors were already spinning. Tristan could make out the rest of the team inside. She ducked her head and vaulted into the cabin. "Sorry to keep you waiting."

Linda pulled the door closed and tapped Jett on the shoulder, saying at the same time, "All aboard, Chief."

Tristan strapped in next to Linda and, keeping her transmitter turned off, leaned close. Under cover of the motor revving, she asked "Who was that?"

"Who?" Linda asked.

"The brunette. The soldier."

"Oh. I don't know. A friend of Jett's, I guess. She showed up in the flight lounge a while ago, asking for Jett."

Tristan frowned. "And Jett brought her up here?" To our favorite place, she almost said.

"I don't think so. I think she came up on her own."

"Pretty fucking good friend," Tristan muttered, "or a pretty ballsy one."

"What?" Linda yelled, signaling that she couldn't hear.

Tristan shook her head. "Nothing. It doesn't matter."

Except it did. It mattered a hell of a lot. Because no matter how much Jett said whatever had happened between her and the mystery woman in the Army was over, her eyes said otherwise. Tristan didn't believe in coincidences, not when they showed up out of the blue and acted like they owned the place. Following Jett to the flight deck. Hell. She stared past Quinn into the cockpit. She couldn't see Jett's face, only her shoulder, one arm, and her hand. She watched Jett's fingers cradle the stick, reading the aircraft through its vibration and pitch, just as she had read Tristan's body as she'd clenched and tightened. Tristan had a quick flash of Jett grabbing Mandy, of her hands skimming Mandy's breasts, and suddenly Mandy became the woman by the elevator. Only this time Jett wasn't just touching the woman, the woman was touching Jett too. The idea made something inside Tristan coil so tightly she felt herself quiver.

A strong hand gripped her shoulder and broke her reverie.

"You okay?" Quinn yelled.

"Yeah. Fine." Tristan tore her eyes away from Jett. "Couldn't be better."

"It's going to get hairy down there," Quinn said, peering into Tristan's face. "Stay focused."

"Always am." Tristan closed her eyes so Quinn couldn't read them, and blanked her mind. They'd be in the field in a few minutes and lives depended on her being sharp. She didn't have time to think about Jett, or why the idea of Jett with any other woman made her furious. She wanted to hang a sign on Jett that said *mine*. What the hell was *that* about?

❖

Jett studied her approach through the wide windows of the glassed-in cockpit. Even from a few miles away, signs of the devastation were clearly evident. The air surrounding the site of the freeway collapse was cloudy with particulate matter, probably concrete dust, resembling what she'd seen in Baghdad after buildings had been reduced to rubble by missiles and bombs. She tensed, half expecting incoming fire, automatically preparing to begin evasive maneuvers. Despite the internal climate control on the aircraft, she was sweating. The closer she got, the more the ground action looked like a war zone. Huge slabs of concrete were standing on end, resembling a jumble of giant dominoes haphazardly tossed about. A section of the overpass had accordioned down onto the highway below. If the collapse had occurred even a half a mile in either direction, there would have been houses buried in the rubble rather than just vehicles.

"Oh my God," Jett heard Linda say over the radio. "There are cars everywhere. In the water...oh my God."

Cars floated upside down in the Delaware River, kept afloat by air pockets inside the vehicles. Jett figured there had to be dozens more beneath the surface. At one spot where two block-long sections of the highway formed a funnel, cars and trucks lay piled at the bottom of the vee. Coast Guard cruisers and smaller boats littered the waterways. Emergency vehicles jammed the side streets in all directions. A news helicopter drifted into view. Jett disliked sharing her airspace with news choppers. Even experienced emergency helicopter pilots occasionally crossed paths midair, but the news pilots tended to be too busy jockeying for camera angles and exclusive shots to adhere to strict safety protocols. Risk takers. Jett might take chances, but she knew her limits. They didn't.

"This is Healthstar 3, two nine nine PMC. Request LZ site." The FAA would have set up a temporary flight restriction above and around the disaster area, so the TV and radio news choppers weren't likely to come any closer. Just the same, Jett slowed and circled, keeping an eye on them while waiting for clearance to land on one of the designated landing zones. The firecrews on the ground would direct her to one.

"Roger Healthstar 3. Your LZ is the Marina parking lot. You have power lines at the southwest corner. Land between the trucks."

"Roger."

Jett set down in the parking lot on the river side of the destroyed highway, a few hundred yards from the center of the rescue activity. She climbed down from the cockpit to help unload the emergency equipment.

"Try to work as a team," Quinn instructed the medics. "If another crew requests assistance, go ahead, but let me know where you're going. We don't want to lose anyone out here, and these situations can be unstable. Don't take any chances."

Jett edged through the people toward Tristan, who was offloading equipment. She had been surprised to see Tristan climb aboard, but her overwhelming response had been pleasure. Pleasure and relief. Gail— Gail who was no longer part of her world—had just appeared out of nowhere and then disappeared just as quickly, and Jett didn't want to think about her, *couldn't* think about her now. And when she'd seen Tristan, Gail's face had faded. Instead she'd remembered waking up with Tristan in her arms and the feeling of peace like none she'd ever experienced. All the while she'd been in the air, she'd thought about Tristan. Tristan, who never seemed afraid to talk about anything, who could get Jett to talk, to *feel*, even when she didn't want to. Tristan, who wasn't afraid of Jett or what she wanted. Jett replayed how Tris's hard, strong body had softened with desire and how her tight, powerful muscles had trembled on the brink of orgasm. Thinking about caressing Tristan, of making her cry out with pleasure and release, fueled the hunger that had never ebbed, and Jett had to fight not to touch her. Like an addict, she craved more.

"You doing search and rescue now?" Jett asked, cramming her hands in her pockets because she didn't trust herself.

"Being out here beats sitting back at the shop waiting." Tristan kept dragging equipment out of the cabin. She was still thinking about the brunette. About who she was and why she'd come looking for Jett. It bugged her that she wanted to know so badly, and she didn't know how to ask, and she didn't know how to stop thinking about her with Jett.

"Look," Jett said hurriedly. "I'm going to be transporting casualties to any available hospital, and from the looks of things, we're going to be out here for a while."

Tristan stopped what she was doing and finally locked at Jett. "Yeah. A very long night. Be careful."

Jett grinned. "I was just going to say the same thing to you."

"I'm always careful." Tristan went back to what she was doing, stiffening when she felt Jett's hand close around her upper arm. Even that casual contact sent her pulse into overdrive. Then Jett moved closer and their legs touched. Tristan started shaking, and for a terrifying second, she thought she might actually fall. She locked her knees and gritted her teeth. She needed some control, and she needed it fast. This thing with Jett, whatever the hell it was, had her so completely turned around she didn't recognize herself.

"I'm sorry about earlier," Jett murmured.

Tristan shook her head. "There's nothing to be sorry about. You're right. I had a great time." She lifted her shoulders and forced a casual tone. "You definitely know what you're doing."

Jett ran her fingers up and down the inside of Tristan's arm, stroking the bare skin below her scrub shirt. "No, I don't. Not where you're concerned."

"I gotta go," Tristan said, aware of Quinn waiting for her nearby. Jett was driving her crazy, not just from touching her, that was bad enough. The slightest caress got her so hot she couldn't think. She was a little sore from all the sex, but she still wanted it. Wanted Jett. And that's what was really driving her nuts. One minute Jett was there, touching her, taking her, pushing her to places she'd never been, and in the next minute she was gone, sequestered behind a wall of perfect indifference, leaving Tristan feeling gutted. Laid open and bleeding.

And all she could think was that she wanted more. "Fuck, I really gotta go."

"Yeah. Go. I'll catch you later."

Tristan didn't go. Instead she turned so her back was to Quinn and only Jett could see her face. "I want to kiss you right now. I want you to do to me what you did last night. How fucking crazy is that?"

"Pretty fucking crazy," Jett agreed. She took a breath. "And about last night. When things settle down, we should do it again."

"We should. I'll call you."

"Yeah, do that," Jett called after her. She watched the team disappear, then headed toward the white van with the flag indicating it was the command post. She needed to let someone know she was available to transport. She rubbed her fingertips. They were warm, and she thought of Tristan's skin. She thought of how easily Tristan had recognized what she needed, and how effortlessly she'd given it.

I know what you need, Gail had said. But maybe she'd been wrong.

❖

Quinn squatted next to a fire rescue van, twisted off the top of a plastic bottle of water she'd snagged from a cooler filled with them, and punched in Honor's cell phone number on hers. After three rings the call was picked up.

"Hello?" Honor said, sounding harried.

"Hi, love, it's me," Quinn said.

"Baby," Honor replied softly. "How are you? How are things out there?"

"Pretty grim," Quinn said. "They've been pulling cars out of the river for the last six hours, and it still looks like there's more down there or under the rubble."

"If we get many more, we're going to have to close," Honor said. "We've converted half the fifth floor to an intermediate care unit, and all the intensive care units are full. We're boarding patients in the ER. God only knows how much blood we have left."

Quinn could hear the strain in her voice. "You need to go home, Honor. It's been almost eight hours. It's too soon for this."

"I haven't been walking around, I swear."

Quinn said nothing.

"I promise I won't stay any longer than two more hours. Then I'm gone."

"Okay."

"What about you? What's it like out there?"

"Hot." Quinn guzzled the rest of the water. She didn't need to tell Honor about the casualties. Honor was getting them flown in to her. "A lot of cars are burning. If it wasn't August, it would feel like it anyhow. The smoke makes it tough to see. I just talked to the OR. Every room is running. Things are slowing down a little out here. If there are people in those cars, well—there probably aren't many more survivors, and it's going to take a long time to get them out. Most of the acute surgical patients have been transported. I'm heading back to the OR now."

"Are you going to be able to get any sleep before you start operating?"

"I'll try."

"Take care of yourself, baby. I love you."

"I love you too. Tell Arly I said hi, and I'll see her tomorrow sometime. Kiss Jack for me too."

"I will. Miss you."

"Me too."

Quinn put her cell phone away and went to find Jett. She wanted to hitch a ride back to the hospital.

❖

Tristan wrapped a thin strip of tape around the endotracheal tube she'd just placed and secured it to the cheek of a child who appeared to be no more than four. The Coast Guard had pulled her out of the water, just floating there. Tristan wondered where her family was and tried not to think about how long she might have been in the water, how long she'd gone without oxygen, how long her brain had suffered from hypoxia. If Tristan let the pictures of grief and loss into her head, she'd be useless. So she did her job and passed the child off to the next person to do theirs. Two medics strapped the child carefully to a gurney and trundled away. Still crouched down beside her equipment box, Tristan wiped the sweat off her forehead and was surprised to see streaks of blood on the back of her arm.

"Tris!" Jett dropped to the ground beside her and cradled her face. "You're bleeding."

"Can't be much," Tristan said wearily. "I don't feel anything."

"Let me look." Jett rummaged in the open tackle box of equipment and found a penlight and some gauze. The sun had gone down an hour ago, and despite the emergency halogen lights strung around the perimeter, there were still pockets of darkness that swallowed up victims and rescuers alike. Here on the bank of the river, they were in shadow. "Hold still."

"You give up your wings?" Tristan asked.

"Not likely." Jett gently dabbed at Tristan's forehead with the gauze. "You've got a pretty deep laceration. What did you do?"

Tristan started to shrug, then recalled reaching into a mangled automobile to help extract an elderly woman and cracking her forehead on a twisted portion of the frame that shouldn't have been where it was. "Hit my head."

"No kidding."

"What are you doing here?"

"I caught a five-minute break." Jett turned away, searching in the box again. "Haven't seen you in a couple of hours. Aren't you about ready to head in?"

"Soon. What about you?" Tristan liked that Jett had come looking for her. She liked it very much.

"Soon." Jett put on gloves, smeared antibiotic ointment over the laceration, and taped a square white bandage over it. "I think it needs stitches."

"You any good at that?"

"I think someone in the ER should do it. I think you're beautiful no matter how you look," Jett said, "but it would be nice not to have too much of a scar."

"Beautiful, huh?"

Jett rubbed a smudge of soot away from the corner of Tristan's mouth. "Yeah. Very beautiful."

Tristan closed her eyes, giving herself a second to absorb the contact. Jett's touch helped mute the horrors of the last few hours. Then she sighed and looked around. "I feel like I'm in a war zone. Is this what it was like?"

"The destruction. The senseless death. Yeah." Jett smiled bleakly. "But at least no one is trying to kill us."

"I don't think I would have lasted very long."

"Sure you would have. You get used to it. And everyone else is going through it too."

"That must have helped. Not being alone."

Jett busied herself replacing equipment and didn't answer.

"The soldier who visited today," Tristan said. "Was she with you over there?"

"You saw her?" Jett thought Gail had left before Tristan showed up on the roof. She wondered what Tristan had seen. She wondered how much Tristan guessed.

"Talked to her for a few minutes. Who is she?"

"Just someone I knew." Jett stood. "I've got to get back. I'll be making another run soon."

Tristan rose also, surprised when she felt dizzy. She ignored the spinning sensation. She didn't want to ask, but she had to know. "Was she someone special?"

"Special?" Jett laughed, a short, bitter laugh. "Well, I guess you could say she was a special friend."

"Oh. I see." So they'd been lovers, Tristan thought. And now she'd come for a visit, or something more. Tristan had no reason to be jealous. In fact, what she felt wasn't jealousy. It was something far, far more painful.

"I didn't know she was coming," Jett said, although Tristan hadn't asked.

"And if you had, you probably wouldn't have spent last night with me," Tristan said lightly. "You would've had better places to be."

Jett went completely still. "You're wrong, Tristan. You couldn't be more wrong."

"I'm sorry." Tristan knew she'd pushed too far one time too many, but she was exhausted and soul-weary and God damn it, she was jealous. She didn't want to be just a body in Jett's bed. Replaceable. Forgettable. "Jett—"

"I've got a run to make."

And then Jett was gone. Tristan wanted to go after her, to explain, but she didn't move. What could she say? She didn't have any claim on

Jett, even though she was coming to realize she wanted one. More, she wanted Jett to put a claim on her. It didn't make any sense, but then, looking around her, the entire world had gone insane. Why should she be any different?

CHAPTER TWENTY-THREE

E verybody secure?" Jett called, her hand on the throttle.
Linda and Quinn had just loaded a middle-aged man with a broken leg, facial lacerations, and a concussion. He was stable, but the closed head injury combined with serious extremity fractures put him at risk for unseen internal injuries as well. Quinn wanted to get him to the ER faster than he would make it if he was added to the queue waiting for ambulance transport.

"We're set," Linda said.

"Where's Tristan?" Jett didn't like returning to base without all of her crew, especially without this particular crewmember. The disaster scene was even more treacherous now that night had fallen. Shifting blocks of concrete, uncertain tides, and the ever-present fires threatened more than the victims. The rescue crews were exhausted, their reflexes dulled, their judgment slowed. Tristan had been on the ground now for ten hours.

"Tris is staying to check out one of the engine crew," Quinn said, reaching behind her for her shoulder strap. "Smoke inhalation, and the guy is having a fair amount of respiratory distress. She's worried he may need to be intubated out here."

"I should stay and help. Our patient's stable." Linda started to climb back out, but Quinn grabbed her arm.

"There are a couple of medics and a respiratory tech with her. She's got enough help, and I told her to get her butt back to the hospital as soon as this is squared away. She'll catch the next chopper back to PMC."

"Okay," Linda said, settling back down.

Jett scanned the area outside one more time, hoping to see Tristan emerge from the smoke and the dark, but she didn't. After another minute, she took her aircraft up and left the chaos and Tristan behind.

❖

"We have to move these boarders," Honor said to Yale, her new head nurse and Linda's replacement. "We don't have any treatment rooms open for the incoming patients."

"There's nowhere to put them upstairs," the burly redhead answered, frustration putting an edge in his voice. "All the beds are full."

"I don't care if they have to sleep two to a bed on the medical floors. If a patient doesn't need immediate surgery or intensive care monitoring, they go to medicine. And I mean right now."

Yale straightened. "Yes, ma'am. I'm on it."

"Thank you." Honor pressed both hands to the base of her spine and pushed in, trying to ease the stiffness in her sore muscles.

"Very impressive," Quinn said, sidling around the doorway into Honor's small, windowless box of an office. She closed the door behind her. "My residents never move that fast for me."

"God, I love ex-military nurses. I never have to ask them twice. And they never give me any excuses." Honor draped her arms around Quinn's neck and rested her cheek against her shoulder. "You are the best-looking thing I've seen in many an hour."

Quinn stroked Honor's hair and kissed her forehead. "I'm very glad to see you too, even though you're not supposed to be here." She led Honor to the tiny, nearly threadbare couch pushed against one wall, sat down, and eased Honor down beside her. She held her, smoothing her hand up and down Honor's arm. "How are you doing?"

Honor sighed and burrowed deeper into Quinn's arms. "I feel like I used to during my residency. After a while you get so tired you forget that you're tired. Or hungry. Or that there's even a world outside these walls."

"You need to go home," Quinn murmured. She didn't want to let her go. She wanted to hold her, soothe her. She wanted to carry her all the way home and put her to bed. She wanted to grab the kids and gather their family around them. She wanted the joy and comfort and sanity Honor had brought to her life. "If you wear yourself out, it's only going to take you longer to get back to work full time."

"Oh, Quinn Maguire, you are so slick." Honor rolled her head back and smiled wearily at Quinn. "What were you going to try next if bringing work up didn't motivate me sufficiently? The children need me at home?"

Quinn grinned. "Not a bad idea, but I was thinking I'd try sex next."

"Oh really? If I could move, I might actually be interested." Honor ran her fingers through Quinn's hair. "What was the offer?"

"That you should get some rest so that when I got home, all worked up and not able to sleep, you could work your magic."

Honor laughed. "Oh, that's really bad."

"How about, I'm worried about you."

"I know, honey," Honor murmured. "I'm sorry. I'm going, I really am. Tommy Henderson is on his way. I think he can handle things down here, especially with Yale helping."

"Thanks."

"What about you? Are you holding up okay?"

"I'm all right. I'm used to twenty-four-hour shifts."

"Yes, but you were just on call—" Honor stopped at the sharp rap on the door and moved away from Quinn. "Yes?"

Yale burst through the door. "Sorry. I just heard a report over the radio. A couple of choppers collided and went down. They think one of them's ours."

"Oh no." Honor started to rise. "Linda."

"She's all right," Quinn said quickly, keeping Honor seated. "She came back with me. You stay here. I'll find out what's going on." She pressed Honor back onto the couch and lifted her legs until she was lying down. "I mean it." She looked over her shoulder. "Yale? If you see her walking around, I want you to escort her back to this sofa."

"Yes, ma'am. Understood."

Honor held Quinn's hand tightly. "Let me know as soon as you hear anything."

"I will." Quinn didn't want to tell her that Tristan was almost certainly on that second Healthstar helicopter.

❖

Head back, eyes closed, Jett stood under the ice-cold spray as the sharp needles drove the fatigue and sadness away. Per regulations, if she slept for four hours she could fly again, and the way things were looking, she would need to. She and the other pilots had staggered their shifts so that only one of them would be down at a time. She might not sleep, but at least she could lie down and de-stress for an hour or two. Then she'd be ready to go again.

She fumbled for the soap, found it, and rubbed it automatically over her body, her mind drifting back to the night before. She'd been making love to Tristan at just about this time last night. Just thinking about it caused her clitoris to rise. She'd come undone with women before, losing herself in sensation, driving them and herself to the limits of endurance until they both collapsed. Those times, she'd been nearly mindless, blind and deaf, propelled by some urgent primitive need to connect, to declare her presence in a world that ripped life away with heedless indifference. When she lost herself in a woman, she never felt more alive. All of that had been true for her the night before, but for the first time she could ever remember, she was completely present. She heard every one of Tristan's soft moans, every plea and exhortation, every cry of pleasure and release. And because it was Tristan, *Tristan*, she had found something beyond passion. She'd found she wasn't alone.

"Tris," Jett murmured, replacing the soap and turning the water to hot. She brushed her fingers over her clitoris and her hips jerked beneath her hand. She leaned her shoulders against the shower wall, closed her eyes, and imagined Tristan kneeling between her legs. She—

"Jett!" Linda banged on the bathroom door. "Jett!"

Jett shut off the water, jumped out of the shower, and scanned for her weapon. It took her another second to realize she wasn't under attack. She grabbed a towel, slung it around herself, and pulled open the door. Linda stood on the other side, wild-eyed and breathing as if she'd just finished a marathon.

"What?" Jett demanded.

"Two helicopters..." Linda gripped the doorjamb as if to steady herself. "Two helicopters collided—"

Jett grabbed Linda's arm. "Ours?"

"We're not sure. Everything's so garbled. It's crazy. God, Jett..."

"I'll be right there. See if you can raise our aircraft."

Linda nodded wordlessly and hurried away.

Jett tossed the towel aside and pulled on a shirt and pants over her still-wet skin. She kicked into her boots without bothering to put on socks. She was through her door and into the lounge in under twenty seconds. Linda, Juan, Mike, and two flight nurses were crowded around the radio. All Jett could hear were voices talking over one another, shouting names and call numbers of aircraft.

"Who do we have out?" Jett called loudly.

"Cindy and Jeremy," Mike said, referring to two of the other pilots.

"Have we heard from either of them?"

"No, but there's so much chatter, it's hard for anyone to get through. And ground control has diverted a lot of aircraft to other hospitals because so many are full. We don't know who's going where."

Jett gripped the back of one of the metal chairs that ringed the round Formica-topped table in the middle of the room. She'd been in this limbo a dozen times before. Wondering if her fellow pilots, her friends, were coming home again. If anyone had asked her a month before, she would have said she was prepared to lose anything. She'd been wrong.

Tristan was out there. Jett couldn't even let the possibility that Tristan wasn't coming home into her mind. When her thoughts veered in that direction, a loud noise filled her head, like a klaxon roaring, and her stomach threatened to empty what little she'd eaten in the last day. She held on to the chair as hard as she could because she knew her hands were shaking, and she didn't want anyone else to see. Tristan couldn't be hurt. Because if she was, Jett simply didn't know what she would do.

"Wait," Linda shouted, pointing at the radio. "There. There. Those are Cindy's call signs, aren't they?"

"Yes," Mike said. "Thank God. She's okay. She's coming in!"

Jett turned and ran for the stairs. She reached the roof just as the helicopter landed and she didn't slow until she'd reached the aircraft. She grabbed the handle on the side door and yanked it back. A medic she didn't recognize blocked her view and she was forced to step back as a stretcher was handed off bearing a dark-haired woman with a cervical collar immobilizing her head and severe burns to her face and both arms. For a second, Jett thought it was Tristan and her knees wobbled.

She caught herself against the side of the aircraft and fought back another urge to vomit. A second medic jumped out, this one a nurse she knew. The rotors slowed and Cindy climbed down from the cockpit. They were still one aircraft short, and Tristan was still missing.

An enormous chasm opened on the horizon of Jett's heart, threatening to swallow her alive. She closed her eyes.

❖

Tristan jumped out after Cindy. Once she'd secured the patient's airway, she'd squeezed into the space next to the pilot to give the medics in the back of the aircraft room to work. Cindy was already at the stairs on the far side of the roof. They'd all seen the fireball erupt in the sky not far from them. But none of them knew who it was. All the way back, all Tristan could think of was Jett. Jett had said she had another run to make. She should be back already, right? Safe. The fifteen-minute flight had been the longest of Tristan's life. She took two quick steps forward, then abruptly stopped and turned back.

"Babe? Babe!" Tristan grabbed Jett by the shoulders and wrapped her tightly in her arms. "Jesus Christ. I was so scared. You're all right, right? Jett?" She held Jett at arm's length. Jett looked shell-shocked, her eyes completely blank. "You *are* all right, aren't you?"

Jett shuddered and her eyes snapped into focus. She grasped Tristan's head and kissed her fiercely. Then she pushed away.

"Yeah," Jett croaked, her voice sounding rusty and unused. "I'm okay."

Tristan stared as Jett abruptly turned and strode off, her gait slightly unsteady. What the hell?

"Jett," Tristan shouted, running after her.

Jett held up a hand, not looking back. "I need some space. You should probably get some sleep." She pushed through the stairwell doors and disappeared in a clatter of boots on stone.

Tristan hesitated for a second, then shouldered through the door. "Fuck this."

CHAPTER TWENTY-FOUR

Tristan caught up to Jett just as she was opening her on-call room door. Tristan didn't bother to say anything since she didn't think she'd be getting an invite. She just pushed inside behind Jett, slammed the door behind her, and locked it.

Jett spun around in the middle of the small, narrow room. "What are you doing?"

"Never mind what I'm doing. What are you doing?" Tristan edged between Jett and the dresser to lock the second door that she presumed led to the lounge. "What the hell was that all about up on the roof?"

"What?" Jett shoved her hands into the front pockets of her plain black pants and leaned against the wall next to her bed, as far away from Tristan as possible, which was only a few feet. Even though she didn't want to have this conversation, not here, and not like this, she was so glad to see Tristan, she almost didn't care. When she'd finally registered up on the flight deck that Tristan was there in front of her, unhurt, that Tris had come back, she'd just reacted. She'd kissed Tristan because she was so relieved and because she needed the physical contact to be absolutely certain Tris was safe. Then the enormity of just how much she had needed Tristan to come back had hit her with the force of a machine gun salvo. The memory of that crippling need had sent her running, and she still needed time to regain her balance. "Nothing. Forget it."

"Fuck forget it." Tristan stalked over to Jett and gripped her shoulders. "First I find you totally out of it, then you kiss me like you want to swallow me whole, then you tell me you need space and walk away. What the hell, Jett."

Jett shrugged as much as she could with Tristan pinning her to the wall. Tristan was leaning against her, and with Tristan this close, with Tristan's hands on her, Jett couldn't keep from getting excited. She didn't need that now. She feigned nonchalance. "Reflex. Sorry."

"Bullshit," Tristan snapped. "You think I care that you kissed me? You think I didn't want that?" She kissed Jett roughly, driving her tongue into her mouth, bruising her own lips against Jett's teeth. "What were you thinking about? What were you *doing* up there?"

Jett paled. "Nothing."

"You're lying." Tristan's eyes softened. "Don't do that, babe."

"We heard there was a helicopter crash," Jett said quietly. "I wanted to check on the status of our choppers."

"Is everyone okay?" Tristan was determined to get all the answers she wanted, but she was worried about the others too.

"I don't know. I don't know if Jeremy has checked in yet."

"We'll find out in a minute. You didn't answer me. Why did you kiss me?"

"Look," Jett said in a reasonable tone. "Everybody's strung out. Tense. I was worried, I was glad to see you. So I kissed you, okay? Let's not make it more than it is."

"Why not?" Tristan slid her hands from Jett's shoulders down her chest until she cupped Jett's breasts through the thin black T-shirt. She felt Jett's nipples harden beneath her fingers. She watched Jett's eyes as she played with the small tight tips, rolling and squeezing and flicking. Jett's eyes lost focus, but they weren't the blank void she'd seen on the landing pad, they were soft and liquid with desire. "Oh yeah. You like that, don't you."

"You already knew that." Jett gasped and clutched Tristan's hips, her head falling back against the wall.

"Why were you worried?" Tristan murmured, her mouth against Jett's ear. She spread her fingers over Jett's breasts, nearly covering them with her hands, and squeezed. Jett's hips bucked and Tristan's vision narrowed until all she could see was Jett's face. "Why?"

"The choppers...the crash." Jett groaned when Tristan caught her earlobe in her teeth. "I was afraid. Afraid you might be hurt."

"You don't have to be afraid. I'm right here." Tristan yanked Jett's T-shirt from her pants and drove both hands underneath, skimming hot skin and finding soft breasts. She fondled her breasts, teased her nipples, and kissed her way down Jett's neck. Then she replaced her fingers with her mouth, and bit down on a hard nipple.

Jett arched her back, her head rolling convulsively from side to side. "Tristan."

"It's all right, babe." Tristan rested her cheek against Jett's breast and reached down to open her pants. "I know what you need."

Jett jerked as if she'd been shot and grabbed Tristan's wrist, twisting it into a defensive wrist lock. "No."

Tristan cried out more in surprise than pain, and Jett immediately loosened her grip.

"I'm sorry," Jett gasped. "I'm sorry. I didn't mean to do that. But you have to stop. We have to stop."

"For now."

Jett shook her head. "No. We have to stop this thing between us."

Tristan braced her arms on either side of Jett's body. She knew Jett wanted her. It was written in her eyes, on her face, in the way her body responded. She loved the way Jett responded to her. She loved the way Jett made her feel, what Jett unleashed in her. But it wasn't enough. She wanted more than Jett's desire, she wanted her heart, and her wanting made her desperate and foolishly brave. "Why?" She kissed Jett. "Why do we have to stop?"

Jett looked at Tristan and saw Gail. She blinked and forced the image away, but she couldn't force away the pain.

"Oh my God, what are you doing," Gail moaned, shoving Jett back with both hands against her shoulders.

Jett was so lost in the sweet taste of Gail's skin and the softness of her body, she couldn't decipher the words. Had Gail said no? Jesus, she must have said no, but Jett hadn't heard. She hadn't stopped. Jett stared in confusion, trying to make sense of what Gail was saying. She couldn't think, she could barely breathe. Gail's blouse was open. A button was missing and her breast was outside her bra, as if a hand had lifted it free. Had she done that? Gail's nipple was dark purple in the muted light, rigid and erect, and Jett had a faint memory of kneading it against her palm. Or had that been another woman? Another night?

"Gail, I...I..." Jett shook her head but she still couldn't think. Gail had kissed her, hadn't she? Or had she kissed Gail? *I know what you need.* Gail's hands on her back, on her ass. *I know what you need.* Jett's clitoris throbbed. Gail had gripped her crotch while they were kissing, hadn't she? Or had she imagined that too? Was that just a memory from all the nights she'd made herself come thinking about Gail caressing her? *I know what you need.* Jett lifted her hand to touch Gail's cheek.

"Stop it." Gail pulled her head away. "I don't want you to touch me. I'm not a lesbian."

"You kissed me," Jett said numbly. Hadn't she?

"No, Chief McNally. I did not." Gail skirted out from between Jett and the shower wall, rearranging her clothing with trembling hands. "You're mistaken. I think it best if we just forget this."

Jett grabbed her before she could walk away. "I can't forget this. Gail, I love you."

"That's impossible."

"Why? We can be careful."

"You don't understand. I'm *not* a lesbian." Gail wrenched her arm free.

Jett followed her. "Is it something I did? I scared you, didn't I? I'm sorry." Jett reached for Gail's arm again, then hesitated. "I just needed to touch you so much. I'll be more careful. I'd never hurt you."

Gail spun around. "Listen to me. I don't want you to touch me. I don't want you that way at all. If anything like this ever occurs again, I'll be forced to report you."

"I'm sorry," Jett whispered, but Gail was gone.

Nothing that had ever happened to her had been as bad as watching Gail walk out of her life—not her father's beatings, not her brothers' tauntings, not the loneliness and isolation of so many years alone. She'd learned not to care about anything except flying. But she'd let Gail into her heart, and now she'd driven Gail away. When Jett's knees gave way and she fell to the slick wet floor, her eyes were dry. Only her soul cried.

"It's her, isn't it?" Tristan demanded harshly. "It's because she's back."

"No," Jett said quickly, because that wasn't the reason. Gail's unexpected appearance had brought all the uncertainty and pain Jett had so carefully buried right to the surface, like an abscess being lanced. She'd lost Gail because she'd wanted her too much, and she was terrified of wanting Tristan.

"You're lying again. God *damn* it, don't lie to me." Tristan clenched her fists until the tendons stood out on her hands and her joints ached. She wanted to punch a hole in the wall. She'd never punched anything, and always thought it was a stupid reaction, but right now, she wanted to destroy something. She wanted to make some other part of her body hurt besides her heart. "You still love her. I get it."

"I don't…it's not…"

"Never mind." Tristan took a step back and looked wildly around the room—at the perfectly square stack of clothing on the top shelf of the open closet, at the precisely ordered pile of books on the floor by the night table, at the narrow bed where Jett slept. She knew she'd be imagining herself in that bed, with Jett beneath her, with Jett between her legs, with Jett inside her, for months. Jesus Christ. She was losing her mind. She knew about wanting someone so badly it ate you up inside. She knew *now*, when it was the wrong woman, and too fucking late to do anything about it. "You still want to fuck her, and it's eating at you, isn't it?"

"No. Yes. God, I don't know," Jett blurted. "I keep thinking about her. Gail. I keep remembering."

"Ah, babe," Tristan whispered. She brushed her fingers through Jett's hair. "She came looking for you. She must want you." She laughed, although inside it felt like tears. "She'd be crazy not to."

"I don't know why she's here." Jett dropped onto the narrow bed and put her head in her hands. While she'd been flying, ferrying the injured back and forth to the hospital, she'd been able to block out thoughts of Gail and why she had come. Now the past had come roaring back, and she was terrified. Terrified of feeling again what she had felt that night. Gail had been kind to her, Gail had been tender. Gail *had* touched her. But when she'd touched Gail back, she'd needed something, wanted something, *done* something to make Gail run from her. And now all she knew was that she wanted Tristan in ways she had never even begun to want Gail. She couldn't do it again. "I don't know anything."

Tristan knelt in front of her and rested one hand lightly on Jett's thigh, the other on the back of her neck. "You have to find out, babe. Cause she's still got hold of your heart."

Tristan kissed the top of Jett's head, straightened, and went to the hall door. She unlocked it, stepped out, and closed the door quietly behind her.

Jett listened for Tristan's footsteps, but she couldn't hear her. She was just gone.

"You're wrong," Jett whispered to the empty room. "She doesn't have my heart."

❖

Tristan took the stairwell down five flights on the run. She barreled through the door onto the OR floor, punched in her code to the surgical locker room, and stripped down. She pulled on clean scrubs, grabbed a mask and a cap, and walked directly into hell. The OR looked like a MASH unit. Stretchers littered the halls, the floor was covered with discarded tubing, plastic wrappers from IV bags, and half-used rolls of tape. She started down one side of the U-shaped complex, checking rooms until she found one of the senior anesthesia staff.

"I can relieve someone," Tristan said.

"Uh, I think Christopher in room eight...no, nine...is probably due for a dinner break. Six hours ago. You okay? Where did you come from?"

"I went with the first responders. I'm fine."

"Go ahead, then. Tell Christopher to grab a couple hours' sleep after he eats."

"Sure." Tristan headed off. She needed to take her mind off Jett. She needed not to think about the brunette. Gail. A beautiful woman. A beautiful woman who had come halfway around the world for Jett. She stopped suddenly, the pain nearly blinding her.

"It'll pass," she whispered to herself. She'd let her guard down, let things go too far. She'd made a mistake. She'd get over it. She'd work, and while she was working she wouldn't be able to think of anything else. She was too conditioned to give all her attention to the patient to let her mind wander. And when she was done working, she'd make a few phone calls. She'd get over it.

❖

Jett waited until some of the familiar numbness returned, blunting the pain, and then she went into the flight lounge. It didn't matter how much she hurt, she still had crew members somewhere out in the field. And she didn't leave her crew behind.

"Any word from Jeremy?" Jett asked.

"He just radioed," Linda said, her eyes bright with tears. "They're grounded in Atlantic City. Jeremy thinks something's wrong with the hydraulics."

"All accounted for, then," Jett said.

Quinn Maguire came through the door. "All our people okay?"

"Yes," Linda said. "Everyone is fine."

Jett pivoted and started for her room. "Log me back in at oh-two hundred."

"Are you sure?" Linda called after her. "You had a really long shift today."

"I'm fine. I'll be ready." Jett closed her door and stretched out on top of her perfectly made bed, fully clothed, her arms straight down at her sides. She stared at the ceiling, dry-eyed, and waited for sleep.

❖

The lights were out in Honor's office when Quinn returned. She opened the door and stepped carefully inside. The glow from the x-ray light box behind Honor's desk provided faint illumination, and she made her way to the side of the couch and knelt down.

"Honor," she said quietly.

"Mmm?"

Quinn stroked her hair. "Time to go home."

Honor turned on her side and rested her head on her folded arms. She regarded Quinn for a long moment. "I love you, do you know that?"

"I do." Quinn kissed her. "I love you."

"I know. You gave me back my life, Quinn. All of my life."

Quinn kissed her again. "You gave me a life."

"I guess I should go home and take care of the rest of our life, huh?" Honor sat up.

"I'll be there as soon as I can to give you a hand with that," Quinn said.

"We'll be waiting." Honor trailed her fingers down Quinn's cheek. "What a night."

CHAPTER TWENTY-FIVE

Jett sat on the wide stone wall ringing the rooftop, her back to the city, her gaze on the empty helipad, listening for the sound of the chopper returning as if waiting for a lover. A faint breeze played through the hair at the back of her neck, drying the sweat that misted her skin. She'd flown most of the last twenty-six hours, slept when she had to, and now she was done until the following night. Three hours to sundown, another eight until sunrise, another fourteen until her next shift. Twenty-five hours to fill. She felt as empty inside as the hours that stretched before her.

She had not seen or heard from Tristan since they'd parted in the middle of the night. She hadn't expected to. Tristan thought she wanted Gail. Maybe Tristan was right. She hadn't stopped thinking about Gail, dreaming about her, in all the time since she'd left the service. Not until she'd met Tristan. Smiling, Jett fingered the seam on the inside leg of her jeans, running her fingertips slowly along the ridge. Tristan had shouldered her way into her life, refusing to be ignored. Tristan…

Movement on the far side of the roof caught her attention and she straightened, squinting in the glare off the concrete, hoping to see the familiar figure come jogging toward her. Disappointment, sharp and raw, cut through her when she recognized Linda.

"I thought you might be up here," Linda said, shading her eyes with one hand against the slanting rays of the sun.

"I thought you left a while ago."

"I've been checking on friends. I stopped by the ER and the OR. Things are slowing down a lot and the relief crews are cleaning up the rest."

Jett didn't ask if she'd seen Tristan. Tristan wasn't coming back. Why would she? She thought—

"So listen," Linda said, resting her hand on Jett's knee. "No one really wants to go home. I guess after what happened...after everything...people just want to stay together for a while."

"I know."

Linda studied her. "I guess you do. So, my long-suffering partner, God bless her, is throwing together some food and a couple of people are picking up beer. Everybody's heading over to my place."

"You came up here to tell me that?"

Linda nodded. "Yes. I did."

Jett studied her hands, which she'd clasped between her legs. Linda's hand still rested on her knee. Linda touched her a lot, and Jett liked her. But Linda's touch wasn't like Gail's, and nothing like Tristan's. Nothing was like Tristan's hands on her. "Thank you."

"Are you okay?"

"No," Jett said. "Not really."

"Is there something I can do?"

Jett shook her head. "Thanks, but I think I have to figure this out for myself."

"Is it about Tristan?"

Jett tensed. "Why?"

"People can be jerks sometimes when they're jealous. Don't hold it against her."

"I don't know what you mean."

Linda colored. "Oh, I thought...she was asking about your visitor earlier. She seemed pretty bent out of shape about it."

"Gail?"

"Is that her name? The soldier who was here?"

"Yes."

"I think Tristan thought she was your girlfriend. I'm just assuming..."

"She isn't."

"Ex?"

Jett thought about that. What was Gail to her? They'd been friends, she'd thought. She'd thought they'd been more than that—she'd thought what they'd had was special. She laughed, thinking of Tristan and her special friends.

"No," Jett said. "Just a friend."

"So are you going to come?"

Jett was going to say no, and then she thought about the twenty-five hours she needed to fill. There would be others at Linda's like herself, others who had had a bad night, who didn't want to go home with the memories—unable to explain to those who loved them what they'd seen and what they wanted to forget. She wouldn't have to talk to anyone. She could sit, drink, let the time go by. She could try not to think about Tristan, but that would be harder. But wherever she was, she was going to think about Tristan, and with luck, she could find some kind of diversion at Linda's. "I might be late. I need to make a stop first."

"I have a feeling we'll be going a long time tonight. We've got a couple of spare rooms and a lot of floor space, and we like overnight visitors. Come around when you're ready."

"Thanks."

Linda patted Jett's thigh. "I really hope you make it. See you later."

"Right," Jett said softly.

Linda disappeared and Jett was alone again. She thought about Tristan being jealous, and then of Tristan kneeling beside her in her on-call room, telling her to talk to Gail, telling her that Gail still held a piece of her heart. Maybe Tristan was right. Maybe that's why Gail haunted her dreams and her waking moments. Jett didn't know what she felt. She hadn't really been able to think about Gail until now. About what had happened. About what she'd done to make Gail leave.

Jett slid down off the wall and sat on the rooftop, her legs outstretched. Tristan was gone, and she had let her go because of Gail. She'd left the service because of Gail, and now she was running away from Tristan. Running away because of Gail and because of all the things she wanted and shouldn't. She closed her eyes and made herself think about Gail because she couldn't think about Tristan being gone. She'd thought she'd loved Gail. She'd never had a woman in her life like Gail before, a woman who was constantly there for her—waiting for her to come back from a mission, taking care of her when she was tired and hurt, soothing her with her words and her touches. Her touches. Looking back, Jett replayed dozens of moments when Gail had touched her—casual caresses on her shoulders and arms, fingers running through her hair, breasts pressing against her back while standing in line for chow. Gail was always touching her. At the time, Jett had been so beaten down by the constant stress, the unrelenting uncertainty, the ever-present threat of death, she hadn't been able to see what was happening. She thought *she* had been the one who'd wanted too much, who'd asked for too much. But Gail had touched her.

Jett pushed herself up and strode across the tarmac to the stairwell.

Gail had kissed her. Gail had *wanted* her. Now she needed to see Gail.

❖

Quinn knelt down next to Honor's lounge chair. "I don't think you should be doing that out in public. You're likely to get a few people hot and bothered."

"Who?" Honor laughed incredulously.

"Me, for starters."

Honor looked down at her chest to make sure something hadn't come undone that she hadn't intended to be undone. All she saw was Jack's fair hair and a small triangle of pale flesh. "Sweetheart, there's nothing to see. You're just imagining things."

"That works pretty well for me too. The real thing's better, though."

"Will you be quiet," Honor chided, nodding toward Jack. "He'll hear you. If he takes after you, *you* will regret it when he's thirteen."

Quinn laughed and stroked Honor's hair. "Baby, Arly takes after me. This one's all yours."

Honor grasped Quinn's hand. "It's true, you know. She wants to be just like you." She rubbed Quinn's fingers against her cheek. "And I can't think of anyone better."

"Well, from everything I hear, Terry was the real jock. So I think the credit has to be divided on that one."

"Don't make me cry."

"I'm sorry," Quinn whispered.

Honor shook her head. "No, sweetheart. Happy tears. These damn hormones are still not back to normal."

"You sure?"

"Never more." Jack started squirming and Honor handed him to Quinn. "Take him for a second while I get myself together. And no looking."

"Tease," Quinn muttered, settling Jack on her shoulder and patting his back.

"Patience, Maguire," Honor said. "Remember when we get home how you're going to be all restless and not able to sleep and I'm going to—"

"Let's go now."

Honor laughed and held out her arms for Jack. "Arly's inside watching a movie with the other kids. When it's over, we'll go, okay?"

"All right. Can I get you anything?"

"No, but…" Honor pointed surreptitiously to a small group of people sitting on Linda's back porch steps. "Maybe you should talk to Tristan. I'm not sure she's doing real well."

Quinn frowned and looked where Honor was pointing. Tristan leaned against the porch post. She was a little disheveled—her shirttail was hanging out of her jeans, which wasn't like her—but she seemed okay otherwise. "What do you mean?"

"I noticed she's drinking a lot, and that's not usually her style. And she just looks…I don't know, lost."

"I'll check on her on my way inside to collect our girl."

"Don't be long."

"Oh, don't worry. I won't be."

Tristan carefully maneuvered her way through the throng of people congregated on the stairs and Linda's porch. Inside the kitchen she sidled around more nurses and techs and doctors and other hospital personnel, everyone talking about what had happened. She found the scotch and poured another two inches into a small red plastic cup. The first half went down with a bit of a bite, the second was smooth and warm. She lifted the bottle but stopped in mid-pour when she felt a hand on her shoulder. Her heart leapt, and she spun around. Then she kept her smile in place through sheer force of will. Jett wasn't here and she wasn't coming. Fuck, no point thinking about where she was.

"Hey Quinn," Tristan said heartily. "Rough one, huh?"

"Yeah, but we had some good saves too. That fireman you tubed is going to make it. That was good work."

"Well, sometimes you get lucky."

"That wasn't luck." Quinn put her arm around Tristan's shoulder and said quietly, "You doing okay?"

"Peachy."

"You look like shit. Why don't you go home and go to bed."

"I will, as soon as I find some company."

"We're all a little shaky—"

"Nope. Not me. I'm solid."

"Uh-huh." Quinn stared intently. "Is it work or something else? You don't usually drink yourself under the table, and you're about there."

"I'm okay." Tristan swayed and gripped the counter behind her. "I won't drink any more. Word. Just tired."

"Let me walk you home."

Tristan shook her head. "You've got the family here. Not going far. I'll make it."

"I don't think—" Quinn stopped as a truly gorgeous redhead came sailing up and about jumped on Tristan.

"Tristan, baby, I just got your message!" Darla slid up next to Tristan and smiled at Quinn. She looped her arm around Tristan's waist and kissed her on the side of the mouth. "I would have been here sooner, but I was finishing an audit and didn't check my voicemail until just a few minutes ago."

"There you go." Tristan grinned at Quinn. "I'll be fine now."

"Make sure she gets home all right, will you?" Quinn said to Darla.

"Don't worry, I'll take care of her." Darla rubbed Tristan's stomach and nuzzled her neck. "Come on, baby. Let's find someplace to sit down for a while."

"Sure, okay. Night, Quinn." Tristan dropped her arm over Darla's shoulders. She definitely needed to sit down for a few minutes and clear her head. She was having trouble getting her thoughts in order, and something about what was happening didn't feel quite right. If she could just think for a minute, she knew she'd figure it out.

"Take care of yourself, Tristan," Quinn said.

"Always do."

❖

Jett walked past Linda's house three times before pushing through the gate and starting down the path to the back. She knew the impromptu party was still going on because she could hear it. She didn't see Tristan's car, and she looked for it. Tris probably wasn't here. But her apartment had been dark when Jett had driven past. Maybe Tristan was already home and asleep. Even as she thought it, Jett doubted that was true. She knew what Tristan would be looking for right now, what she needed to chase the nightmares away.

The backyard was dark and it took her a few minutes to make her way around, checking out the people standing in groups or sitting at a picnic table and on the porch. She finally saw Linda curled up on an old-fashioned porch swing next to a woman in shorts and a T-shirt.

"Hi," Jett said.

"Jett, you made it," Linda exclaimed. "This is my partner, Robin. Robin, honey, this is Chief McNally."

Jett extended her hand to the other woman on the swing. "Just Jett is fine."

"Good to meet you, finally."

"Same here." Jett peered through the open door into the kitchen. She recognized some faces, but not the one she was looking for. "Have you seen Tristan?"

"She was here earlier," Linda said. "I don't think I've seen her for a while, though. There are quite a few people still inside."

"Okay. Well." Jett rocked on her heels.

"Go check and see," Linda said gently.

"Right." Jett nodded to Robin, smiled at Linda, and ducked into the kitchen.

Jett found them in a room on the first floor that might be a den, but she wasn't taking inventory of the contents. The only light came in through the open door from the hallway, but she didn't need much light to tell what was happening on the couch. Tristan was mostly upright, sprawled with her arms outstretched on the back of the sofa and her legs splayed. Darla lay half on top of her as they kissed. Darla's hand rested in Tristan's crotch, her fingers circling lazily. Neither of them knew or apparently cared if they had company.

Jett felt the same burst of adrenaline and anger and fear she experienced when someone on the ground opened fire on her aircraft. She had learned through bitter experience that the only way to survive the firefight was to fly through it. When Darla's hand crept up Tristan's fly and opened the top button, Jett moved. She walked to within a foot of the couch and cleared her throat.

"Sorry to interrupt," Jett said, "but I need to talk to Tristan."

Darla shifted to look up at Jett, her fingers still toying with Tristan's fly. "We met before, didn't we?"

"Briefly." Jett kept her attention on Tristan, whose eyelids were heavy and her gaze unfocused. Jett waited until she was sure Tristan saw her. "I fucked up. I'm sorry."

"No harm," Tristan said, her words slightly slurred.

"Yeah, there is." Jett squatted down next to the sofa opposite Darla and spoke directly to Tristan. "You need to go home."

Tristan looked around and grinned lopsidedly. "Aren't I?"

"No." Jett glanced at Darla. "I'm taking her home."

"She seems to be pretty comfortable right here," Darla said, rubbing Tristan's thigh.

"She's not. She's hurting. My fault—or a lot of it is."

"I take it you're friends." Darla eased away from Tristan just a little.

"Special friends," Tristan mumbled. Then she laughed.

"No, we're a lot more than that. Excuse me." Jett leaned over, slid both hands under Tristan's arms, and heaved her up. She held her for a few seconds tight against her body until she was certain Tristan had her legs under her. Tristan rested her head on Jett's shoulder and Jett hooked an arm around her waist. Then she said to Darla, "She's special to me, but not the way she thinks."

"I can see that." Darla stood and straightened her skirt. "She shouldn't be alone tonight."

"She isn't going to be," Jett said.

CHAPTER TWENTY-SIX

"Okay," Tristan said, "I'm okay now. Head's nice and clear. I'll just head on home." Tristan patted her pockets. "Keys? Did you see my keys?" She spun in a slow circle on the sidewalk. "Have you seen my car?"

Jett grabbed her when she started to sway and leaned her against the front end of her Jeep. "Stay right there. Don't move."

Tristan frowned. "The last time you said that to me, you just about fucked my brains out. That was nice."

"I remember." Jett opened the passenger side door, collected Tristan, and, with a hand on the top of her head, guided her inside. Then she leaned in and hooked her seat belt. "Don't move."

"Are you going to do it again?" Tristan yelled as Jett closed the door.

Jett slid in behind the wheel, started the engine, and pulled out into the deserted street. Linda lived in a residential neighborhood and most of the houses were already dark. She glanced at Tristan, whose head lolled back against the seat. Her eyes were closed. Jett smiled. Even half drunk and dead tired, she was the most beautiful woman Jett had ever seen.

A few minutes later, Jett pulled into an empty spot along the curb a few doors down from her apartment building. She reversed the process, opening Tristan's door, releasing her seat belt, and slipping one arm behind her back. "Let's go, baby."

Tristan turned her head on the seat and opened her eyes. "Did you go see Gail tonight?"

"We'll talk about that later," Jett said gently. "Right now, we're going to bed."

"Together?" Tristan frowned. "Nope. Bad idea."

"All right." Jett reached into the car, lifted Tristan's legs out onto the sidewalk, and pulled Tristan out. "Up. That's good."

Tristan slung her arm around Jett's shoulders. "Sorry about Darla."

Jett shook her head and gripped Tristan's waistband. "Come on, we're right down here."

"You mad?"

"No."

Tristan sighed. "No, I guess not. We're just fuck buddies."

"We'll talk about it later."

"Nothing to be mad about. Nothing," Tristan echoed.

Jett unlocked the outside door, keeping her arm around Tristan's waist, and then the inner door. Three flights of stairs awaited them. She tightened her hold on Tristan, and they made it all the way up with only one missed stair that almost landed them in a heap.

"This isn't my house," Tristan announced.

"No, it's mine." Jett opened the door, reached inside for the light switch, and tugged Tristan into the apartment.

Tristan looked around. "It's very neat. Very clean." She turned and studied Jett intently. "Like you."

Jett laughed. "Come on. The bathroom and the bedroom are down here."

"Did you kiss her?" Tristan asked.

"No." Jett took Tristan's hand and pulled her down the hall. She pushed open the bathroom door. "Everything you need is in the medicine cabinet. All the toothbrushes in there are new."

"Did she kiss you?" Tristan leaned against the doorjamb and spread her legs for balance.

"Yes."

"I knew she would. I would. I'd come back for you too." Tristan skimmed her fingertips over Jett's cheek. "She got there first. God damn it."

Jett gripped Tristan's shoulders firmly and kissed her mouth very, very softly, then the line of her jaw, then below her ear. "No, she didn't. Now shut up and get ready for bed."

"You love her, though."

"Shut up, Tris. We'll talk later." Jett pushed her over to the sink, and Tristan braced herself with both hands on the sides of the vanity, her head lowered. Jett found a toothbrush and put toothpaste on it. "Here."

"She's beautiful."

"So are you. Here."

Tristan took the toothbrush. Jett stood with her arm around Tristan's waist while Tristan brushed and splashed cold water on her face. "Thanks."

"You're welcome," Jett said.

Tristan looked at Jett in the mirror. "I want you so bad."

Jett closed her eyes because she recognized the longing in Tristan's. She'd seen it in her own eyes for years and never knew quite what it meant. Tristan was in no shape to hear anything right now, and if Jett kept looking at her, she was going to have to touch her. She opened her eyes, dropped her arm, and backed away. "The bedroom is right next door, Tris. I'll see you in the morning."

Tristan watched Jett's reflection waver and fade in the glass and she panicked. She spun around. "Jett. I'm sorry." The sudden motion made her dizzy and her stomach took a nasty dive. She closed her eyes and fought to stay upright. "Always push you away. Don't mean to."

"You don't." Jett steadied her. "It's okay."

"Please don't go."

"Come on."

In the bedroom, Jett turned down the covers. "I'll stay for a while. Get undressed so you can sleep."

"I'm okay now," Tristan muttered.

"I'm not." Jett kept her eyes on Tristan's face as she kicked off her shoes, unzipped her pants, and took them off. Then she pulled her T-shirt over her head and let it fall behind her. She slid between the sheets and Tristan hurriedly followed.

"Turn on your side," Jett murmured, and when Tristan complied, she spooned against her from behind and wrapped an arm around her. She nuzzled her face in the bend of Tristan's neck. "Now go to sleep."

"I'm so fucking tired." Tristan found Jett's hand and molded it to her breast.

"I know you are." Jett kissed her neck. "I know."

"No," Tristan protested, sounding on the verge of sleep. "Of all of it. Being lonely. Being alone."

"I know, baby." Jett kept her hands still, even though Tristan's nipple was a hard knot against her palm and Tristan rocked her hips slowly in the curve of her pelvis. Desire pounded through her, warring with a tenderness so profound she wanted to weep. She squeezed her eyes tightly closed and rubbed her face over Tristan's shoulder. She needed her in a place so deep she had no name for it.

"I can hear the way you're breathing," Tristan muttered. "You're hot, aren't you? Hard, too, like you were before."

"Yes," Jett said thickly. "You do that to me. Now shut up, and go to sleep."

"Make yourself come," Tristan whispered. "Do it for me."

Jett shuddered. "Tristan."

"Please, babe. Hold me while you do it." Tristan clasped Jett's hand and squeezed Jett's fingers around her breast. "I need you and I'm so fucking tired."

"It's about more than just being hot, Tris," Jett whispered.

"Yeah. For me too." Tristan released Jett's hand and rolled onto her back. She hooked her arm around Jett's shoulder and pulled her close. "But that's part of it. Isn't it?"

"Yes."

"Do it." Tristan kissed Jett's forehead. "Do it."

Jett slid her thigh over Tristan's and reached down. "Hold me."

"You too."

"I will." Jett turned her face against Tristan's neck and filled her mind and senses with Tristan. She moaned when she came, and Tristan, sighing with pleasure, finally relaxed into sleep.

❖

Five hours later Tristan opened her eyes, sat up in the strange bed, and took stock of her surroundings. The room was spartan. A single dresser with items arranged in orderly rows on top of it. A double closet, the doors closed. A chair beside the closet with a pile of neatly arranged clothes, probably waiting to be put away. Books on the bedside table. Sunlight just beginning to break through the windows. A small electric clock reading 6:32.

She pushed the sheet aside and swung her legs to the floor. She was naked. She ran her hand over her chest and down her abdomen, and then she remembered Jett. She remembered Jett shuddering in her arms, softly whispering her name as she trembled and came, and the memory took her legs out from under her. She ended up back down on the bed, her limbs shaking and her heart doing somersaults. God, she couldn't think of another night, another woman, another moment that had felt so special.

The rest of the evening came back in a flash, and she remembered pretty much all of it. Except how she'd ended up on the sofa with Darla on top of her. For a few minutes there she'd checked her sanity at the door. Christ, and Jett had found her that way. Now Jett was missing. She looked around again and saw her clothes folded on a battered locker at the foot of the bed. She was certain she didn't do that. Jett must have done it after she was asleep. Jett had taken care of her. Not the way Darla would have, but Darla would only have done what she knew Tristan wanted. Only now, Tristan realized that *this* was what she wanted. A stack of folded clothes, the safety of being held, someone to look in on her in the night. No, not just someone. Jett.

Tristan stood again and waited for a few seconds for her stomach to settle. No headache, but she was queasy. She'd been too strung out and tired the night before to eat. No wonder a couple of scotches had practically put her on her ass. On her ass with Darla in her pants. Jesus. She picked up the pile of clothes and frowned. Sorting through them, she realized that they were not only neatly folded and stacked, they were clean. She tucked them under her arm and crept quietly down the hall in the direction of the living room.

Jett sat on a stool at the table in a faded green T-shirt and matching boxer shorts—Army issue, probably—bent over an array of tiny gold workings and several empty watch cases. She wore magnifying glasses built into a visor around her head. She held tiny screwdrivers and tweezers in a delicate grip. Tristan felt a twinge in her belly remembering what those hands were capable of doing to her body.

"You did my laundry," Tristan said.

Jett swiveled in her direction and took off her visor. Her eyes scanned Tristan's naked body. "It was either that or burn them. Mine too."

"Thank you." Tristan walked toward her. "Did you sleep at all?"

"An hour or two." Jett leaned back on her stool until the table stopped her from easing away any further. "How are you feeling?"

"I'm feeling like I don't know what's going on." Tristan dropped the clothes on the floor next to Jett. She held her hands out at her sides, palms facing Jett. "I feel like one of those watches you've got there, with my insides scattered all over this apartment. I need you to put them back."

Jett rose abruptly and pulled Tristan into her arms. She kissed her, one hand on the back of her head, her fingers laced through Tristan's hair. She was trembling. So was Tristan.

"Tris," Jett whispered, her mouth gliding down Tristan's neck. Her skin was so soft, sweet and salty. She rested her forehead on the top of Tristan's shoulder, watching Tristan's nipples tighten as her breasts rose and fell rapidly. "I want you, but—"

Tristan groaned. "Please. You want casual, I'll do casual. Just, please…please don't tell me to go."

"No!" Jett jerked her head up and cradled Tristan's face. "No. No. Not ever. I can't."

"Then what?" Tristan cried. "You love her? Is that it?"

"No," Jett exclaimed again. "Jesus. No. I'm in love with *you*."

"Are you going back to…" Tristan flinched. "What did you just say?"

Jett took in the absolute confusion and disbelief on Tristan's face, and she understood. She finally got it. Tristan didn't expect to be loved. She didn't believe she'd ever be more than someone's "friend with benefits," a temporary diversion. Tristan was so wrong.

"I said," Jett repeated softly, "I love you."

"Oh fuck." Tristan buried her face in Jett's neck. After a second, Jett realized she was crying.

"Hey. Tris. Hey." Jett led her to the sofa and pulled her down. She fumbled for the thin blanket she kept folded up on the back for the nights when she slept there and draped it around Tristan's shoulders. "Just listen, okay." She pulled Tristan into her arms and rubbed Tristan's back through the light cotton covering.

"Listen."

"I'm in room 1017," Gail said. "Come up."
Jett rode the elevator, not thinking about much of anything at all.

She'd never once been alone with Gail anywhere except on the military base. She couldn't quite believe she was going to see her, here, now. After all this time.

She walked down the hall and stood in front of the door, contemplating why she had come. Wondering if it was another mistake she would regret for a lifetime. Before she could knock, the door opened. Gail stood in the entrance in a light blue silk robe that came to mid thigh, tied loosely at her waist. Her hair was damp and tousled, the way it used to look just after she'd showered.

"I'm sorry. I wasn't expecting you," Gail said.

"I should've called." Jett backed up. "I'll call you tomorrow."

"No!" Gail hurriedly grasped Jett's hand and pulled her into the room, then closed the door and locked it. "I was afraid you wouldn't come."

"I almost didn't." Jett took several steps and stopped abruptly. She could see the bed now. The covers were turned down and the sheets were very crisp and very white. She felt awkward and out of place. She did not belong in this room with this woman like this.

Gail turned back when she realized Jett was no longer following. She grasped Jett's upper arms and ran her hands up and down them, as if afraid if she stopped touching her, Jett would disappear. She leaned into her and kissed her softly. "I'm sorry about what happened. About our misunderstanding."

"Misunderstanding."

"Yes." Gail cupped Jett's cheek. "You must know how terribly fond of you I am."

Jett nodded. "I'm a lesbian, are you?"

Gail couldn't have looked more surprised if Jett had slapped her. "Of course not. I told you that."

"Then why did you kiss me?"

"We're friends. I'm glad to see you."

"No. That night."

"I didn't."

"All right. Then I apologize. Good night." Jett turned and reached for the door. Gail might not be able to admit the truth, but Jett could. Gail had wanted Jett to kiss her, and she'd kissed her back. But Gail had never loved her, and she…she had loved a dream.

"Jett!"

Jett didn't turn around.

"I can't risk my career." Suddenly Gail was behind her with her arms around Jett's waist. Her breasts were firm against Jett's back as her hands roamed over the front of Jett's body, caressing her breasts, her stomach, the length of her thighs. "But we could have these ten days. They could be our secret."

"A secret."

"Yes," Gail said urgently, turning Jett to face her. Her robe was partially open, her breasts nearly exposed. She pressed against Jett, her arms around Jett's neck. "God, I've dreamed about this."

"I thought I frightened you. I thought I hurt you." Jett caught Gail's hands and stopped her from pulling her shirt from her pants. "I wanted you so much, and I thought I hurt you. I thought that's why you left."

"I couldn't, not there. But here. Here." Gail kissed Jett again, her breath coming fast. "No one ever needs to know."

Jett gently pushed her away. "I would know."

"Please, Jett," Gail pleaded. "You need it. I know you do."

"No, I don't. Not like this." Jett opened the door and left her sorrow where it belonged, in the past. "Good-bye, Gail."

"I want to kill her for hurting you," Tristan said when Jett finished telling her.

Jett lay back on the couch and pulled Tristan with her so they were side by side. She kissed Tristan softly. "It's over. I'm okay—sad, maybe, but for her more than me. But thank you."

Tristan, her expression solemn, traced a fingertip along the edge of Jett's jaw. "Do you still love her?"

"I told you this morning. I love you. I never loved Gail—I never loved anyone—the way I love you."

"But you said *but* earlier...if it's not Gail, then what?"

Tristan's voice held so much uncertainty and pain, Jett's insides hurt. She didn't want Tristan to doubt how special she was, but she was afraid of her own feelings. She shifted uneasily and pulled away. "It's me, Tris. The way I am."

Tristan gripped her harder. "Don't. Don't pull away from me. What do you mean, the way you are?"

"That night with Gail, I lost it," Jett confessed. "I was kissing her, and then something snapped and I was just crazy out of my mind to have her. I thought that's what drove her away. I'm like that with you, only worse. It's like…I feel sometimes if I can't get inside you, own you, make you want *me* that way, I'll die." Jett pressed her face into Tristan's hair. "God, Tris, I can't help it."

"And you think I want that to change," Tristan asked, her voice husky. "Don't you know I *want* you to want me that much?" She straddled Jett's thigh, her naked center against Jett's leg. "Can you feel how hot I am? How wet I am? I'm soaking you, aren't I?"

"Mmm, yeah. Now look who's hard." Jett gripped Tristan's hips and pressed her leg harder between Tristan's thighs. Tristan rapidly slid down the length of her thigh and back up, then moaned and did it again. "Keep that up and you're going to come."

"I want to." Tristan threw her head back, gripping Jett's wrists. She looked down, her eyes hazy, searching Jett's face. "Can I?"

Jett eased one hand between Tristan's legs and stroked her clitoris. "Say please."

"Oh, Jesus, please." Tristan rocked harder, rubbing herself on Jett's hand. "Please, babe, please. Help me get off."

"Why should I?" Jett countered, speeding up her hand action between Tristan's legs.

"Because I need you," Tristan cried.

"Why else?" Jett demanded.

"Because I love you." Tristan ground into Jett, her eyes flickering between Jett's face and Jett's hand between her legs. "I love you. Oh God, babe, you're going to make me come."

"That's all right, baby, that's what I want." Jett finally understood what she'd always needed. "Because I love you too."

CHAPTER TWENTY-SEVEN

Jett couldn't believe she'd actually fallen asleep and slept without dreaming. Judging by the slant of sunlight coming through the windows on the opposite side of the room, it was late morning, close to noon. She never slept that many hours in a row. And she never slept without part of her mind being aware of her surroundings. Tristan was still curled up beside her, her head on Jett's shoulder. Jett stroked her hair.

"Hey," Tristan murmured, rubbing Jett's stomach with her hand underneath Jett's T-shirt. "You don't move when you sleep."

Jett laughed. "Did you stay awake the whole time to check?"

"You don't relax completely, either."

"Oh, I don't know. I feel pretty relaxed right now."

Tristan cupped Jett lightly between the legs. "Oh yeah?"

Jett hissed. "Easy there. My trigger's pretty tight where you're concerned."

"Yeah?" Tristan eased up on her elbow, slid two fingers into the opening of Jett's boxers, and worked a finger around either side of Jett's clitoris. "That's nice."

"That's teasing." Jett's stomach pitched and rolled. She hadn't come since last night and she needed to. Wanted to. Wanted Tristan in so many ways she was almost paralyzed.

"You look worried. Why?" Tristan kissed her and continued to slowly fondle her.

"I'm...not." Jett couldn't stop her legs from trembling and she realized her fingers must be digging into Tristan's arm. She consciously loosened her grip.

"You don't get it yet, do you?" Tristan flicked her tongue over Jett's mouth, then down the center of her chin. She bit her neck, then licked all the way down to her collarbone. "I like the way you are. I like what you need. I want to give it to you."

"Too much." Jett shook her head, trying to make sense of her jumbled thoughts. "I might want too much."

Tristan laughed and pushed up to her knees. She spread open Jett's boxers, leaned down, and kissed the swell of her clitoris. "I wouldn't worry about that." She closed the material and patted Jett lightly between the legs. "I need a shower. Come with me."

Jett narrowed her eyes. "What the hell? You do me like that and then walk away?"

"Got to keep you interested." Tristan pushed off the couch and disappeared down the hall.

"God damn it." Jett bolted up and almost fell over, her legs were so weak. She steadied herself on the sofa, then took off. By the time she reached the bathroom, the shower was running and Tristan was standing under the spray, her head tossed back and water cascading through her thick dark hair and over her muscled shoulders and back. Jett stood completely still with the glass door open and drank her in. She forgot about needing to come. She forgot about worrying that what she needed would drive Tristan away. She couldn't think of anything except what a miracle it was to have Tristan here, and how much she loved her. She slid in behind her and kissed her neck.

"Took you long enough," Tristan murmured. She turned, pressed Jett against the wall, and kissed her, slipping one wet thigh between Jett's legs. "I love you. Have I told you that?"

"Yes," Jett said. "A few hours ago."

"That long? I'll be sure to repeat myself more often."

"You were also about to come, and when a woman is about to come, she'll say anything," Jett teased, sucking a drop of water from the end of Tristan's chin.

"You'll notice I'm not coming now," Tristan said. "And I love you. Okay? I'm not in this just for the sex." She grinned. "Although I won't pretend I don't think about it a lot. Like all the time."

Jett smoothed her hands over Tristan's shoulders, then gripped her firmly and held her at arm's length. "About Darla."

"Oh, Jesus." Tristan took a deep breath. "I don't even have an excuse, babe. I—"

"You don't need an excuse—not for last night." Jett continued her caresses over Tristan's chest, around the sides of her breasts. "But I'm not going to be happy if it happens again."

"It's not going to happen again," Tristan said quietly. "Not with anyone. I love you. I want you, so much I can hardly breathe. You're it for me, babe."

Jett leaned her head back against the wall, feeling completely centered for the first time in her life. "For me too."

"That's good." Tristan knelt between Jett's legs. "Because I don't think I could stand it if anyone else touched you."

Jett looked down and watched Tristan take her into her mouth. The slow pulse of her heart beating between Tristan's lips was nothing like she'd imagined it would be. She could feel herself opening, pouring into Tristan's mouth, her soul flowing to meet Tristan's as surely as her body yielded to Tristan's insistent demands. Jett pushed herself deeper and Tristan used her teeth, the tip of her tongue, her lips, biting and circling and sucking.

"I'm getting close to coming. Really close." Jett steadied herself with her hands on Tristan's shoulders. She would come, if Tristan wanted her to. She would wait, if that was what Tristan wanted. "Whatever you want, Tris," she gasped. "Whatever you want. It's yours."

Tristan glanced up and took her mouth away for an instant. "You. That's what I want. I want you."

"I'm yours."

Then Tristan put her mouth back and Jett came.

❖

"Feeling better?" Honor asked as Quinn came into the bedroom, toweling her hair after her shower.

"Couldn't be better." Quinn grinned, leaned over to kiss her, then smoothed a hand over Jack's head. "Thanks."

Honor laughed. "Believe me, it was entirely my pleasure."

Quinn pulled shorts from the top drawer of the dresser. "How about you? You were on your feet a long time. Is your incision bothering you?"

"I'm a little achy, but nothing serious." Honor sat up on the side of the bed and put Jack back in his bassinet. "It's almost time for me to go back to work anyhow."

"Take the last week you've still got coming to you." Quinn slipped into her T-shirt, then sat down in the big overstuffed chair to put on her sneakers and socks. "You don't want to go back to work on Labor Day weekend. It's always crazy."

Honor padded across the room and sat on Quinn's lap. "You just want to keep me at home, barefoot and pregnant."

"I do think you're really sexy when you're pregnant." Quinn leaned back and pulled Honor against her chest. She kissed her and lightly cupped her breast. "Very sexy now too."

"I'm not getting any younger," Honor whispered.

"That's okay, baby." Quinn kissed her forehead, then her mouth again. "I'm happy just exactly the way things are."

"But I think I could do another one in a year or so."

Quinn searched Honor's eyes. "You're sure?"

"Uh-huh."

Quinn grinned. "I'd like tha—"

The door burst open and Arly raced in. "Hey, Quinn! We're going to be late."

Honor shifted on Quinn's lap and fixed Arly with a stare. "The door? What are the rules?"

"Oh." Arly threw a beseeching look in Quinn's direction, then ran out, slammed the door, and knocked.

Honor gave Quinn a long look. "Are you positive you want more of *that* for another couple of decades?"

"Never more certain." Quinn kissed Honor quickly one more time, then called, "Come on in, Arly. We're all yours."

❖

"Hi, Tris." Linda, curled up in the corner of the couch with a cup of coffee and a novel, greeted Tristan with a smile when she walked into the flight lounge. "Are you on call again?"

"Nope. Just visiting."

Linda raised her eyebrows and gave Tristan the once-over. "Looking for Jett?"

Tristan grinned. "How did you guess?"

Linda tapped the side of her neck with two fingers.

"Huh?" Then Tristan rubbed her neck in the same spot and felt a twinge of pain. She laughed. "Oh. What did she do, leave her initials?"

"I saw you two leave last night," Linda admitted. "You're good, but how many women could you have in one night?" She held up her hand quickly. "Don't answer that question."

"Don't worry, I wasn't about to," Tristan teased back.

Linda stared at the coffee cup she was holding for a few seconds, then back at Tristan. "She's a real sweetheart, you know."

"Believe me, I know that." Tristan leaned a hip on the arm of the couch. "I guess you saw Darla too, huh?"

"Ah, well…"

"I'm not going to hurt Jett."

Linda blushed. "I'm being nosy. Jett's an adult. I'm sure she—"

"I'm totally crazy about her," Tristan said softly.

"Oh!" Linda's face lit up. "Well, in that case. Does she know?"

"I think so. But just to be sure," Tristan stood, "I'm here to tell her again."

❖

Jett initialed the last box on her preflight checklist and stowed the clipboard next to her seat in the cockpit. She sensed someone behind her and turned. Tristan stood a few feet away, her hands on her hips, watching her. She wore jeans and a pale blue shirt with the sleeves rolled up. Her expression was part appraisal, part ownership. Jett's heart speeded up. "Hi. I thought you were off tonight."

"I missed you."

"I've only been gone an hour." Jett leaned back against the aircraft because seeing Tristan look at her that way pretty much knocked her out.

"Is that all? Seems like a lot longer," Tristan murmured, moving closer. She unzipped Jett's flight suit, opening it from neck to crotch, and slid her hands inside. She kissed Jett's neck. "You'll be careful tonight, won't you?"

"I'll be careful every night." Jett gripped Tristan's wrists and drew her hands away from her body. Then she zipped up. "I'm officially working now. Sex is against regulations."

Tristan dropped her forehead to Jett's shoulder and groaned. "I think I'm going to hate night call."

"Just think of it this way," Jett whispered, rubbing the back of Tristan's neck. "You get to have all the morning sex you can handle."

Tristan clasped Jett's hand and leaned back beside her, their shoulders touching. "Does that mean you're going to come home to me every morning?"

"Are you asking me to?"

"Yes."

Jett cradled Tristan's hand in both of hers and kissed her knuckles. "Then that's affirmative."

Tristan rested her head against Jett's shoulder. "I'm pretty sure I could learn to love night call."

About the Author

Radclyffe is a retired surgeon and full-time award-winning author-publisher with over thirty lesbian novels and anthologies in print. Five of her works have been Lambda Literary finalists, including the Lambda Literary winners *Erotic Interludes 2: Stolen Moments* ed. with Stacia Seaman and *Distant Shores, Silent Thunder*. She is the editor of *Best Lesbian Romance 2009* (Cleis Press) and has selections in multiple anthologies including *Best Lesbian Erotica 2006, 2007, 2008,* and *2009; After Midnight; Caught Looking: Erotic Tales of Voyeurs and Exhibitionists; First-Timers; Ultimate Undies: Erotic Stories About Lingerie and Underwear; Hide and Seek; A is for Amour; H is for Hardcore; L is for Leather;* and *Rubber Sex*. She is the recipient of the 2003 and 2004 Alice B. Readers' awards for her body of work and is also the president of Bold Strokes Books, one of the world's largest independent LGBT publishing companies.

Her forthcoming 2009 works include *Radical Encounters* (an all-Radclyffe erotica anthology), *Justice for All, Secrets in the Stone,* and *Returning Tides*.

Books Available From Bold Strokes Books

truelesbianlove.com by Carsen Taite. Mackenzie Lewis and Dr. Jordan Wagner have very different ideas about love, but discover truelesbianlove is closer than a click away. (978-1-60282-071-5)

Justice at Risk by John Morgan Wilson. Benjamin Justice's blind date leads to a rare opportunity for legitimate work, but a reckless risk changes his life forever. (978-1-60282-059-3)

Run to Me by Lisa Girolami. Burned by the four-letter word called love, the only thing Beth Standish wants to do is run for—or maybe from—her life. (978-1-60282-034-0)

Split the Aces by Jove Belle. In the neon glare of Sin City, two women ride a wave of passion that threatens to consume them in a world of fast money and fast times. (978-1-60282-033-3)

Uncharted Passage by Julie Cannon. Two women on a vacation that turns deadly face down one of nature's most ruthless killers—and find themselves falling in love. (978-1-60282-032-6)

Night Call by Radclyffe. All medevac helicopter pilot Jett McNally wants to do is fly and forget about the horror and heartbreak she left behind in the Middle East, but anesthesiologist Tristan Holmes has other plans. (978-1-60282-031-9)

Lake Effect Snow by C.P. Rowlands. News correspondent Annie T. Booker and FBI Agent Sarah Moore struggle to stay one step ahead of disaster as Annie's life becomes the war zone she once reported on. Eclipse EBook (978-1-60282-068-5)

Revision of Justice by John Morgan Wilson. Murder shifts into high gear, propelling Benjamin Justice into a raging fire that consumes the Hollywood Hills, burning steadily toward the famous Hollywood Sign—and the identity of a cold-blooded killer. Gay Mystery. (978-1-60282-058-6)

I Dare You by Larkin Rose. Stripper by night, corporate raider by day, Kelsey's only looking for sex and power, until she meets a woman who stirs her heart and her body. (978-1-60282-030-2)

Truth Behind the Mask by Lesley Davis. Erith Baylor is drawn to Sentinel Pagan Osborne's quiet strength, but the secrets between them strain duty and family ties. (978-1-60282-029-6)

Cooper's Deale by KI Thompson. Two would-be lovers and a decidedly inopportune murder spell trouble for Addy Cooper, no matter which way the cards fall. (978-1-60282-028-9)

Romantic Interludes 1: Discovery ed. by Radclyffe and Stacia Seaman. An anthology of sensual, erotic contemporary love stories from the best-selling Bold Strokes authors. (978-1-60282-027-2)

A Guarded Heart by Jennifer Fulton. The last place FBI Special Agent Pat Roussel expects to find herself is assigned to an illicit private security gig baby-sitting a celebrity. (Ebook) (978-1-60282-067-8)

Saving Grace by Jennifer Fulton. Champion swimmer Dawn Beaumont, injured in a car crash she caused, flees to Moon Island, where scientist Grace Ramsay welcomes her. (Ebook) (978-1-60282-066-1)

The Sacred Shore by Jennifer Fulton. Successful tech industry survivor Merris Randall does not believe in love at first sight until she meets Olivia Pearce. (Ebook) (978-1-60282-065-4)

Passion Bay by Jennifer Fulton. Two women from different ends of the earth meet in paradise. Author's expanded edition. (Ebook) (978-1-60282-064-7)

Never Wake by Gabrielle Goldsby. After a brutal attack, Emma Webster becomes a self-sentenced prisoner inside her condo—until the world outside her window goes silent. (Ebook) (978-1-60282-063-0)

The Caretaker's Daughter by Gabrielle Goldsby. Against the backdrop of a nineteenth-century English country estate, two women struggle to find love. (Ebook) (978-1-60282-062-3)

Simple Justice by John Morgan Wilson. When a pretty-boy cokehead is murdered, former LA reporter Benjamin Justice and his reluctant new partner, Alexandra Templeton, must unveil the real killer. (978-1-60282-057-9)

Remember Tomorrow by Gabrielle Goldsby. Cees Bannigan and Arieanna Simon find that a successful relationship rests in remembering the mistakes of the past. (978-1-60282-026-5)

Put Away Wet by Susan Smith. Jocelyn "Joey" Fellows has just been savagely dumped—when she posts an online personal ad, she discovers more than just the great sex she expected. (978-1-60282-025-8)

Homecoming by Nell Stark. Sarah Storm loses everything that matters—family, future dreams, and love—will her new "straight" roommate cause Sarah to take a chance at happiness? (978-1-60282-024-1)

The Three by Meghan O'Brien. A daring, provocative exploration of love and sexuality. Two lovers, Elin and Kael, struggle to survive in a postapocalyptic world. (Ebook) (978-1-60282-056-2)

Falling Star by Gill McKnight. Solley Rayner hopes a few weeks with her family will help heal her shattered dreams, but she hasn't counted on meeting a woman who stirs her heart. (978-1-60282-023-4)

Lethal Affairs by Kim Baldwin and Xenia Alexiou. Elite operative Domino is no stranger to peril, but her investigation of journalist Hayley Ward will test more than her skills. (978-1-60282-022-7)

A Place to Rest by Erin Dutton. Sawyer Drake doesn't know what she wants from life until she meets Jori Diamantina—only trouble is, Jori doesn't seem to share her desire. (978-1-60282-021-0)

Warrior's Valor by Gun Brooke. Dwyn Izsontro and Emeron D'Artansis must put aside personal animosity and unwelcome attraction to defeat an enemy of the Protector of the Realm. (978-1-60282-020-3)

Finding Home by Georgia Beers. Take two polar-opposite women with an attraction for one another they're trying desperately to ignore, throw in a far-too-observant dog, and then sit back and enjoy the romance. (978-1-60282-019-7)

Word of Honor by Radclyffe. All Secret Service Agent Cameron Roberts and First Daughter Blair Powell want is a small intimate wedding, but the paparazzi and a domestic terrorist have other plans. (978-1-60282-018-0)